BITTEN BY BLOODMOON

MATELESS SHIFTERS BOOK 2

ELLA MILES

PROLOGUE

NYX

"*A snow wolf will be the one to break the curse,*" the seer's voice plays over and over in my head as I watch Lumi and Ambrose descend the stairs.

They look powerfully regal in their all-black attire and golden crowns in a way that makes my stomach churn. If they want to rule the packs, so be it. I couldn't care less, as long as they leave me and the Bloodmoon wolves alone after the curse is broken.

The crowd watches them in silence, all breaths collectively held until the ceremony is over and the curse is broken. My own breathing remains normal until I catch a full glimpse of her.

Stunning.

Lumi looks good in black lace. It's a harsh contrast to her fair skin and white hair winding around her golden crown. Her hair grips the crown tightly, as if it were an extension of her. She's been destined to become a queen this whole time.

In the short month since I first saw her, a confidence has grown in her. She holds her head high, and though her heartbeat has increased, it's nothing compared to the others sitting on this hillside watching her.

I can't take my eyes off her; all the air has escaped my lungs.

And then, she's looking directly at me like she knows the thoughts playing in my head. I shut off all emotion, attempting to keep her out of my thoughts, but her eyes are sharp and full of determination. She'll try to kill me as soon as she gets the chance.

I smirk. *I look forward to it.*

Her eyes dart to Kael, who is standing next to me. She does a full once-over of him, looking for any sign of injury, but I'm a man of my word. Our deal seemed to have inspired her to take action and get here. I kept her silly secret about being a Wintermoon wolf, and I kept Kael alive. In exchange, she learned to shift so she could complete this marking ceremony.

I raise my eyebrows at her as she glances back at me one last time before turning her attention to Isolde.

"A snow wolf will be the one to break the curse..." the words repeat again.

She's the one, I have no doubt.

Ambrose—I still have my doubts about him. I know he wants to break the curse, just like me. But...

"...she will fall in love with an alpha, and that alpha will love her with everything he has. A love strong enough that it almost destroys the world instead of saving it. Together, they will find a way to break the curse."

Does he love her? Has their love really had time to grow to that level in a month?

I stare at their interlinked hands, and an uncomfortable feeling rises in my belly. I know nothing of love, and I probably never will. They put on a good show, I'll give them that. They present a united front, as if they are already joined together.

Isolde speaks, but I'm not listening. I'm too focused on finding any details of the prophecy that has or hasn't been fulfilled. With a blink, an entire coven of witches surrounds them, and the crowd around me gasps.

Gods, this better work. Otherwise, a lot of creatures are going to end up dead tonight.

I glance over my shoulder to my beta, giving her a look that tells her to prepare—*now*.

She sends the message through my pack, and one by one, I see my pack shifting into their wolf forms. We aren't taking any chances if this goes south. I won't lose a member of my pack tonight.

I look to my right and bare my fangs at the vampires hidden in the crowd. They need to be reminded of their place and to follow my orders.

The witches raise their hands together, and golden threads flow from their fingertips, weaving an intricate design until a see-through cage forms around Lumi and Ambrose, locking them in.

"The moon will soon be at its peak. It's time to start." Isolde holds up her hands. "Do you, Lumi, accept Ambrose as your mate?"

"Yes."

"Do you, Ambrose, accept Lumi as your mate?"

"Yes."

"Very well, we shall see if you both chose correctly. There are two parts to the ceremony. Part one is to join as your human selves. Part two is to shift into your wolf forms and for Ambrose to mark Lumi's upper shoulder. If you both survive, then the mating bond should make itself known."

With a flick of her hand, an altar appears in the center of the stage.

Gods, there is no way that Lumi will agree to this. No way the curse is broken here.

And then suddenly, the cage seems to fog over, preventing any of us from seeing what's happening.

Ambrose.

For once, I'm glad the bastard has magical powers. I may hate him, but this—this is too much.

Murmurs ripple through the crowd, with some asking, "How can we confirm that they are really joining together if we can't see?"

"We'll know they did when they break the curse," I snap at the crowd, shutting them up.

We don't have to wait to see if the curse breaks or not to know what they are doing as Lumi's soft moans and whimpers echo through the air.

My body stills harder than rock as a chill races over my skin. A strange ache shoots through me, and I get the urge to break through the magical cage and rip Ambrose from her body.

My hands are fists beside me, and I anchor my legs to the ground. It's been too long since I've been with a woman, and my emotions are heightened right now— that's all it means.

"The snow wolf has to complete the marking ceremony no matter what happens—it's the only way to break the curse. She has to complete the marking and survive. Then the curse will be broken."

She doesn't need saving. The sounds she's making prove she's enjoying herself thoroughly. *Maybe they really are in love?* I wouldn't know anything about such a thing.

I glance at Kael, who looks pale, but he doesn't speak

or try to stop this. He knows what the prophecy says, just like I do. He knows she's strong enough to finish this.

Ambrose's roar rips through the air, claiming what's his.

I close my eyes for a second, trying to block out the sound that seems to burn my ears, but there is no escaping it.

It's over.

They joined as humans.

Now, they just need to join as wolves.

I open my eyes as the foggy cage becomes visible again. Lumi is standing glued to Ambrose's body with flushed cheeks and matted hair, but the crown still sits atop her head, and her dress is barely wrinkled. But her scent mixed with Ambrose's invades my nostrils, making it crystal clear what happened.

Fuck me.

I shake my head, confused as to where these emotions are coming from. It must be because of my history with Ambrose. I want to fuck what's his.

"Move on to part two," Ambrose snarls.

Isolde nods. "Shift."

"We are doing part two without shifting," he says.

Isolde smirks like she knew that's what he'd say. "That's not your choice. I know she can shift now."

Suddenly, Lumi begins screaming, magic flooding her body.

I twitch for just a second, trying to stop myself, before I take a full step toward her.

I can't stop this. The prophecy says she has to complete the marking ceremony to break the curse and survive. She has to shift. She can do this.

One by one, the entire Moonfire coven pours their

magic into her, until I don't know how she's not burning alive from the power flowing through her.

"Shift, Lumi, shift," Kael whispers with wide-eyed panic next to me. He starts toward the stage, but I grab onto his arm, shaking my head.

"I have to do something. She can't survive this," he says.

"Give her a chance. She's destined to be the one. She's stronger than you know."

He frowns at me.

"Lumi!" Ambrose screams. "Stop this, Isolde! She can shift on her own. Just give her a minute."

"We don't have a minute. The moon is cresting. It has to be now," Isolde says.

Lumi collapses to the floor, and a shockwave spreads through the crowd.

Get up, get up, Lumi. I send all my strength to her, like that will somehow save her.

Lumi stands with fierce determination. "I will complete the ceremony in my human form."

"You'll never survive," Isolde says with cruel intentions.

"Watch me," Lumi growls before turning to Ambrose. "Shift."

A second later, Ambrose has shifted into his massive dark wolf speckled with golden flecks. He's impressive, I'll give him that. But so is she. She doesn't cower, doesn't even flinch at the thought of the pain she's about to endure.

"Do it," she says.

Ambrose lets out a low growl.

"Do it. Mark me as your mate," she says, her words full of power.

Ambrose stalks toward her in a predatory way, and every hair on my arms stands to attention.

Something's wrong.

I look around the crowd, but everyone is looking at them with hopeful anticipation.

"The snow wolf has to complete the marking ceremony no matter what happens—it's the only way to break the curse," I hear the seer's voice more clearly than before. I look to my left and see her hiding among the forest with a soft smirk on her lips.

I narrow my eyes. I'm missing something, something important.

I turn back in time to see Ambrose open his massive jaw as his teeth brush against her flesh, barely touching her before I feel the pain.

Fire-hot pain shoots through her, and she sends it out to me in waves, almost as if I'm feeling the same pain she's feeling. He's barely pricked her skin and already the pain is too much for her to handle in her human form. She needs to change to survive. I examine her more carefully and take a deep breath, gathering all the information I can about her. She's lost a lot of blood recently. She's weak, and I'm unsure if she can shift to save herself. The energy it would require might overwhelm and kill her.

A jolt shoots through my body, with a power I've never felt before.

What the hell?

I start to move—

"The snow wolf has to complete the marking ceremony no matter what happens—it's the only way to break the curse," the seer snaps at me, her magic directing her voice into my ear. Her power shoots through me, holding me still as a statue.

Gods, I hate witches.

I can't let her die.

"This is the only way to break the curse," the seer says.

I can't let her die.

The words come stronger and stronger, overpowering the seer.

I won't let her die.

"Stop! I'm your mate, not Ambrose," my words fly from my mouth as if I have no control over them. And I have no idea why I say them, no idea if they are true or not.

But my words save her at the cost of saving my pack, and of saving me.

CHAPTER 1
LUMI

He bit me. Nyx's teeth sank into the exact same spot on my neck where Ambrose had started to mark me, and in one quick bite, he completely erased what Ambrose had started, making the mark his own. And then, with a gentle pull of his lips, he drank my blood.

A creeping coolness spreads into my body as the last of my warmth drains away. With a jolt, I'm pulled from my dream—no, my nightmare. This can't be real. This can't really be happening. Rowena can't be dead. We couldn't have failed. And I—*am I dead?*

I blink, and bright lights illuminate the room.

I'm not dead. And I'm not in a dungeon either.

I'm lying in the largest bed I've ever seen. It's pillowy soft, with crisp sheets indicating a high thread count. Floor-to-ceiling windows expand the entire wall opposite me, and my breath falters at the sight of the cliff and valley below. It looks as if I were to take one step toward the windows, the house would tilt and we'd all plummet to our deaths below. It would be worth it, though, because I've never seen anything so beautiful in all my life.

"How are you feeling?" Nyx asks.

I snap my head toward the sound on my left and find Nyx leaning against the closed door, watching me intently. He's adorned head to toe in black that squeezes over his honed body. A whisp of his hair falls over his blackened eyes that stare at me like he wants to eat me.

"You don't care how I feel."

He blinks. "You're right, I don't."

I sit up and the covers slip down my body—down my very naked body.

I clench the cover and yank it up, tucking it tightly under my armpits.

"I'm naked," I growl at him.

He raises an eyebrow in the annoying way he does. "And?"

"And, I should have clothes on."

"You wanted me to dress you?"

"No," I snap.

"That's what I thought. Clothes will be provided when we are done with this conversation."

I narrow my eyes at him, a silent promise of violence. "Now."

His lips tilt up. "You need to work on your alpha commands. It really could use some work. But then, me being who I am, I doubt you would ever be strong enough to command me to do anything."

"I hate you."

"I know. Most people do."

"Maybe you should change that."

"Maybe, but I won't."

"Where are we?"

"My house."

I swallow and quickly glance around the room. It's large, bright, and beautiful. Not at all what I would expect for a room in a vampire's house. His room must be dark and windowless in comparison. But I'm not sure why I'm in this room if the sunlight prevents him from getting closer to me.

"That's why you're standing in the shadows, you can't step into the light. Why put me in the brightest room in your house then?"

His attention drifts to the window, distant and unreachable, as he stares out, deliberately silent when it comes to answering my question.

"How? How are you a vampire?"

"How is Ambrose a witch?"

My mouth falls, remembering Nyx's earlier confession. He's part vampire; Ambrose is part witch. *How could any of it be possible? How could I have not realized what Ambrose is?*

"How?" I ask again.

He shrugs.

Blood boils in my veins. "Are you going to answer any of my questions?"

"Are you going to answer any of mine?"

"No."

His shoulders lift again as if to say, *Same.*

I exhale in a sharp rush. Leaning back against the thick, black headboard, I feel something scratch against my neck. There's a small bandage there, covering my wound. I brush my hand over the bandage for just a second before I feel Nyx watching me and stop.

"You drank my blood. You could force me to talk to you. Alpha commands aren't always strong enough to get people to talk, but vampire mind control...you could force me to talk to you—spill every secret I have."

"I could, but what fun would that be?"

I frown as I look at him. "You're toying with me. I don't like it."

"Sorry, love, but you'll have to get used to it."

"I'm not your love. I'm Ambrose's mate."

"Are you?"

"Yes," I hiss.

His lips curl into a mischievous grin. *"If you say so,"* he whispers into my mind.

"Fuck!"

"Do you always curse so much?"

"Get out of my head!"

The silence returns, and he's standing there, leaning against the wall with his arms casually crossed in front of his chest. Gods, I forgot how good-looking the man is. But everything about him is a warning.

There's danger in his stance; it coils in the way he moves his muscles and in the silent precision of his movements. Darkness fills his eyes and clings to every part of his body in a lethal beauty. There's a raw magnetism to his deliberate grin that draws me in. The kind of beauty that's irresistible and perilous. He's a god in devil's clothing. It doesn't matter how devastatingly beautiful he is; he's not my mate.

"How?"

He cocks an eyebrow. "How?"

"How did you speak to me in my head? Is that a trick all vampires can do?"

"No, vampires can't speak to others in their head. At most, I can get a single word, phrase, or quick feeling out, but it's nothing like this. I'm not in their heads, able to see and feel everything they're feeling. Or talk to them as freely as I can with you. It's a strange sensation being in your head, speaking to you, and hearing you in return."

"Then how?"

"How do you and Ambrose speak to each other in your heads?"

"We're mates."

His eyes loom large as if he's waiting for me to answer my own silly question.

"We are *not* mates," I protest.

"Logic would say otherwise."

I shake my head. "This must be Isolde fucking with me, messing with my head. She hates me. This can't be real. I can't have two mates."

"Isolde isn't capable of magic like this. But I agree, it's strange of you to have two mates."

I stare at him. "What aren't you telling me?"

"Plenty, same as you."

I roll my eyes. "Start talking."

"Hmmm."

"Hmmm?"

"Hmmm."

"Gods, just use your mind control and force me to talk. This conversation is insufferable."

He smirks. "I'm quite enjoying it."

I huff and start to move out of the bed, before I'm reminded of my nakedness and sink back under the covers. He left me naked just to force me to stay in this bed without even having to use mind control.

"Or has the mind control worn off already? Need to drink more of my blood to control me?" I tease.

He just stares at me, and it's clear I'm not going to get any answers out of him. But I have to try, I have to get him talking. I have to find out everything I can about him and about where I am—it's the only way I'll be able to escape.

But there is one question that bubbles above all others in my mind as my heart aches at the very thought.

"Did you kill Ambrose like you did Rowena?" I ask in a monotone voice devoid of any emotion. I will not let Nyx see my pain.

Nyx pauses for a second, and I think the bastard isn't going to answer me, just like he hasn't answered any of my other questions.

"When I took you, Ambrose was still very much alive. There is no reason to doubt that he still lives, as there was no one left powerful enough to kill him after we left."

My heart beats again, as if it still has a reason. But Rowena...she's gone. I know it without asking. I saw her body with my own eyes. And I'll never forgive Nyx for that. I'll get my revenge—he dies.

"Where is Kael? What of our deal?"

"I honored our deal. And as you were prepared to die in the marking ceremony to break the curse, Kael is free to go where he wants."

"I wasn't going to die. You were the reason the curse wasn't broken. Where is Kael?"

"Last I saw him, he was with the Moonlight pack."

Thank gods, he's safe.

"So what now? You're going to keep me in some dungeon somewhere until the next ceremony? I'll never let you mark me. I'll never agree that you are my mate."

"A dungeon, huh? That's your kink?"

I glare at him. "I'm going to kill you."

"Probably."

This man is insufferable. But there's a twinkle in his eyes that tells me he's amused by the idea of me trying.

"What I want is for us to figure out how to break the curse," he says.

"I'm not your mate. I'm not completing the marking ceremony with you."

"I'm not asking you to…yet, at least. I'm asking for us to share knowledge. We both know pieces of the prophecy that no one else knows. Maybe I can talk to you in your head because you need to know the final pieces of the prophecy to break the curse."

What he says makes sense.

"Or, maybe, it's because I'm really your mate and not Ambrose."

I growl at him.

He barks out a laugh.

"Then tell me what you know," I demand.

He shakes his head. "That's not how this is going to work. We share information. We seek out the rest of the prophecy together. Then we decide what needs to happen at the next marking ceremony."

"I'm not sharing anything with you. And there is no *we*. You killed Rowena! I don't want anything to do with you unless it's putting a stake through your heart."

He tilts his head as he watches me. I know he's a wolf shifter—I've seen him shift with my own eyes and ridden on his back. But right now, all I see is the vampire, my enemy.

"Rowena's death was unfortunate."

"Stop! You don't get to act like you cared about her, you cold-hearted killer. You're an abomination, a predator. You go against your own kind to help the vampires."

"I'm sorry about your friend's death. And I am, as you say, a killer. You shouldn't trust me. You shouldn't like me. You shouldn't fall in love with me. You shouldn't mate me. But I'm your only chance at breaking the curse now."

"I will never work with you. And you'd better lock me in a dungeon because I'm not staying here. I'm going back to my pack—to Ambrose."

He shakes his head. "You're not going to kill me until the curse is broken, and I'm not locking you in a dungeon. I do not need to. I tasted a drop of your blood. You want to know how long the mind control lasts after I taste your blood?"

I freeze, terrified I already know the answer.

"Forever," he chuckles.

CHAPTER 2

LUMI

orever—that word is going to live in my fucking head forever. *Gods, it can't be true.* He must be bluffing. But then, why would he? He's a vampire and an alpha wolf shifter; if he had to drink a drop of my blood every day to control me, he easily could.

Forever—that's how long I'm under his control.

I have to kill him.

It's the only way.

But what if...

No, no what ifs—Nyx dies.

Nyx stares at me as if he can read my mind. As if he knows the plan that's slowly forming in my head.

I wait for him to attack me or to command me not to kill him.

Instead, with the blink of an eye, he vanishes and returns before I can even process that he's moved.

I gasp when I see clothes on the bed and a small tray of food on the nightstand next to me. He put them there so quickly, it was as if they instantly appeared.

"Get dressed and eat something. Then you can plot my death more easily," he says.

I frown. "Is that your mind control telling me to?"

"Does it feel like my mind control is forcing you?"

"No."

"Well, then."

"Alpha command?"

"No. Unlike Ambrose, I rarely use an alpha command on anyone."

"Sure you don't."

He huffs. "Get dressed, eat, or don't—it's up to you."

He's gone before I can get in another word.

I scramble for the clothes, pulling the first top and pants off the pile I find and yanking them on my body as quickly as possible. I'm not going to be vulnerable again.

And then I eye the tray of food as I climb back into the sunlight-drenched bed. I'm safe in the sunlight, or as safe as I can be around a vampire that has drunk a drop of my blood and could tell me to jump out the window to my death at any moment.

There are eggs, oatmeal, waffles, and fruit. I glance at the cups—coffee, tea, orange juice.

It's thoughtful of him to include choices in my food when I don't get to pick where I live or who my mate is.

Nyx can't be my mate; he can't be. I don't know why he can talk to me in my head like Ambrose can, but it doesn't matter. He's not my mate.

I pick up the cup of tea and take a long sip, letting the warmth of the liquid sink into my body like a warm hug.

The tears fall.

And fall and fall and fall.

I pull my knees up to my chest and grip the cup of tea like it's the only thing holding me together.

Rowena's gone. I can't bring her back.

Ambrose is hundreds of miles away.

As much as I love him, how much do I really know him?

And Kael, my best friend, who I would have talked to about all of this, isn't here.

My body shakes as grief overtakes me, wracking through my entire body.

When I've cried all the tears my body could possibly produce, I get up, use the ensuite bathroom, have my breath taken away by the bathroom's beauty, of course, and then make a plan.

I don't hear anyone outside my door, but I can't tell how many people are in the house. I don't feel any compulsion, any mind control, or a command holding me to this room. I don't feel any magic when I place my hand against the door.

I don't know where we are, but based on the oversized sweatshirt and sweatpants I'm in, I'm guessing north.

I swallow at that thought.

But I can shift now. I just need to find my way out of this house, then I can shift and run until I find Ambrose and the rest of the Moonlight pack. Killing Nyx will have to wait.

I open the door, surprised to find no guards posted outside. But I can hear soft voices echoing through the hallways—the house is far from empty. There is no way that their wolf or vampire hearing could have missed me opening the door.

I have to try. I can't hide in this room, crying for a month until Nyx drags me to the next marking ceremony under the full moon and uses his compulsion to force me into mating with him.

Energy surges through my body, roaring with a single determination: I kill Nyx tonight.

I like the idea even though I know it's not possible.

I don't have a plan—not really. Still, I keep walking down the maze of hallways in this house that feels more like a castle. I walk toward the voices instead of running away from them. Running never gets me anywhere. I'm not going to make that mistake again. I'm going to face them head-on.

I stop as the voices grow closer and listen.

"What are you doing with the girl, Nyx?"

"Lumi's the key to breaking the curse."

"I know that—but she's Ambrose's mate. Holding her hostage doesn't seem like the best way to break the curse."

"If I had let Ambrose mark her, she'd be dead, and the curse would never be broken," Nyx answers before pausing. "Are you going to join us or just hide behind the wall all night, Lumi?"

My heart jumps in my throat, but I step around the corner of the wall. I inhale sharply at the sight of five pairs of eyes in what appears to be the living room, all with a different drink in their hand and all staring at me like they want to kill me.

Vampires—all of them.

Shift.

I'm not powerless, not this time. I can shift.

I let the feelings flood my body as I tell my wolf to come out. But nothing happens. No claws form. No canines lengthen. No fur or thick muscles appear.

Nyx cocks his head at me as if he knows I'm trying to shift but can't.

Did he fuck with me? Compel me to not be able to shift? What's going on?

But if I can't shift, then I'm defenseless against them. Any one of them could kill me with a single bite, and there is nothing I could do to defend myself.

Fear overtakes me in a way I haven't felt before. It wraps around me, suffocating me under its merciless weight.

I'm not afraid I won't survive the night—I will. Nyx has made it clear that he doesn't want me dead—at least not yet.

No, I'm petrified that I'm irrevocably broken, and I won't ever be able to break the curse. Even if I escape Nyx and return to Ambrose, the same situation will repeat itself.

I won't be able to shift when it matters most during the marking ceremony. Ambrose won't be able to mark me as his mate. He'll never be able to love me without risking killing me.

We'll never be able to break the curse.

Nyx opens his mouth to speak to me, but I don't hear him. Nothing matters if I can't shift when I need to, nothing.

"Lumi? Are you okay? What's wrong? Your fear is over-whelming me. What's wrong?" the voice is clear and sharp in my head, but it's not the man in front of me speaking into my head. It's Ambrose.

I blink, once, twice, unsure if I imagined his voice or if it's really him.

"Lumi? Talk to me," Ambrose says again.

"Is it really you?"

"Yes, my queen. It's me. Thank gods you can still talk to me. Are you okay?"

"I'm okay. Nyx has me at his house. Are you close?"

Please, gods, let him be close. Let this nightmare be over before it really begins. I need him. I need him to help me figure out why I can't shift.

But his answer comes in a single word that stings deep into my heart.

"No."

CHAPTER 3
LUMI

Nyx stares at me curiously as if he's part of the conversation with Ambrose, but he can't be. *Can he?*

Or maybe he's just confused as to what I'm doing here. *Can vampires read minds? Is it part of their mind control powers?*

I should ask Ambrose. But the millions of questions I have for Ambrose are going to have to wait.

"You're all vampires," I say, shuddering at the very thought of living in a house filled with predators.

The room erupts in laughter at the first words I've spoken.

A woman sitting to Nyx's right whips her long brown curls cascading over her shoulder, her eyes cutting into me with piercing intensity.

"You really are clueless. How? How could you not know?" She's breathtakingly beautiful with sharp, feminine features that give way to bands of muscles at her biceps.

Beneath her gentleness lies a sharp edge with a

dangerous charm. She's the kind of woman who can lure men in and kill them in equal strides. A perfect balance of power and beauty. "You're either a naive, foolish girl or playing dumb to hide the truth from us."

"Enough, Sylara," Nyx says.

"We're doomed if she's the one who's destined to save us all," Sylara continues.

All of their dark black eyes lock in on me as if they can discover my truth just by looking at me.

"Lumi? You okay? Your fear?" Ambrose says in my head.

I'm done being afraid.

Done being naive and foolish.

"You should have told me the truth. You should have told me everything," I let the pain lace my voice.

"I'm sorry."

"What do I need to know about Nyx? About his pack? His vampires?"

"Don't trust a word he says."

"You're vampires. Don't lie to me and call me naive in the same breath."

Sylara's jet black eyes drill into me with a glare that could kill. "We're not vampires. And I don't lie. I know who stands before me, and I don't mince my words."

"Then what are you?"

Sylara looks to Nyx, waiting to see if he wants to answer.

"I'm the only one who is half-vampire, half-wolf shifter. Just like Ambrose is the only half-witch, half-wolf shifter," he tells me.

I stare around the room at Sylara and then at the three men who have yet to speak. I hope to the gods that by just looking at them, I'll be able to tell if Nyx is telling the truth or not.

"I don't believe you. I don't trust a word you say. How do I know that you aren't lying to me so that I won't suspect when your friends here have vampire abilities as well as wolf shifter ones?"

"You believed him," his voice lashes in my head in a cold and unyielding frost, in sharp contrast to Ambrose's, which feels like an earthy, warm embrace.

I glare at Nyx. "Stop talking in my head."

Sylara raises an eyebrow at him, shocked that he can talk in my head. The other men exchange glances.

"You shouldn't trust me. You shouldn't trust anyone. You shouldn't trust any facts that you haven't verified with your own eyes. The world has been hidden from you your entire life. Now you've had a few glimpses of it, but it's not enough. You have to find the truth. Don't trust me. Don't trust Ambrose. Don't trust anyone," Nyx sneers.

"Does it matter if we have vampire abilities or wolf shifter abilities? I could kill you easily either way," Sylara says.

My blood boils at her words, but her sculpted form tells me she could kick my ass without any otherworldly powers. Not to mention it's five against one. I turn inward, once again begging my wolf to make an appearance. Not that she would save me when it's five against one, but I just need to know she's still there.

Sylara shakes her head at me in disgust.

"Why can't I shift?" I send to Ambrose, my words desperate.

"What do you mean you can't shift?"

"I can't shift."

There's a pause. *"Fuck."*

"So what now? You kill me to ensure a new mate is found for Ambrose or Nyx?" I ask the group.

"If only," Sylara says.

"I really don't like you," I tell her.

An irritating smile spreads across her face, and she folds those honed, muscular arms across her chest. "The feeling is mutual."

"As I said before, we aren't going to kill you. I need the information you have," Nyx says.

"You're just going to hold me prisoner," I snap at him.

Sylara glares at me. "You really don't know Nyx at all, do you?"

"Sylara," Nyx warns, and she closes her mouth with a huff.

"Where are my manners?" Nyx changes his tone and claps his hands together. "I should introduce you to the Bloodmoon pack. This is Sylara, my beta."

Sylara barely acknowledges me.

"That's Riven, Brax, and Talonis," Nyx points to each man as he speaks their name, and they all silently stare at me. Each has a shade of dark brown or black hair, with equally inky eyes. The entire pack must share similar traits.

Riven stands, each fluid motion of his muscles exuding power and strength as he walks toward me with clear intention. The air intensifies between us in sharp crispness. I'm not sure what's going to happen until he holds out his hand to me. I gape at it like it's about to transform into claws at any second.

"I know you grew up isolated in a small pack, but you do know what a handshake is, right?" Riven asks with a knowing smile.

I frown. "I don't shake hands with vampires."

"Good thing I'm not a vampire."

"Or of people holding me hostage and trying to kill me."

Riven shoots Nyx a knowing glance before turning back to me.

"Maybe there's hope for you after all," he says before returning to his seat.

I look across at the other two guys. Both are studying me with a curious fascination on their faces. Brax is the largest of the three men. Stockily built with a physical weight large enough that I doubt he'd need to shift to take on another wolf shifter. He looks like he's built for the battlefield. Talonis's muscles are small in comparison, but no less intimidating.

"Where am I?" I ask, hoping someone will answer me.

"With the Bloodmoon pack," Sylara answers with exasperation in her voice as if she's already annoyed with me.

I look from her to Nyx, who is awfully quiet as he watches me, seeming to weigh each of my movements and thoughts.

"And where is that exactly?" I demand.

"Does it matter? You can't escape back to your mate, as you call him, no matter where you are," she responds.

"If it doesn't matter, then just tell me. Are we still in the state of Washington? Oregon? Canada?"

"Your mate will come for you no matter where you are. Though why you'd want him to after he lied to you and obviously failed to prepare you for breaking the curse is beyond me," Sylara says before standing up abruptly. Her head snaps to Nyx. "I'm done with this. Let me know when you make a decision regarding our earlier conversation."

Nyx nods as Sylara leaves.

"Don't mind Sylara too much. She's like that with everyone," Brax says, running his hand over his buzzed head.

"So why is she the beta then?" I ask.

"She's the strongest besides Nyx," Brax says.

"The most cunning," Talonis says.

"And Nyx, as well as the rest of us, is a bit afraid of her," Riven chuckles, the braid in his thick curls swinging as he moves his head.

All eyes turn to Nyx. "She's the obvious number two. My reasons for choosing her as such are abundant. But that's not what we are here to discuss."

"I'm not telling you anything. You'll have to torture it out of me or use the mind control you vampires love so much."

The guys exchange glances. "Maybe we should leave the two of you alone for a bit," Riven says. The other two nod, and suddenly it's just me and Nyx in the living room.

"He lied to you," Nyx says gently.

"It doesn't change anything." *It changes everything.* I know that, but I don't know what to do about it.

"He lied to you. He didn't tell you he is part witch. He didn't tell you I'm part vampire. He didn't tell you the truth about our history. He didn't tell you everything he knows about the prophecy. He didn't tell you why you can't shift now."

"Stop."

"*Why didn't you tell me you were part witch?*" I shoot through my bridge to Ambrose.

Maybe if he explains himself, it will make it all better. There has to be a good reason, something that can make Nyx's words sting less.

"I'm sorry," the words float back to me, but they aren't enough.

"Why?"

"I want to explain...in person."

"You don't have to like me. We can still be enemies, but when it comes to breaking the curse, you should realize that we are on the same side. We both want the same thing. So whatever it takes to get us to work together to put the pieces of the prophecy together is what we should be focusing on."

"Then you'd better find me fast."

"I will. I'm already looking."

"Tell me what you can."

"I should talk to you as little as possible until the curse is broken."

"Why?"

"So that I don't let my feelings end up being the death of you."

Oh, right—the whole if you fall in love with me, you kill me part of his curse.

"That would take trust, and I don't trust you. You're holding me hostage," I return my attention to Nyx, watching as he spreads his legs casually on the couch despite the formidable weapon he is.

"Am I? I didn't realize that was what I'm doing. I thought I was saving your life and trying to help you break the curse."

"I don't believe you."

"Then what would it take for you to believe me?"

"I don't know."

Nyx's lips dip as he watches me, but he does not move an inch toward me. He seems to know I need the distance between us to continue the conversation.

"I'm scared," I send to Ambrose as I watch the predator in front of me, waiting to see if he'll kill me at any moment.

"We all are," Nyx responds.

Fuck, did I send my thought to Nyx instead of Ambrose? Does he know I've been talking to Ambrose this whole time? Has he listened to our entire conversation?

"But you should trust me when I say all I want, all any of us want, is to break the curse. I know Ambrose suffers from a curse that just affects the witches, although I don't know his individual curse. However, I suffer from one that specifically affects vampires. And my curse is far worse than anything Ambrose has ever suffered. That's why you should trust me when I say I'll do anything to break the curse."

CHAPTER 4

NYX

sk me. Ask me about my curse. Ask me anything.

Lumi doesn't. She's still standing in the same spot she's been standing since she entered my living room in a pair of oversized grey sweatpants and a sweatshirt that might as well be a dress on her. I wasn't sure what clothes she would pick when I scrounged up clothes from what I could find that the others had left lying around my house. But she somehow managed to find the only pair of clothes that belonged to me. And she's wearing them like a shield.

As she stands, her shoulders cave inward, and her eyes are sunken from exhaustion. Without even dipping into her head, I can sense how broken and fragile she is. Whatever Ambrose did to her, I want to kill him for that alone.

But I can't worry about that right now. I have to find a way to get through the shattered glass that she's barely holding together. I need to find a way to earn her trust enough to work with me. To understand why I can communicate with her in her mind the way Ambrose can.

To figure out who her mate really is and how she can break the curse.

Ask me.

She doesn't.

I run my hand through my long tendrils, brushing them out of my eyes, my frigid body coiling under my own touch. My body still feels foreign to me even after all this time. It always will.

I stand, careful to walk through the shadows and not where the sunlight shines through my windows toward her. To her credit, she doesn't cower away from me when I approach her.

"Want to go for a run with me?" I ask.

"A run?"

"Yeah, a run."

"Um…I guess."

She didn't immediately turn me down. *That's good. Progress.*

"Let's go, then." I lead her out of my house, careful to walk along the shadows. She walks like a zombie on autopilot, just going through the motions. I doubt she even knows what she just agreed to. We keep walking until we get to the thickest part of the forest near my house. The trees are so thick here that almost no sunlight can get through.

Even so, I prefer to be in my wolf form during the day. It's the only way I can enjoy the sunlight. When I'm in my human form, my vampire side takes over, and the sunlight refuses to allow me into it. If I accidentally step into the light, the sun overpowers me, weakening me with unthinkable pain until I step out.

I transform into my towering midnight-black wolf with striking red eyes—the mark of a Bloodmoon wolf. I turn my head, expecting to see Lumi's majestic white wolf streaked with the golden markings of the Moonlight pack.

Crystal blue eyes blink back at me as she stands frozen in her sweatsuit.

"You going to shift?"

"No," she says aloud.

"Why not? I heard that a healer told you not to shift when you were healing, but that's stupid. Your wolf can heal you; it won't hurt you. It would strengthen you to transform into your wolf. Might even help you with your grief."

She glares at me. "No."

I'm rooted to my spot, uncertainty clawing at me as I have no clue how to help her. I barely know this woman. I don't know what she's been through. So, I do something that is becoming increasingly natural the more time I spend with her—I reach out through our bond.

If she senses me in her head, she doesn't react. I'm not sure if she even realizes the bond is more than just a way to communicate telepathically with each other. It can also be used to read each other's emotions, to send each other feelings, messages, and probably more. I suspect I've barely scratched the surface of what our bond can do.

As soon as I'm in her head, I want to pull away. White-hot, brutal, relentless pain gnaws at me like a dull blade through flesh. The pain is endless in its vastness. The longer I spend in her head, the more likely it is to engulf me, too.

There's also a throbbing ache consuming her from the inside out.

For Rowena.

At Ambrose.

At me.

And at her wolf.

Her wolf?

Why is she mad at her wolf?

I force myself to push past the pain and anger that's threatening to burn me alive. With each push, I want to retreat to the safety of my ice-cold body. But I have to know. I have to find her wolf. Talk to her. Understand her.

Nothing—I find nothing.

I pull out suddenly, realizing exactly why she won't shift. She *can't* shift.

That fucking bastard.

I want to tell her why she can't shift. I want to tell her everything. But she doesn't trust me. She wouldn't believe me. And it wouldn't help for me to be the one to tell her.

So I shift back into my human form, feeling the heat of her eyes over my naked body as I do. Hungrily, she peruses me up and down, unable to get enough of the sight of me.

I'm used to others looking. Despite it being a daily occurrence in pack life, other shifters still appreciate my naked form. Their eyes heat over my body unapologetically, but it's nothing like what I feel when she does it.

"Like what you see?" I can't help but quip before realizing it's not going to win me any awards with her.

She rolls her eyes. "Put some clothes on."

But maybe it's exactly what she needs to bring her out of her pain.

"Nah, I think I'll stay like this. Enjoy the cool breeze on my skin."

Her eyes narrow into bullets. "You wouldn't dare. Vampires can't walk in the sunlight."

"No, but it's one of the reasons I picked this area of

the forest. The trees are thickest here, and besides, the gods decided to bless us with a cloudy day. Doesn't seem like I need to shift into my wolf after all."

"In your wolf form, you can walk in the sunlight?"

I smirk, happy that she's asking questions. "Yes."

Ask more.

She doesn't.

"You could still put some damn clothes on."

"I could, but why would I when it irritates you so much? Afraid you're going to like what you see too much and betray Ambrose?"

"I'll never betray him."

"Because he's your mate?"

"Because I love him." *There it is—the truth.*

My stomach sours. Not because I want her or truly think she's my mate. I think the gods are playing games with us. Lumi is nothing more than a way to break the curse to me. But because I can't imagine anyone loving Ambrose.

"Well, then, my being naked won't be a problem, then."

She huffs. "Wolf shifters."

My smile broadens.

"What?" she asks.

"You called me a wolf shifter, not a vampire." I start walking, and she follows in step next to me.

"Whatever, you're still an asshole either way." Her eyes turn to the small village nestled among the trees. When I turned vampire, we found the castle I now call home nestled in the trees, but the rest we built home by home. Each is as unique as the next.

"You could join the Bloodmoon pack if he ends up not being your mate."

Her head snaps in my direction, and she rubs her hands over her arms as if she got a chill at that thought. "Never. I barely survived Moonlight's initiation. I would never survive yours."

I narrow my eyes at her, trying to read her, and I once again am pushing into her mind. But whether she realizes it or not, she's blocked me out. There's a solid door up where I can usually just stroll right through her mind.

"What was Moonlight's initiation?"

"Not as bad as yours."

"I doubt that, since ours is a simple vow after you've been granted the alpha's permission. And since I'm the alpha, you already have permission. So a simple, yes to the question of if you'd like to join the Bloodmoon pack and be loyal to us is all it would require."

Her eyes widen at me as she stops in her tracks, staring at me like she's never seen me before. She's not gaping at my naked body. Just peering into my jet-black eyes.

I open my mind, hoping she'll probe to find the truth like I did with her, but she doesn't. She probably doesn't realize she can do it yet.

"I'm telling the truth. I don't like to lie."

"No, you just kill innocent people and send your vampire friends to torture me."

I wince at the pain in her words.

She starts walking again, her gaze fixed on the empty houses as we walk. The pack went hunting this morning.

"Visit a seer with me."

"No," she says.

"We have to know how to break the curse. It's the only way you get rid of me."

"No, a stake through the heart gets rid of you. And the

only ones who need to know how to break the curse are me and Ambrose."

"Did you tell him?"

"What?" She snaps as she stops.

"Did you tell him everything you know about the prophecy?"

"I told him everything I was told by a seer. The rest is just dreams."

I raise my eyebrows. *Now we're getting somewhere.* "You've had dreams about the prophecy?"

"I'm not telling you anything."

I sigh. "What is Ambrose's curse?"

Her face pales. "I'm never telling you that."

"That bad, huh? If I knew, could I destroy him?"

She growls. "I'll never let you hurt him."

I scoff. "Your frail, human body couldn't stop me."

"I could."

"Fine, don't answer me. I know he has a personal curse, just like all the witches. And I know each Moonlight pack member has their own curse as a result of their alpha being a witch. Don't you want to know what the vampires' curse is? What mine is?"

"No, I hope whatever it is is very, very..." she stops as if something has interrupted her thought.

"Very, very?"

She shakes her head as if she can focus again. "Painful."

"You have to ask if you want to know."

But Lumi isn't listening to me. Her mind is elsewhere occupied, which could only mean one thing—Ambrose is communicating with her in her mind.

I test the waters, gently pushing against her mind, but I'm locked out.

They are talking.

Which means he's close by. I don't think the bond has limitless abilities to communicate from any distance.

"We should head back," I say, turning toward the castle.

She nods, reluctantly.

We walk back in silence until we reach my home. When we reach the grounds, I turn toward the woods.

"What are you doing?" she asks.

"Going hunting with the rest of the pack in the north woods. I trust you can find a way to occupy your time while I'm away."

"You're not going to lock me up?"

"No." And before she can question me further, I shift, running into the woods toward my pack. I don't stop until I reach Sylara, and then I shift back into my human form.

She shifts into her human form next to me.

"Where is Lumi?" she asks, staring behind me like she expects her to come running up behind me.

"She's going after Ambrose."

"What? Are you crazy? You're just going to let her escape with him?"

I'm not sure if Lumi is my mate. In fact, I'm pretty sure we're not. The only reason I can communicate with her in her mind is that we need to find a way to break the curse first. We are missing a giant piece of the puzzle that only we can discover together.

Ambrose is her mate.

There is only one thing I'm more sure of than the fact that I'm not her mate. "She'll come back."

CHAPTER 5

LUMI

I'm alone.

Nyx just left, without locking me in a room or using his mind control to tell me to stay.

I could go anywhere, do anything.

It's a trap. It has to be a trap. But at the moment, I don't care.

Ambrose.

I have to get to Ambrose.

"I'm coming," I say to Ambrose, making a split-second decision.

"Run east. I'll find you," he says back.

I turn in the opposite direction that Nyx and the rest of the pack went and start running. The sweatpants and sweatshirt I'm wearing sag as I run, barely clinging to my body. My breath clouds in front of me as I run in the chilly air. But all I can think about is Ambrose. I have to get to him. Just keep running. Everything will be okay if I can reach him.

The world narrows as I run, my heart clinging to the hope of him. Of finding him. Of being with him. A restless

39

energy dances through my veins with every step I take closer. Wild butterflies dance in my belly, unsure of how I'm going to feel when I finally reach him, yet also fearing that Nyx is going to come for me again before I can reach Ambrose.

Suddenly, hands reach out, wrapping around my forearm, snatching me mid-stride.

I scream, but it's muffled as I'm pulled into a man's shoulder. I bury my nose in his shoulder and take a deep breath—evergreens.

Ambrose.

My arms slip around him, and I fold into his body, as his arms cling onto me with a desperation that says he'll never let go again. Home—his body feels like home.

"You're safe. I've got you," Ambrose says into my head like a gentle caress as his lips kiss the top of my head.

I close my eyes, letting his words infiltrate me—*I'm safe.* For a moment, I let myself believe it. But I want to be more than safe. I angle my head up and press a hungry kiss against his lips. A piece of my soul heals the second our lips touch. He'd been holding onto it the whole time we were separated, and returned it to me when our lips brushed together.

I want more, so much more from him. I want to surrender to the kiss and let myself forget everything. The rise of heat flames in my belly, and I know how easy it would be to do just that. To forget. To ignore. To return to the fantasy world I was living in before.

As much as my heart could do it so easily, my brain won't let it be tricked again.

He's a witch.

He lied to you.

My eyes fly open, and I break the seal between us. "You're a witch."

His body tenses around me, but he doesn't let me go. *"I am."*

I frown as I push out of his arms.

He reluctantly lets me go, and I get a better look at him. Dark circles have formed under his eyes, and there's a heaviness to his body that I've never seen before. Like, for once, being an alpha weighs on him. But damn, is he as beautiful as ever. The gold in his eyes and hair shines as brightly as ever.

"Why didn't you tell me?"

"Because—"

"No, not in my head. I need to hear the words out loud."

He frowns. *"I don't want Nyx or anyone else to hear."*

I shake my head. "I need to hear the words."

He sighs and then nods. "At first, it was because I couldn't trust you with a secret that big. Other packs wouldn't trust me if they knew what I was."

"Just like they don't trust Nyx because of what he is."

He nods.

"But why didn't you eventually tell me? After everything we've been through?"

"Because I couldn't. When I became a witch, the pack made me vow to keep it a secret from anyone who wasn't initiated into the pack. I couldn't tell you. I wanted to so many times, but I couldn't."

"But I initiated. I became part of the Moonlight pack." The memories of that night swirl in a tornado of darkness threatening to overtake this conversation and feelings if I let them. But I slam that mental door quickly, refusing to let them in.

He takes my hand in his and gently kisses my palm. "I planned on telling you the second you were initiated, but then I was afraid. I'm afraid of sharing something so vulnerable with you. I'm worried you might not want me. But mostly, I'm scared that you'll accept me for who I am, and that would cause me to fall in love with you. I couldn't let myself love you. I refused to let my curse kill you."

I suck in a breath. *His damned curse.* The one only he and I know. The one that Nyx seems desperate to find out. The secret I will guard with my life. Because the curse could kill me if he doesn't keep his feelings for me in check at all times.

"I'm sorry. I'm sorry for everything. I'm sorry that I didn't tell you. I'm sorry that I failed to protect you against Nyx. I'm sorry that you had to find out from him. I'm so fucking sorry, my queen."

My eyes water when I hear how authentic his words are. I can feel the pain with every word. And as he stares back at me, I know he's one step away from loving me with everything in his being. We're walking a fine line, and possibly the only thing keeping me breathing right now is that he hasn't said the words out loud.

He's terrified. I should be, too, but seeing him and knowing he's my mate—knowing we are destined to break the curse makes me feel the complete opposite.

"I forgive you."

"Don't—don't do that." He looks away, like it pains him that I forgave him so quickly.

I caress the side of his face, turning him back to look at me before I gently kiss the corner of his lip. I don't say anything else. There is nothing else to say.

"How is the pack? How is Emeric? Kael?"

"They're safe. Although everyone will feel better once you are back home."

My heart does a little flip when he says that. He still wants me, still considers his home my home.

"And Rowena? Is she really...?" I can't finish the words.

"Yes." He blinks back tears. "She's gone. I did everything I could. Tried every healer I could, but she was already gone before they started working. Their powers are immense, but they can't bring people back from the dead. I'm sorry, just another way I failed you and the pack."

"You didn't fail me or her. It wasn't your fault. You didn't know that Nyx was going to kill her."

"But I should have. I should have protected her. I should have known that he would have pulled something like this and not let him at the ceremony."

Tears run down my cheeks in quiet surrender as my grief etches itself deep into my soul.

"You're really okay? Nyx didn't hurt you?" Ambrose's voice trembles a little as he speaks.

"Nyx didn't touch me," I say firmly through the tears before I wipe them away, needing Ambrose to know that he didn't fail to protect me. None of this was his fault.

His eyes trace over me in a frantic search, cataloging every detail of my body as if he's going to find some sign of an injury on me that he missed when suddenly his ears perk up.

"We need to go. It's not safe here," he says, slipping back into my head like it's his home.

My ears perk up as I try to catch whatever sound caused Ambrose to change the subject so abruptly. But my hearing and senses are nothing compared to his, so I hear nothing out of the ordinary. But I trust Ambrose's hearing. *"Let's go."*

"Head east, follow my scent. Even if you aren't in your wolf state, you'll be able to smell the path I've created for you. Emeric is waiting a couple of miles from here. He'll help you get back to the pack."

I narrow my eyes, trying to make sense of the words flowing in my head. *"What are you talking about? We are going back together."*

He shakes his head. *"No, we're not. I have to face Nyx. I have to kill him. He took what was mine. He threatened you. He could have hurt you. He could have..."* His teeth sink down into his bottom lip until blood spills out, running down his jawline. I see the shift even though no physical traits have changed. Heat rolls off his body and warms me without even touching him. Muscles have gone rigid, and his eyes have glazed over with his thoughts of vengeance.

He's going to kill Nyx.

Yes.

No.

I want to kill Nyx.

We could kill Nyx together.

But I can't shift.

And Nyx is a vampire. Possibly his entire pack is, even though he claims they aren't. He can't be trusted.

I'm useless to Ambrose. It would be nothing more than a distraction if I went with him. But I can't bear to leave him. I know their history. I know how badly Ambrose wants to kill Nyx. But Nyx is a vampire—a fucking vampire.

And Ambrose is a witch.

I don't know who wins in a fight. But Nyx will have backup. Ambrose won't.

I can't lose him.

There's also a weird flick of intuition growing in my chest, warning me that we can't kill Nyx. We may really need him to end the curse.

My mind is swirling, but all I see is the blood and his pain. I have to stop it. I have to stop him from hurting. I can't stop the anger. I can't stop the pain of losing Rowena. I can't stop anything else, but I can stop him from feeling this pain.

I cup his face with my hands, wiping the blood from his chin with my thumb. He freezes at my touch, barely breathing anymore as the heat of his body almost burns through me. Our eyes lock, but we don't speak as his teeth somehow sink deeper into his lip.

I move my thumb up, brushing gently over the lip he's biting.

He shivers under my touch, but doesn't stop looking at me like he's waiting for something.

A lump forms in my throat because I know what he's waiting for—a sign that I forgive him. That I still want him. Still choose him as my mate.

I shake my head ever so gently in disbelief that he would ever think that anything could tear me away from him.

He lied, but then again, so did I. I'm still lying about what pack I belonged to before I met him. We're still hiding so many truths from each other. That doesn't change my heart; maybe it should. Maybe I'm a fool for still loving him, but I'm a fool in love.

I raise myself on the tiptoes of my bare feet and tenderly kiss that lip that he's so brutally biting. The metallic taste of his blood floods my mouth, but I don't stop. I sweep my tongue across the broken seam until he finally releases his grip on his lip and surrenders it to me.

I grin as I suck that lip brutally into my mouth, running my tongue across his wound as if my saliva can heal him.

He whimpers in submission. *"I would do anything for you, my queen."*

I suck again, pulling a painful groan out of him. And suddenly, this man—this alpha is on his knees before me. I barely have to crane my neck down to keep the kiss going with how large he is. But I'm still in shock to see him practically bowing in front of me. He truly sees me as his queen.

"I'll kill for you. Die for you. Spend the rest of my life groveling at your feet for all the mistakes I've made."

Gods, he's so close. So close to fucking loving me. So close to letting the words slip out, killing me, and dooming us all.

And yet, I trust him completely, even though he lied. He'll do anything to protect me. There is no way he's going to let his witch curse cause me to die. He'll stop himself short of actually loving me. I don't know how he's doing it—magic, maybe. There is so much I don't know about him being a witch.

He's a witch—a thrill shoots through my body. I want to know what that means. What he's capable of. What it would feel like for him to unleash himself on me. The word doesn't terrify me if it's attached to him.

I kiss him again, knowing that we need to get going. We need to be running, not making out in the forest. Nyx could discover us at any second. But each time I kiss him, the intensity grows until I'm barely clinging to control. My primal instincts take over. He's my mate, and after everything we've been through, I need him more than I need to breathe. I need this moment with him. I need him to feel alive. I need him.

Fuck me, show me who you really are.

Ambrose's eyes widen into large golden orbs. I must have actually sent my desires to him. *Oops.*

I grin, catching his lip between my teeth.

"You're the devil," he says seductively in my head.

My chest rises and falls hard with each breath as the anticipation rises. And then the bastard winks at me, and I'm putty in his hands.

Power shoots out in every direction, almost knocking me on my ass as it pushes through me. But Ambrose grabs onto my hips, holding me steady as darkness descends all around us.

I gasp, unsure what the hell just happened. My fingers cling to the soft fabric of his shirt.

"Open your eyes, my queen."

I shudder, not even realizing that I had closed them. But I obey, opening my eyes to see the sky has descended into night, lit by thousands of stars and a full moon. It's incredible, but it shouldn't be dark. It's mid-morning at best, not nightfall.

"How?"

"Me."

I blink my eyes wider, not believing he or anyone is capable of such magic.

"It's a shield to protect us. Like a bubble surrounding us. No one will be able to find us while we're here."

"The blackness? The moon?"

"A natural part of my magic since I'm the alpha of the Moonlight pack. It's the easiest form for my magic to take —moonlight."

"It's beautiful." I look at him again. "You're beautiful."

"Afraid of me yet?"

"No."

He smiles, but it's not a full smile I'm used to from him. He's hiding all his pain from me, but then in a blink, it's gone as if I imagined it. "That's right, you're not afraid of anything."

I frown. "I'm afraid of a lot of things. But never you."

He sighs. "Then maybe I'm not doing it right."

In a blink, absolute darkness surrounds us. The moon and stars blink out, and I can't see the hand in front of my face, let alone Ambrose.

I shiver, knowing he's near. I can still feel his warmth, and the magic he's using caresses me like a warm blanket, even though my heart begins to thunder in my chest. "I'm not afraid of you, Ambrose. You're my mate. My equal. My love—"

His lips crash down on mine like I knew they would the second my mind started to mention the word love. I grin, finally getting what I want—all of him.

He growls. "You're naughty for taunting me."

"And you're cruel for holding back on me."

I still can't see him. It's like a blindfold has been pulled down over my eyes, but I don't beg him to let me see. I trust him. He has my life in his hands. He could kill me with his hands or his heart. A bite of his teeth or his words. Either way, my life is completely his to decide.

He angles my head to kiss me this time, his tongue sinking deep into my mouth until I'm about to combust from the kiss. I need, need, need...I'll probably die from lack of coming at this point. Or maybe my impending orgasm will be what kills me. But my death will come because of this man. Now or in a hundred years, it doesn't matter. And I'd willingly sacrifice it for him again and again for one more night with him.

I shiver as I feel his sharp nails scrape down my back. His fingers are now claws, but as I feel no fur beneath my hands, I know he hasn't fully shifted, just enough to let his wolf play with me. The nails travel back up my back and then over my shoulder before sinking into my thick sweatshirt.

I hold my breath in anticipation.

"This smells like *him*," he growls before shredding the front with a simple swipe of his claws.

My skin bears itself to the cool air. I wasn't wearing anything under the sweatshirt, and my nipples pebble.

"Fuck, I'm so sorry I let him take you. His scent is all over you. He—"

"He didn't touch me. These are just his clothes. He didn't touch me. You didn't fail me."

"I'll never forgive myself either way." Another swipe of his claw, and the sweatpants I'm wearing fall to a heap at my feet. I'm naked. But it's so dark that I doubt even his sharp wolf eyes can make out my body.

"I could stare at you all day."

I blush. "You can't even see me."

"Look down."

I do, and then gasp. My body is glowing. The runes that were marked into my upper body during the Moonlight initiation are glowing brightly as if highlighting every curve of my body.

"Not fair," I say when I can't see him.

"Hmm, who said anything about fair?" I nearly jump out of my skin as he plants a tender kiss on my bare shoulder from behind me. I don't know when he moved, but when he pulls me back against his body, I can tell that he's naked too.

I run my hand up and down his thigh. "I want to see you, too."

"Do you?"

"Yes," I breathe.

"But I'm enjoying teasing you so much." A crisp breeze runs over the front of my body. An unnatural wind that starts at my toes, curls around my cunt almost like a hand would, before swirling over my nipples in a teasing motion until their peaks are hard and stiff.

It takes me a second to register what just happened. "That was you?"

"Yes, my queen."

My head falls back against his shoulder as the wind runs over my body again. If my brain could process anything, I might realize how immense his magic is, but all I can think about is how incredible it feels. How incredible he is.

Golden light draws my attention forward as a crescent moon takes shape as if being drawn by hand in the air. The light begins to dance outward in intricate runes, illuminating the muscular man beneath the design as it slowly lights up all of his features through the darkness.

I gasp at the sight of him, almost losing my balance and falling backward, but a gust of wind pushes me upright in a warm embrace.

I raise an eyebrow as my lips curl up. "Now you're just showing off."

He grins back. "Is it working?"

I lick my lips, my eyes running up on down the hardened body in front of me. "Yes."

My chest rises and falls as his darkened eyes fall to my

chest. We both are silent for a moment, just staring in the darkness that Ambrose created for us. We are in our own little world. Nothing exists here but the two of us. No curses or vampires or pack problems. No worries of danger lurking nearby. No tragedies to mourn. Nothing but us.

"I need this," I send to him. *"Please."*

"I need this to last forever."

I suck in a breath. I need that too, but that seems impossible. It seems like a fantasy that neither of us will live long enough to experience. We may be mates, but we're fated to break a curse. And we've yet to realize the consequences of breaking it.

He steps toward me as the wind he created swirls around my body, heating me to my core. I close my eyes as a hand reaches out, stroking my cheek. I don't know if it's his actual hand or the wind that touches me, but it doesn't matter. It's all him. All intense. All I want.

"I could stare at you all day. The runes on your body mark you as a Moonlight pack member, as *mine*," he growls out that last word.

I shiver as his hand runs down the curves of my body, and then I'm pulled into a deep kiss. Our bodies press together as we both put everything into the kiss. His tongue sweeps through the seam of my lips, and I open wider, letting him in deeper. His large hands grab onto my hips, pulling me against him until I can feel his thick cock, desperate to enter me.

I grab onto his hair, refusing to let him go, no matter what. I won't let the outside world in. I won't let the intrusive thoughts win. There is no stopping this moment. The world could be burning all around us, and it wouldn't matter. I need my mate. I need Ambrose. I need to love him and let him love me in the only way we can until the curse is broken.

I moan around his lips as his hand sinks between our bodies, rubbing over my sensitive bud.

"I can't believe you're mine."

A zip of electricity dances around my back, electrifying the very air around us. For a moment, it makes me jump until I remember it's Ambrose. It's his magic doing this. Suddenly, I'm falling onto my back. I cringe at the thought of how hard the ground will feel and how heavy Ambrose's weight will be on top of me. But a cloud of softness greets my back, and Ambrose's full weight never hits me despite his body being on top of mine.

"Open your eyes, my beautiful queen."

I do, and my mouth falls open in awe. A thousand fireflies are dancing around us as we lie on a bed he produced out of thin air.

"You're incredible, my mate."

He smirks knowingly. "I can't wait to show you all of me. Everything I can be. I don't want to hold back anymore."

"Then don't."

He sucks in a sharp breath, and then I remember his curse. He can't love me; if he does, he'll kill me. So no matter what, he won't be able to fully be himself. He can't let go fully, not until we break the curse. Soon—soon he'll be able to, and that's enough for me. For now, I get to have him. His body and power.

"No more hiding," I say.

"No more hiding," he agrees and then lowers his mouth to mine.

I squirm underneath him as his kiss deepens, awakening all of my primal urges. Gravity pulls me to him with an unrelenting burn. I'd probably kill countless innocents just to be with this man; that's how desperate I am for him in this moment. It's like the mating bond controls me. There is nothing I wouldn't do for him. That should scare me, but it doesn't.

"There is nothing I wouldn't do for you," I whisper.

His eyes sear into mine. "I'll ask no such thing of you. *Ever.* Just being with me is enough."

His cock slides through my wetness in one swift motion, at the same time his tongue presses deep into my mouth, and his magic swirls around us, pressing against every nerve ending on my body. It's too much and not enough at the same time. It's overwhelming in the best way possible.

And then we both open our eyes, staring at each other with all of his magic surrounding us. I grip onto his muscular back until I'm sure my nails must be drawing blood. But he doesn't pull away.

"Gods, you feel incredible," he says through a pained whisper.

"Fuck me."

He rolls his hips, hitting deep inside me as I arch my back up, letting my own hips match his thrusts. I try to hold onto this memory. Try to cling to it like this is my life now, fucking my mate in a magic dome he built just for us, but I know even in my magic bubble that this moment is fleeting. Soon it will be a memory I have to hold onto to get me through everything else.

It just makes me grip onto him harder. I hold my breath, trying to keep my orgasm from coming. From letting this moment end too soon. But Ambrose doesn't need magic to build me. He doesn't need any special powers to bring me to the edge, just him. His body is more than enough.

He strokes my hair so tenderly as he thrusts deep and hard into my body. The combination undoes me. My teeth clamp down onto his shoulder, but it doesn't stop me from screaming his name as an earth-shattering orgasm rips through my body.

Ambrose doesn't stop thrusting. He picks up speed, fucking me harder as my orgasm rolls through me, continuing in one long, powerful spark as if I can create my own magic. I combust over and over, not even realizing that he pumped his seed deep inside me, that he slowed and collapsed on top of me. He had stopped fucking me for a while now, but we both just lay on the magical bed he created in a dark bubble protecting us from the outside world.

The fireflies' light has gone out, and nothing but darkness surrounds us. I can feel Ambrose's heavy breath on my neck, but neither of us speaks. We don't need to after what just happened, and as soon as we speak, we know we'll leave this bubble both literally and figuratively. The magic that happened here will soon be nothing but a distant memory.

So neither of us speaks. We both want this moment to last forever. Speaking would ruin everything.

I love him.

I want to say the words out loud to him even if he can't reciprocate. I want him to know this because I'm uncertain about our future and the dangers we'll face. I might never have the chance to say those words to him again.

I forgive him. I forgive him for everything. Hiding that

he was a witch from me was nothing. A small fib that doesn't matter.

I should tell him my own truth. That I grew up in the Wintermoon pack. That my pack caused the curse, which is why I'm destined to be the one to break it.

But I know it won't matter to him. Not anymore, not after everything we've been through.

I love you—the words almost leave my lips, but then I pull them back. Maybe I can tell him in his head. Just whisper them through our mental bond so that he has to second-guess if he even heard them at all. But I will have said the words I needed to say.

I'm still fighting with myself, though, when Nyx breaks the silence.

"You're very loud when you come, love."

CHAPTER 6

LUMI

I shake my head back and forth as if that will somehow knock Nyx from my head. His words in my head are the worst kind of invasion. I want him out—now. But I don't know how to push him out. Even though he stopped speaking, I still feel his presence creeping around in my mind, leaving a chilling metallic taste in my mouth.

Ambrose and I are still tangled up together. Nyx shouldn't be in my head right now. This can't be happening. This can't be real. It must be a nightmare I've imagined.

"Lumi? What's wrong?" Ambrose asks, but as soon as he asks it, I can tell his own senses have picked up on Nyx.

"Nyx," he hisses.

Nyx's cocky chuckle echoes through the bubble we've created.

My cheeks flush red with a mix of embarrassment and anger. We should have run instead of fucking in the middle of the woods. *What were we thinking?*

I look at Ambrose, who has his arms bound tightly

around me. We were doing the only thing we could do. We couldn't have left this spot without being bound together again as mates. We needed to trust each other again to face Nyx and whatever comes next. We didn't make a mistake.

"Get the fuck out of my head!" I scream to Nyx through our bond that makes zero sense to me.

"Why, when being in your head is so much more fun."

I growl.

Ambrose's head snaps to me. *"You okay?"*

"Yes," I hiss to him and Nyx.

"Hmm, you broke out of the aftershocks pretty quickly. Are you sure Ambrose is your mate? Give me twenty minutes and I'm pretty sure I could change your mind."

Anger boils to a breaking point, and I hurl all of my anger into his words, shoving them as hard as I can off a cliff in my mind. Until his presence is tumbling out of my head. For a moment, my head feels empty, and I know he's gone. I pushed him out.

"That was good, but you have to do better than that to keep me out," he says, slipping back in so easily, like a cockroach I can't get rid of.

"I need you to run, Lumi. I have to kill Nyx. And I need to know you're safe while I do it."

"I bet I could have you coming so loud that it would wake the entire forest. I know this trick with my tongue—"

"Get out!"

"Never," Nyx chuckles in a low, dangerous promise.

"What?" Ambrose says at the same time.

I grab my head, hating having both of them in my mind at the same time. The number of voices in my head makes me feel like it's about to explode. I have to figure out how to get Nyx out for good. There has to be a way to block him out.

"I'm not leaving you. Wherever you go, I go," I say to Ambrose out loud.

"No, I need you safe. I can't lose you," Ambrose says in my mind.

"And I can't lose you either, but I won't go. We need to face Nyx together."

"Don't speak out loud. He can hear you."

I frown. If I speak in my mind, he can probably hear me just as easily, since it's hard for me to send my words just to Ambrose and not Nyx, too.

I sigh, unsure of what to do next. I look around at the magic that Ambrose has created. I don't know much about witches' magic. I don't know how real this bubble is. *Is it more like a glamor that is masking us, or physical walls that Nyx can't penetrate?*

I still don't know why Nyx can speak in my mind like Ambrose can. *Is it because he's a vampire and has some abilities that he's not sharing? Is it something else?* It's not because we are also mates. I don't believe that for a second.

He killed Rowena.

He's the reason Ambrose and I didn't complete the marking ceremony. The reason we aren't mated together. The reason the curse still survives.

It's all him.

"I can't keep Nyx out of the bubble much longer. Please, run. Please, I can't bear to lose you."

I swallow hard, hating that I'm causing Ambrose any pain. But I can't leave.

"I can't lose you either," I whisper back.

Sweat coats his brows, and I can see now how much he's straining to hold his magic together. I'm unsure what Nyx is doing to break through the magic, and I don't know how Ambrose's magic works beyond its immense power. Whatever Nyx is doing to break Ambrose's magic terrifies me.

I look Ambrose in the eye as I say, "Let's kill him—together." I don't care if my words reach Nyx as well as Ambrose. He dies for what he did at both of our hands. Now that Ambrose is by my side, I know I'll be able to shift again.

The corner of his mouth twitches upward as he searches for words to convince me to leave him. To let him kill Nyx on his own. To keep me safe.

"My queen, please..."

"Queens don't run from danger. And they definitely don't leave their mates alone to fight their fights for them. We are doing this together."

"You're incredible." He takes my hand, giving me a warning look, and then the world shifts around us. Like a vacuum on full suction, pulling Ambrose's world away—the darkness, moonlight, and stars are ripped from us. His hands grip onto my waist as the bed vanishes into thin air. Suddenly, we're standing on the floor of the forest with the sun peeking through the thick branches down onto us.

Air rushes into my lungs in a sharp punch. I blink, slowly adjusting to the light. Ambrose's arms are still wrapped around me like a shield, while his jaw is clenched firmly shut. I should be preparing for the battle ahead, but I need another moment of being in awe of this man.

He's not just an alpha; he's a witch forged in an abundance of magic that radiates from him like moonlight in the sky. I barely even realized magic existed at all, and yet his is vast, almost boundless.

"Finally decided to stop hiding," Nyx says, drawing my attention away from Ambrose.

Nyx stands under the shade of a tree, leaning casually against it, as if he hadn't just interrupted a moment of intimacy between two mates and sparked a battle that will end in his death. His dark hair and eyes blend into the shadows in which he is hiding. Black molded clothes help him blend even more seamlessly into the shadows he prefers to hide in.

"You shouldn't have come, Nyx. There is nothing stopping me from killing you this time. Not after what you did. You killed a pack member. You kidnapped my mate. We're going to kill you and turn you into nothing but ash after I drive a stake through your heart."

"Are you?" Nyx says in a condescending tone.

"You know we are," I answer.

Nyx smirks, his eyebrows raising as his attention is drawn to me. His eyes run up and down my body, my body warming under his intense gaze. And it takes me a second to realize why he's staring at me so intently—I'm naked.

Ambrose ripped them up. Although Ambrose is shielding most of my body, Nyx still has an unobstructed view of the rest of it. Ambrose's instinct isn't to cover me. There is no shame in being naked around other shifters. But the way Nyx is drinking me in with an unrelenting, all-consuming gaze has me wishing I were fully clothed.

"Where are your vampire cronies?" Ambrose asks Nyx.

"I didn't want to involve them in something so trivial. They have more important things to do today than watch me destroy you," Nyx answers.

"You're the one about to be destroyed," Ambrose says.

Nyx just shakes his head in an unbothered way. He clearly doesn't think that we are capable of killing him. Probably because he doesn't realize how immense Ambrose's magic is, or that I know my wolf will be able to come out now that Ambrose is near. He gives her the confidence to come out. Together, we are unstoppable.

"Why did you come, Nyx? What do you want?" Ambrose asks.

Nyx's eyes cut to me. "To lay claim to what's *mine*. Lumi is my mate, not yours."

Before Nyx can even get all of his words out, Ambrose launches a bolt of magic from his hand, like a lightning bolt, and aims it at Nyx. But Nyx was anticipating the outburst. He ducks nanchaulantly, the bolt hits the tree behind him, setting a small branch aflame.

The next second, Ambrose leaps into the air, shifting into his glorious black fur with golden flecks of light that seem to sparkle under the sunlight. My eyes linger on him for far too long before my gaze cuts back to Nyx—he's vanished.

Where the hell did he go?

I spin, feeling completely bare and vulnerable. Ambrose lands on the empty spot that Nyx just occupied.

My ears perk up, my wolf eyesight cutting through the thick forest to look for the bastard. *Did he run?* I wouldn't put it past the coward to start a fight but not continue it. A pit in my stomach forms, though, when I hear the tiniest rustle of leaves behind me. I begin to spin, but an icy chill brushes up against my back.

"Hello, love. Or should I call you *my queen*? Did that show of his magic really impress you? I'm pretty sure your mate would make you scream louder when he makes you come, don't you?"

My fists are clenched, and I turn, swinging my arm like Emeric taught me. I make contact with his upper chest, but he doesn't budge. He doesn't even move an inch backward while my hand explodes in pain.

"You can call me Lumi," I snarl at him.

"If you're going to fight like a human, then someone should have shown you how to be effective against other-worldly creatures like myself," Nyx says.

"Still isn't going to stop me from killing you."

He chuckles. "So cocky, my naive snow wolf. Shift if you want to have a chance at killing me."

With a blink, he's shifted. Midnight fur and piercing red eyes stand before me in a monstrous frame. And then he winks at me a second before Ambrose's large wolf slams into him.

Growls are thrown back and forth between the two alphas as their claws swipe at each other's throats. I stand frozen as I watch the two fighting. Their wolves are so large, so fierce that I ultimately don't know who will win. As much as I hate to admit it, they are evenly matched. But Ambrose's witch powers have to be stronger than Nyx's vampire powers.

At the moment, I won't be finding out. Neither seems intent on using anything except their wolf abilities. The growls turn to snarls and howls, and yet, they both seem to understand what the other is saying in those snarls.

Suddenly, Nyx takes a bite of Ambrose's neck. I scream.

"Ambrose!" I cry out. *Please, gods, no...*

Nyx releases Ambrose, but there is no gash with blood

oozing. He didn't break Ambrose's skin with his teeth. He didn't drink his blood. He can't mind-control him.

For a second, I can breathe again.

Ambrose snaps his teeth in Nyx's direction before he pounces on him, knocking him to the ground beneath him, before he tears into Nyx's neck. A high-pitched yelp spills out of Nyx.

I grin, knowing it is a tiny piece of payback for what Nyx did to Rowena. But I'm tired of waiting on the sidelines. I want a piece of him, too. I want to hear him yelp and scream because of the pain I inflict on him. I want to have Ambrose's back and ensure that we are an unstoppable team together.

Shift, I think, closing my eyes. *Shift*. Change into the beautiful white snow wolf with gold flecks that match Ambrose's. That shows the world that we are mates. *Shift*, I command her.

I wait and wait.

But nothing happens. I don't even feel a stirring in my belly, or an inkling of her coming to life inside me.

I open my eyes and realize in horror that Ambrose is now the one beneath Nyx as Nyx bares his teeth at Ambrose, almost as if he's giving him a chance to surrender instead of just outright killing him.

Shift! I scream to my wolf. *I need you! Ambrose needs you! Our mate needs us!*

No magic swells in my body. Nothing happens. I feel as human as I've ever felt in my life. My mind swirls in confusion over how I haven't shifted. *How could I have lost my wolf after working so hard to get her? She's always come alive to save our mate. Why is she so silent now?*

"You can't shift, can you?" His cold, slimy voice slithers into my head.

"Get out of my head!"

"Make me. Or better yet, shift and save your mate," he says.

"Ambrose doesn't need me to save him."

"Maybe not." Ambrose freed himself and is now on the attack again.

I take a deep breath that I didn't realize I had been holding.

"But you should ask him why you can't shift."

"He doesn't know any more than I do."

"Then ask him," Nyx taunts.

"No," I say the word out loud, and it draws both of the males' attention to me.

"Are you okay?" Ambrose asks.

"Yes, I just can't get Nyx out of my head."

"He's in your head? He can talk to you like I can?"

Fuck, he didn't know. But I can't lie to him. Not now, not about anything. I want complete honesty between us.

"Yes," I breathe back.

"Fuck."

If Ambrose's previous attacks were vicious, these are completely driven by animalistic rage. He's not thinking as he attacks, just using his raw, limitless power. His wolf fights, yes, but so does the part of him that's witch. The part of him that he had been holding back before, for some unspoken reason.

He shifts into his human form to shoot a blast of his power at Nyx before instantly shifting back into his wolf form to attack again. Back and forth he shifts between his two selves—wolf and witch. It appears he can't use his witch powers unless he shifts. And I quickly realize that he's going to burn out and risk losing all of his power if he continues like this. There is no way that fighting like this is sustainable.

I have to help him. I have to put a stop to this.

Shift, dammit.

I concentrate with everything I have, but nothing happens.

Nyx moves so fast from underneath Ambrose to on top of him that it looks like he teleported. Vampires are impossibly fast.

One bite. One taste of Ambrose's blood by Nyx, and this will all be over. Nyx will be able to use mind control on Ambrose. He could kill him, and Ambrose couldn't even defend himself. I can't let that happen.

My mind whirls, trying to form a plan. Anything that I can do to help Ambrose get the upper hand. I wish I had a weapon. Not that I'd be any good using it. But I need something—anything to help me since my wolf is so hell bent on not making an appearance.

I stare at the two alphas tangled together, and I know what I have to do. I take a step forward, then another on the mossy floor. Neither of them seems to notice me moving as they are laser-focused on the other. I have no doubt they would fight until one of them dies or both of them. But I can't risk losing Ambrose. I hoped that with the two of us fighting together, we'd have the clear upper hand. But since my wolf decided not to show, they are too evenly matched. Nyx has been too close to tasting his blood too many times. I have to stop this. We have to find another way to take down Nyx.

Slowly, I creep toward them, my feet so light that I know that neither of them hears me approaching. When I'm within striking distance, I take one final deep breath and I leap. The second my feet leave the ground, I know how stupid my plan was. I'll be lucky if I leave here alive, let alone with minimal injuries.

I see the dark of their fur blending together as I land against both of their bodies. The impact is hard, rattling me all the way down to my bones. I'm going to hurt for days after this. But the pain of the impact isn't the only thing I feel. Something sharp swipes at my side, and I cry out in agony.

With a whoosh, I'm pulled hard in one direction—into a strong male's arms. The fighting has stopped. But the question is, *whose arms are these?*

My head is spinning, and I can't see anything in front of my face. I'm biting down on my bottom lip so hard that I taste blood, but I can't stop. It's the only thing keeping me from screaming in pain.

"Lumi, gods, Lumi!" I hear Ambrose screaming, and I know exactly whose arms are holding me.

Nyx.

His hand is pressed against my side, where my wound is.

"I'm fine," I strain, getting the words out before clenching my teeth together again to keep the pain from escaping in a scream.

"You're not fine, love," Nyx whispers in my ear.

I growl at him. "Let me go!"

"If I remove my hand from where it currently rests, you'll die."

I frown, looking down to see that he is, in fact, correct. His hand is holding firm against the gash on my side, stopping the blood from spilling out in all directions.

"Let her go. I'll do anything. Let her go," Ambrose says firmly and calmly.

I shake my head. "No. Go. I'll be fine. Nyx won't hurt

me. He thinks we're mates. He wants to break the curse as badly as we all do. He won't hurt me," I say the words even though I'm not sure I believe them. But I say the only thing that comes to mind to get Ambrose to leave. To be safe again.

"I'm not leaving you," Ambrose says through clenched teeth.

"Please," I beg him, but as I speak, a cry comes out as well from the pain.

"If you believe she's your mate, let her go, Nyx. She'll die if she stays with you. I'm the only one who can heal her," Ambrose says.

Nyx just shakes his head. "If you love her, you'll heal her regardless of whether I let her go or not."

Love—there's that word. Nyx doesn't realize that if Ambrose admits to loving me, it all but assures that I'll die anyway, whether he heals me or not.

I stiffen in Nyx's hold, and I can feel his cold stare on me.

"Let her go," Ambrose says again.

Nyx sighs and then whispers to me. "It seems that your 'mate' isn't willing to use his magic to heal you, so how about you shift? Your wolf will help you heal. You don't need him."

"I can't," my voice is shaky.

"Shift," Ambrose says. His words are gentle and yet firm. *An alpha command?*

Within a heartbeat, I can feel my body changing. It feels like I'm being flayed alive from the inside out. My organs twist and burn, taking a different form as my bones bend, my back arching. Long claws shift where my fingers were, sharp canines cut through my gums, and long, thick, white fur springs up, shining bright with the golden marks of the Moonlight pack.

Time slows. I don't know if it takes seconds, minutes, or hours for me to shift. The world seems to have stopped entirely around me as my body slowly transforms. The pain seems to linger just as long before completely trumping the pain I had felt in my side. For a second, I wish I would just die to stop the pain from consuming me, but as quickly as I think it, the pain stops.

I shifted into my wolf form.

I'm standing on the ground on my four paws between Ambrose and Nyx. I'm much closer to Nyx, and I know with his speed, I can't take a step toward Ambrose without him stopping me, so in a way, he might as well still have his arms around me, holding me in place. I'm as captured as I was before, but I shifted.

I shifted!

Ambrose's alpha command worked. He—

I pause.

I shifted because of Ambrose. Isolde's words come back to me. *If a witch is the one to cause a wolf to shift for the first time, then that witch is the one who controls that shifter's wolf forever.*

I stare at Ambrose, and my world collapses around me. I can forgive him for not telling me he is a witch, but this...this can't be true.

My breath quickens as I put the pieces together. Ambrose caused me to shift. Ambrose controls my wolf, not me. That's why it's so painful. That's why I couldn't shift when he wasn't around.

I don't have control of my wolf. I never will. He will always be able to control me. He's not my mate. He can't be. And if he is, I'll reject the bond. Refuse to complete the marking ceremony.

"You control my wolf!" I scream at him in my mind. My body is shaking. The ground seems to be shaking beneath me. The world shifts. My rage explodes out of me, and it's enough to let go of the wolf holding me captive.

I shift back into my human form. My weak form. The only version of me that I can control. My anger gets the best of me, and I feel compelled to lash out in a vicious manner.

"I reject the bond. You aren't my mate!"

CHAPTER 7
NYX

Lumi's words crack through my mind like a lightning bolt—frying everything in its path. For a moment, my mind is left stunned, unable to think. The world seems to shatter around us. I'm left in awe of this female with incredible powers—maybe not physical or magical powers, but she has powers all the same. I've never felt such formidable strength in my mind before, never felt anything so extraordinary.

Her words weren't meant for me. It's clear she sent them to Ambrose, but in her exceptional rage, they also flew through the bond we share. Though technically speaking, she could be rejecting both of our bonds simultaneously. But her words felt more like a lovers' quarrel, laced with raw disappointment.

She's standing between us, closer to me than Ambrose, completely naked in her human form. The gash on the side has closed some, enough that she's not going to drop dead at any second, but it could still use a healer's touch to close completely. She doesn't care. The pain doesn't even seem to faze her at the moment. Her long mane of white hair blows in the breeze as she locks eyes with Ambrose in a stance that displays her undeniable power. She'll fight the most dominant wolf shifter alpha in existence with nothing more than her fragile human hands to get her wolf back.

I knew she'd figure out what I had already pieced together—Ambrose was the one who granted her her wolf, which means he's the one who controls it, not her. I can't think of anything worse in the world than not being in control of part of myself. He took the most precious part of her and decided it was his without her consent. I want to kill Ambrose for many reasons, but I'd kill him for that alone.

"Get out of my head, Ambrose," Lumi says through grinding teeth.

Ambrose looks stunned for a second, and then finally says, "I'm sorry. No, I'm more than sorry. Sorry doesn't even begin to cover it. I never meant to control your wolf. When it happened, it was an accident. It was part of my magic reaching out involuntarily to you to save us."

"To save *you*, you mean," she snaps.

He flinches.

If I weren't so angry on her behalf, I'd be amused watching him squirm. I've been waiting for a moment like this for years. And finally, this scrawny girl is the one to bring the mighty Ambrose to his knees. I can't help but let a tinge of a grin lift my lips.

"We're mates. You know that. You can hate me all you want. I hate myself, but it doesn't change the fact that we are mates. We were chosen to break the curses. We don't have a choice." Ambrose speaks with cool conviction, as if he already knows that she'll eventually come to the same conclusion herself.

"We're not anything. We're not mates," Lumi says firmly, sadly.

Ambrose runs his hands through his hair. "Just come back with me. Come back, talk to Kael. See Emeric. Let me talk to Isolde and the other witches about how I give you your wolf back. We can fix this." His words seem to indicate he's forgotten that I'm even here. *I'll* decide whether to let him walk off my territory without another fight first.

"I'm not going with you," she says.

"My queen, please. Give me another chance. You're my mate," Ambrose's composure turns to begging as he begins to move toward her.

"I belong to no one." She takes a step back, and I've had enough.

"Don't take another step," I snarl at Ambrose.

Ambrose's head snaps up at me, and he growls, revealing his canines. "*You.*"

I stay where I am in the shadows, watching him glare at me with more hatred than I've ever seen him look give me. Like him taking away her autonomy over such a huge part of herself is my fault.

"You did this," he growls at me.

I cock my head like he's insane, and he probably is. "Did what exactly? Forced you to use your magic to control Lumi?"

"No, you're using your mind control against her now."

Lumi inhales sharply, and her head whips to me, eyes flashing with the same blistering fierceness she unleashed on Ambrose. She hates us both, not that I blame her. But I need her to break the curse. My pack and the vampires don't deserve what they've been through.

"He's in my mind. He's in my mind. Push him out.

Is that why I feel this hatred for Ambrose? Is he controlling my feelings?

No, Ambrose is a liar. He's controlling.

But Nyx is no better. He killed Rowena. He's controlling my mind too.

Push them out!"

Lumi's thoughts are so loud that I hear them as clearly as if she were just standing right next to me speaking them aloud. She doesn't realize she's doing it. I focus on Ambrose, trying to figure out if he is also being blasted by her every thought or if their bond was severed when she rejected him as her mate. He's looking from Lumi to me in horror.

I make a split-second decision. One that I know I'll probably regret.

"I drank her blood. You may control her wolf, but I can control her mind—forever."

"You fucking bastard!" Ambrose screams.

But I have Lumi pulled against me in less than a millisecond. My arm is hooked around her neck as I hold her against my chest.

I pull back my lips, revealing my overly sharp fangs that are twice the size of his canines as I run them over her neck. Her smell is intoxicating to me, a heady mix taunting me to bite her, taste her. I can feel her pulse drumming in her neck. How easily I could drain her with one tantalizing bite. I've only tasted a drop—one single drop. But that was enough to leave me physically in pain whenever I'm reminded of how good she tasted.

"Leave or I'll kill her."

Ambrose's eyes widen. "You wouldn't. You think she's your mate. You need her to break the curse."

"Let me fucking go!" Lumi screams, elbowing me hard in the stomach. But I don't budge or acknowledge her.

"I'd rather see us both cursed forever than let you have her," I say.

Lumi sucks in a breath like she can't believe I just said that.

Ambrose looks from me to Lumi. "Nyx won't kill you. He wants to break the curse too badly. Whether he incorrectly thinks you're his mate or mine, he knows you are the key to breaking the curse. He won't kill you."

Lumi just stares at him, not speaking.

"I'll find a way to break his mind control. To give you your wolf back. To fix everything. You're my queen. My mate. I fucked up. But I'll fix it. I'll come back for you. I'll save you. I promise." Ambose looks at her with such longing, but it's not enough. Not enough for her to apologize or take back her words.

"Get out of my territory," I say in a low, menacing voice, using the full weight of my alpha command as I do. It's like stretching a muscle that I rarely use. It's hard to use on other alphas, but when I'm this angry and he's in my territory, the command is a potent one. He doesn't have a choice but to obey.

He looks at Lumi one more time, and I know he's trying to communicate with her through her bond. I have no idea if he is successful or not, but my command isn't patient. I don't give him any more time to say his goodbyes.

The second I feel Ambrose leave my land, I release Lumi.

She stumbles back, caught off guard as she sucks in a rattled breath. I watch her struggle to breathe for a second before she spins around, throwing a punch at me.

I let her hit me, knowing she has enough anger inside her to destroy the world if she decided to. But even with all the rage inside her, it's a weak punch. One without any form or technique, so when it hits me, it feels like a fly brushing against my skin.

"That's all you got?" I ask.

She throws another punch and then another and another. Each with more rage and less accuracy than the last, until she's wildly flinging her arms at me. I see the idea forming in her mind as she decides to try with her leg instead of her arm. I watch in what feels like slow motion as she sweeps her leg out. But instead of kicking me, she collapses onto the floor. Her body is void of all breath.

"Did you get that out of your system?"

"No. You're a fucking bastard. You used mind control against me. You killed Rowena. I'll never be done with you until I kill you."

"Fair enough, but why don't you pause your efforts until you've seen a healer so you don't die. Then you can continue your pathetic attempts at whatever it is you're doing."

She bares her teeth. "I hate you."

"I know, but you're still bleeding."

She looks down at her side as if realizing for the first time that there is an immense wound on her side stretching from the bottom of her rib cage to her hip. Shifting into her wolf form helped somewhat, but she wasn't in it long enough. Her wolf would never have been able to fully heal her, but if she'd stayed in that form longer, it might have been enough to avoid needing a healer. We'll never know.

It's not the only thing she realizes. She's naked, as am I.

She hastily covers herself with her hands, but the quick movement shoots pain through her side. She flinches, her hands landing over her wound instead.

"I don't trust any of your healers. They probably aren't medically trained, and they will just try to turn me into a vampire. I'm fine." The smallest attempt at movement draws a cursed wince. The adrenaline that was coursing through her when she was throwing punches my way is long gone, no longer providing any pain relief.

"You trusted Ambrose's healers even though they could have turned you into a witch."

She opens her mouth to argue back, and then it's as if the world has tilted on its axis in her expression as she realizes another truth. Her previous medical attention wasn't medical at all. It was magic—that's what had healed her.

"Fuck. But I still don't trust you not to turn me into a vampire."

"Why would I turn you into a vampire? You're a human whose ability to shift into a wolf is tied to an asshole alpha. You're powerless against me. I don't even need to use my mind control to control you. Why would I want to give you vampire abilities? That seems foolish to me."

She scoffs, and I take the opportunity to inspect her body, looking for any other injuries I missed. But my eyes betray me, straying from her wounds to the curve of her naked ass, then up her slim waist to the swell of her breasts that I want to bite. Everything about her is a magnetic desire being served on a platter for me. Kill her, taste her, fuck her—she has to be mine.

"Stop looking at me like that."

"Like what?"

"Like you want to fuck me. I will never sleep with you. I'm going to kill you."

I nod my head. "Then stop looking at me like you want me to bed you."

She scowls. "Why would I ever want to fuck a man who nearly killed me?" She points to the gash on the side of her body.

I clench my jaw, remembering how foolish and brave she was jumping between Ambrose and me to stop us from killing each other. It's a miracle neither of us killed her.

"Speaking of that, you shouldn't ever interfere with a fight between Ambrose and me again."

"Stop telling me what to do! I'll do whatever I want."

"I'll stop telling you what to do when you stop almost getting yourself killed."

She glares at me stubbornly.

"Now, will you follow me back to the Bloodmoon village? Or would you prefer I carry you?"

"Neither," she says stubbornly.

I scratch the back of my neck, trying not to explode on her. She's infuriating. All I'm trying to do is keep her alive so we can figure out how to break the curse, and she's making everything as difficult as fucking possible.

"Do you have a death wish? If you stay here, you're going to die. You'll bleed out or die of infection. And that's if another animal or vampire doesn't come along and finish you off first."

That gets her attention. Her eyes widen when I say the word vampire, and she suddenly sees the woods very differently.

"You can't keep me as your captive."

"I can," I remind her. "But then again, I think you're going to stay willingly."

"Why would I ever stay with you?"

"Because right now, you hate Ambrose more. And Ambrose can't get to you as long as you are here."

"He did before."

"Only because I allowed him on my territory. I won't again."

She frowns, but doesn't ask any other questions.

I sigh. "Let's take this one step at a time. For now, come back to the village. Let a healer look at you. Get some clothes on. Eat some food. Then we can talk."

Take a bath and wash Ambrose's stench off you...

She doesn't agree so much as she begins walking in the direction of the village, and I take that as her consent.

We walk at a steady pace, Lumi doing her best to act like the slash in her side isn't bothering her when I can hear her little winces with each step she takes.

"I could get you back to the village in seconds if you let me carry you."

"Fuck off."

I smirk. "Just offering to help end your suffering."

She growls back at me, and I chuckle.

"You'd better watch your step, you wouldn't want the sunlight to accidentally touch you," she tosses back.

I take another step, easily dodging the flicker of sunlight that breaks through the branches. The sun has begun to set, so I won't have to dodge the light much longer. Not that it's much of a hassle for me anymore. It's become so second nature to me that I find myself doing it even when I don't have to, even in my wolf form.

"This way," I say when she makes a wrong turn.

She begrudgingly follows me, and we walk the next half mile in silence until the village comes into view. I alert Sylara that I'm going to need her and a healer, which is about all I can communicate with pack members, especially while I'm not in my wolf form. I can't talk to them clearly in my head like I can Lumi.

I lead Lumi back into my house, back into my bedroom.

She's fighting for every breath when she finally makes it up the three stories of stairs, but she refuses to let me help her, and I'm too tired to argue with her.

"Sylara will be here with the healer any minute now. Rest in the bed. I'll have some food and more clothes brought up."

Lumi collapses onto the bed, too exhausted to argue with me. But she's not so tired to resist sending me one last searing look. "You can try to control me all you want. Force me into completing the marking ceremony with you and becoming your mate. But I will find a way to break free. And I will kill you. I loved Ambrose and rejected him. Just think about what I'll do to you."

"Do you want to kill Ambrose, too?" I ask because I'm curious what she thinks about him.

She pauses, and I know her answer. There is still a part of her that loves him. Still part of her that views him as her mate. Still part of him that she hasn't fully severed from her body yet.

A hint of disappointment crosses through me, but then I shake it away. She's been through a lot. It doesn't matter that she doesn't immediately demand revenge against a man she loved and was willing to die for an hour ago.

"Ambrose was the one who caused that gash by the way, not me, if that helps at all."

She frowns. "It doesn't matter whose claws sliced through my skin. You're both controlling bastards. And I want nothing to do with either one of you."

I nod and walk to the door, but before I leave, I say one more thing.

"I didn't use mind control back there. Just because I have the ability to doesn't mean I will."

I know what it's like to be controlled, and I will never take away anyone's free will unless there is no other way. I'm afraid Lumi will give me no choice but to eventually use it against her. The curse has to be broken, and she's the key to breaking it.

CHAPTER 8
LUMI

The room spins as I watch Nyx soar out the door, as if he can literally fly. It's just a combination of him moving fast and my brain not being able to keep up with his movements, given how much blood I've lost. As soon as he's gone, I let out the blood-curdling scream I've been holding in since I got this gash.

Fuck, it hurts.

I stare down at the large cut oozing blood on the left side of my abdomen. It's large, raw, and painful, but not as agonizing as it was when I first got it. Shifting did help partially close the wound. I can see spots where my skin has started pulling together to close the wound and keep my blood loss to a minimum. But without treatment, it will definitely get infected being this open.

I lay my head back on the pillow, waiting for the healer Nyx will send my way. He said Sylara would be bringing them. Nausea rises in my throat at the thought of having to interact with her again.

He didn't use mind control.

At least, that's what he said. I don't know what to

believe anymore. All I know is that I need this pain to end in order to think at all.

There's a knock at the door, which isn't something I expected. I expected Sylara to just rudely enter.

"Come in," I strain through another agonizing scream.

The door flies open, and Sylara and Riven are standing in the doorway.

"Where's the healer?" I ask through gritted teeth. I'm pretty sure I'm going to pass out soon from the pain, and I'd rather know and agree to who's working on me before I do. I can't handle any more of my bodily autonomy being taken from me.

"That would be me," Riven says with a happy smirk and a braid through his long, thick curls that hang down his back.

I frown. "You? I thought you were a wolf shifter? Aren't healers witches?"

"Ambrose isn't the only wolf shifter with witch powers. Although I'm pretty sure Ambrose made a deal with the witches to gain his powers, mine I acquired through my blood relations. My great-great-grandmother was a witch. I have powers, but have really only focused my energy on healing. The rest of it I'm not interested in."

Ambrose made a deal to gain his witch powers. *Why didn't I realize that sooner?*

I move to sit up, but the sharp pain shoots through my body like a freight train, knocking me back down.

Riven frowns.

"Am I needed here?" Sylara asks curtly, speaking for the first time.

Riven and I both answer in unison, "No."

She rolls her eyes before spinning out of the room.

"Don't worry about Sylara. She's like that with everyone except Nyx."

I raise an eyebrow at that. "Are they an item?"

Riven chuckles. "Hell no, more like brother and sister." His gaze finds my wound, but if he has any thoughts about how hard it will be to fix, he keeps them to himself.

His eyes meet mine, completely ignoring the fact that I'm naked. He hasn't glanced anywhere except my wound and my eyes. But I can see his gentle request to heal me.

I nod, and his smile returns to his face.

Standing over my body in his large, intimidating frame, he seems better suited to a battlefield than healing.

"How do you take your coffee?"

"What?" I ask in confusion.

He chuckles. "How do you take your coffee, Lumi?"

"Um..."

"You don't know? Or you don't drink the stuff? I don't usually bother. I find there are far better energy sources to wake me up if you know what I'm saying," he says with a wink.

I roll my eyes at him.

"But most shifters still prefer the stuff. So how do you take it?"

"With a lot of milk."

He nods. "Me too if I have to suffer through drinking the bitter sludge. Alcohol of choice?"

"Tequila shots."

He smiles. "So you'll burn to get drunk, but not to wake up in the morning. I like your thinking."

A twinge of a smile tugs at my lips.

"Hot or cold shower?"

"Hot, who prefers a cold shower?" I ask in disgust.

"Lots of wolf shifters do since we run hot and need a way to cool down after shifting."

"Oh," I say, realizing I've never really had that problem since I can't control my own wolf. My entire mood shifts.

He sighs, the sound laced with thoughts he doesn't dare to speak. "I'm sorry, I didn't mean to bring that up."

I shake my head, not wanting to talk about it.

"I'll bring you some clothes you can put on and some food. You should take it easy tonight, but by tomorrow morning, you should be back to your full strength after a night of rest. No reason to have to lie around in bed after that unless you need to sulk."

"What?" I stare down at the gash, or rather, where the gash once was. Other than a small pink line on my skin, there is nothing to show that there was even a wound there a few moments ago.

"You healed me," I say, my eyes wide as I stare at the faint scar.

He chuckles. "That was what I was sent in here to do."

"Yes, but...I didn't even notice what you were doing. And I didn't expect that to be so painless or quick."

He shrugs. "What can I say, I'm good at the art of distraction. And flesh wounds like this are pretty easy to heal. No major organ damage, just needing to convince some tissue and skin to pull back together and not much else. Easy enough."

I blink several times, still in disbelief. "You must be a pretty powerful witch."

He grimaces when I say that. "I'm a healer, not a witch. My powers are limited to healing. I don't belong to a coven. The amount of witch blood in me is small. I'm a wolf shifter through and through."

"Sorry." I run my hand over my smooth skin. "Thank you."

He nods. A few minutes later, he returns with all of my favorite foods and a new pile of clothes to choose from.

"How?" I ask when I spot the pad thai and bowl of miso soup.

"I'm good at reading people, and I'm a good cook."

I stare down at the food in disbelief. He leaves before I can say anything else, and despite having wanted to clothe myself for hours, I dig into the food first. It tastes divine.

I scarf it down quickly, then pick out some leggings and an oversized black T-shirt to still have access to my scar just in case.

The second I get my clothes on, the tears hit hard, spilling fast, steady, and unyielding. My body is done trying to hold them back.

I cry for the loss of my wolf that I can't access. I'll never be able to control when I shift. Ambrose will always control her.

I cry for the loss of my mate. A man I still love despite everything. That didn't just vanish when he betrayed me.

I cry that Nyx has the power to control my mind whenever he wants. I believe him when he says he didn't earlier, but it doesn't mean he won't as soon as he needs something from me.

I cry at everything I've lost. Rowena. My father. My pack. I don't even have Kael to talk to.

I cry about my haunting memories of the Moonlight pack's initiation. A pack I no longer want to belong to.

I'm nothing but a human—a pathetic, weak human.

"Fuck!" I scream at the top of my lungs, letting every-thing out. The tears slow, only because there are no tears left in my ducts.

I snap my mouth shut. I will not be weak. I will not let anyone else control me, not anymore.

I don't know what I'm going to do, just that I have to do something—anything.

I leave the room in a flurry, not really sure what I'm doing, just following my intuition. I don't know my way around this huge castle. I don't know where I'm headed or why, but as I move, I just know that I'm headed in the right direction. So I keep going.

I find myself in the basement, standing in front of a set of closed double doors. I don't know what's behind them, but I know this is where I'm supposed to be right now. Whatever is behind it is exactly what I need.

I don't knock; I just push the doors open.

The lights are turned off, but my wolf eyesight still works. It's the only part of me that is better than a human.

It's a massive gym.

There are weights and cardio machines on one far side, a sparring ring in the middle, and a few punching bags on the other.

I walk toward the punching bags, not even bothering to turn the lights on. When I reach the first one, I let my hand run down the cool leather. Emeric taught me the very basics of how to throw a punch, but I never got very good at it. I never had enough time. Even if I did, I never had the will to take my training seriously enough.

Now, it's all I have. I'm human. I live in a world of wolf shifters, witches, and vampires. I can't rely on my wolf abilities. I have to learn how to rely on my human strength. It's all I have left.

I throw a punch.

The bag barely moves, and my hand already feels bruised, but it also feels satisfying. So I do it again. I feel a gentle tightening of my skin across my scar, but it barely aches. Riven healed me well. The minuscule amount of pain doesn't stop me from hitting the bag again and again. I don't think as I throw punches, but if I hadn't cried earlier, I know this release of sorts would have done it. I keep going until I'm breathless and hugging the bag to keep myself from collapsing.

"It's not going to be enough," his voice sounds in my head.

I squeeze my eyes shut and clench my teeth at the invasion. *"Get out."*

"It's not going to be enough," Nyx says out loud this time.

I don't have to open my eyes to know where he is in the room.

"So why should I even bother, right?"

"That's not what I said. You should train every day. Learn all of your strengths and weaknesses. We all should. But it alone won't be enough to protect you."

I open my eyes and turn, watching him circling me in the dark. The question that's been bothering me the most escapes my lips. "Can you use your mind control to control when I shift? To control my wolf?"

He pauses for a second. "Yes."

I shake my head, hating that the universe sent me two mating bonds to choose from and then gave both of them the power to control me. *Fucking unbelievable.*

He doesn't bother to tell me he won't. I know he will if he needs me to. And I hate it.

"And you still think you're my mate if you're willing to control me?"

He doesn't show me any of his feelings. His expression doesn't change. "I think the gods are playing games with us. Making it as difficult as possible to break the curses. I'm not sure what to believe anymore."

I frown, but he's right. I'm also completely lost when it comes to who my mate is or if I even have one. I share a link with Ambrose and Nyx that allows me to communicate with them mentally. That doesn't mean anything. I fell in love with Ambrose, but that doesn't mean anything either.

"I do think there is a reason that the three of us are linked, though."

My frown deepens at his words. "Pretty sure it just means we were meant to kill each other. Be mortal enemies and all that. Entertainment for the gods."

He shakes his head. "Tell me what you know. Help me find the way to break the curses."

I stare back at the punching bag covered in my sweat. "And why would I do that? I'm not cursed. I'm not a wolf shifter, or a witch, or a vampire. I'm a human. Seems like you all being cursed would actually help me."

"You're still a wolf shifter. Nothing has changed, snow wolf."

"Don't call me that. I'm not."

"You are. A part of you was stolen from you, that's all. It doesn't mean you can't get it back."

"How?" I ask, hating that he's giving me hope.

"Help me break the curses and I'll help you regain control of your wolf."

"I don't trust you. You're a vampire. You can control my mind—what I think, everything I do. You have no reason to make a deal with me when you can just control me or succumb to your bloodlust and drain every drop of blood I have."

He sniffs me and wrinkles his nose. "For one, you didn't shower and smell of that wretched alpha, so you don't have to worry about me wanting to drink your blood. And two, I'm giving you a choice for me not to use my mind control on you. If you prefer I use it and you get nothing out of it, then fine by me."

"I hate you," I snap. I should have showered. I should have washed Ambrose away, but I'm not ready yet.

"I know."

"You're not really giving me a choice. You're still controlling me. You're no better than him," I say, not able to say Ambrose's name.

"I know."

"I don't care about the curses. I should go live my life with the humans and forget about helping any of you." Maybe my father was right, or had seen some premonition, some prophecy of my fate, and he was trying to save me from this outcome. A tear wells in the corner of my eye at the thought of never getting to talk to my father again. Not being able to get his advice. Not even really knowing how he died.

"Only one species can break the curse. Vampires, witches, or wolf shifters—not all three. The first to break the curse gets their curse lifted, the rest are destined to live with their curses forever until their species dies out," he says.

My jaw falls slack. He can't be speaking the truth. *Why would he share that with me? Why trust me?*

"I know you have your own pieces of the prophecy that no one else has shared with you. And I'm not asking you to share anything—yet. Just visit a seer with me. See if you can work with me long enough for us to start putting together the pieces of the puzzle."

His circling is starting to make me dizzy, but it doesn't stop me from hanging on to his every word.

"You're lying when you say you don't care about the curses. You do care. And you're going to want to ensure the wolf shifters break the curse first, because if they don't, they're doomed. Whether you can control your shifting doesn't matter—you're still a snow wolf. And you are the key to breaking the curse."

I'm so silent that I can pick up the steady beat of his heart through the silence, even with my very human ears.

And then, it quickens.

"Fuck," he says.

He turns from me and goes to a cabinet behind him, unlocking it. He digs through it before coming up with something shiny, glinting through the limited light in the room. He walks over and holds it out to me, a blade coming into my view.

I grasp the handle, unsure of what's happening.

"We have to go, but you should carry a blade with you at all times, to act as your claws when you can't shift. I'll train you in the best way to use it soon enough."

He turns toward the door, expecting me to follow.

"Where are we going? What's happening?"

"Vampires," he says the single word, and then vanishes.

CHAPTER 9

NYX

"Keep Lumi in this house. Don't let her leave, no matter what," I say to Sylara, Riven, and Brax as I do the last button on my dark dress shirt, which I changed into when I realized I'd be dealing with vampires tonight. I can still hear Lumi's footsteps climbing up from the basement floor, where the gym is. I'll be gone before she reaches the top step. I don't want to have an argument or use my mind control to get her to do what I want. I'm trying my best not to piss her off any further.

"I'm not her babysitter. Besides, it's not like she's going to leave this house as soon as she realizes there are vampires outside," Sylara says.

I look to Brax and Riven, knowing I don't have time to argue with Sylara about this right now.

"We won't let her out of our sight," Brax says.

Riven nods his agreement.

"Let's go," I say to Talonis as he slips on his dress shoes. For some gods forsaken reason, the vampires now expect me to dress up when I hold court. Not that this is really court per se, but they will see it that way. And if I want to keep the power I've worked my ass off to get, then I'd better play the part.

Talonis is the only one who ever comes with me. He's the only one willing and who actually understands this part of my life. He's not a vampire, but unlike the rest of the Bloodmoon pack, he doesn't look down on them.

As we walk out the door, I say, "Let's handle this quickly before Lumi shows up."

"She won't actually show up. I know Sylara doesn't like Lumi, but Riven and Brax will keep Lumi safe," Talonis says.

"Yeah, but who is going to keep them safe from Lumi?" I ask.

He raises his eyebrows. "Is she really that dangerous?"

I shake my head. "No, but she's stubborn, determined, and sly. She'll find her way out of the house and into trouble if we don't make this quick." Plus, I'll be distracted. I still can't shake the conflicting smells on her body from my mind. Her sweet cum is still smeared on the inside of her thigh, but it's mixed with *him*—an instant turn off. But I can also smell *me* on her. Once again, out of all the clothes that Riven brought her to choose from, she chose my shirt to wear.

He frowns. "Then we'd better hurry."

I nod.

The sun has set, making it easy for me to move in my vampire form. Talonis does his best to keep up without having to shift, but my vampire speed is unmatched. Even if he shifted, he still wouldn't be able to keep up with me. It's one of the things I enjoy about being a vampire—the otherworldly speed.

Honestly, there is a lot to enjoy about being a vampire.

The speed, the agility, the heightened connection to my emotions. I halt suddenly, waiting for Talonis to catch up, needing at least one ally at my side to report back to the Bloodmoon pack if things go south.

For every pro, there are as many cons about being a vampire. And I don't need exceptional intuition skills to understand exactly why I was called to court. Nor superior hearing ability—I can hear vampires from outside the cave.

"Fuck," I say under my breath.

Talonis appears next to me, out of breath, gripping his side. "What is it?" he asks between breaths.

A tortured scream rings out, echoing off the walls of the cave.

"Gods, what are you going to do?"

"I don't know." But I can't wait outside the cave any longer. The appalling scream slams into me, shaking me to my core. This one singular con about being a vampire makes even the best of pros taste sour in my mouth. For this reason alone, I believe vampires were never meant to exist. We aren't a natural balance in this supernatural world. We are an abomination.

I enter the cave, my face turning neutral as I mask any feelings I have. There is no room for emotion when it comes to what I have to become and do tonight. Talonis walks solemnly behind me. Despite his smaller frame and less intimidating posture, he's the best in these types of situations. His particular skills lend themselves perfectly to it, and he'd protect me with his life. I just hope it doesn't come down to it. We walk through a narrow entrance that quickly opens to an expansive chamber. Darkness blankets the room, vaulted ceilings and jagged stalactites loom above me in breathtaking columns as a touch of light glistens off them. But it's what I see in the pooling shadows that has my undivided attention—dozens of vampires.

One intake of air and I know exactly what's driving the frenzy.

Humans.

Three of them—clinging to one another in the center of the room, beneath a single ray of light, shaking, blood already streaking down their necks. I don't know who they are, nor do I care. I'm a vampire. Vampires feed on humans to survive. Most kill them, unable to control their bloodlust. But the humans are not what I was called here to address. No one is upset that a vampire is about to kill three humans.

I scan the room, looking for the cause of the room exploding in a ruckus. A deafening roar rips through the room, and all heads snap in that direction. A vampire throws a rope around the neck of another, tightening the rope to add to the three others that are tied to his wrists and legs. The four vampires holding onto the ropes are pulling with all of their might, trying to restrain the vampire, but with each rope being added, he becomes more feral, more lost to his bloodthirst.

The room is split into two. Those trying to tie up the savage vampire and those on the other side of the room, demanding that the vampire be released. While the humans are stuck in the middle, too stunned and losing too much blood to attempt a getaway.

This isn't going to end well for anyone involved.

The feral vampire struggles against the ropes like a wild animal. With one grunt, he pulls free of the ropes and runs right toward one of the humans, pulling him apart limb by limb as easily as if he were ripping paper to shreds. The vampires trying to hold him back look terrified, while those wanting him free cheer.

I study the numbers, trying to gauge which side has more support, but it seems there's a pretty even divide among the vampires, with no clear path to take when it comes to the cursed vampire.

"My lord, it's good to see you. Although I'm not sure there is anything to be done except letting them battle it out," Raul says.

I scour the room, tending to agree that I can't get involved, at least not yet. I'm a brand new lord, still proving myself to the local vampires. Most still loathe that I was the one to win the title since I'm also a wolf shifter. They don't trust my loyalties. They don't trust me to do the right thing.

The crowd charges with electricity, and it feels like a battle is looming.

"You have to do something," Talonis says.

I agree, but I need to wait for the right moment. I need to give them a minute to let the fight get physical. To express their initial emotions to each other. Hopefully, if I let them fight a little before I put an end to it, they won't be so charged the next time it happens.

"Not yet," I say, stepping into the shadows to watch the impending fight play out. I hope my instincts are right, but I'm not sure. I know how to handle the Bloodmoon pack. I know how to lead them, but vampires are different. They don't have the same loyalty to the pack. They are more individualistic creatures who believe in the powers of the individual.

Talonis and Raul stand on either side of me like guards willing to protect me with their lives if I ask them to. But I would never ask.

I study all of the players as the first fangs are drawn. There will be no winners, not until the curse is broken.

"Why are you letting them fight, again?" Talonis asks me.

"Because there is no right side. There is no right way to handle the cursed one. I understand both sides. The emotions are heightened on each, and they deserve a chance to fight their opinion." And despite what Lumi says, I'm not a controlling bastard. My goal in life isn't to control others. I want to give them as much free will as possible.

"What is his name?" I ask Raul.

"Benson. He wiped out an entire village of humans. He's lost complete control of himself."

"I'll make sure the human situation is dealt with," I say, looking to Talonis.

He nods curtly.

An opposing vampire rips out one of the human's throats, leaving the last trembling, hugging her knees to her chest in the center of the cave as she squeezes her eyes shut. The cursed vampire has another rope wrapped around his waist, and several other vampires are yanking hard, trying to control him, while the others are fighting to break him free.

None of them is a match for Benson in his cursed state. He's ten times stronger than any of them. With one more yank, he breaks free, going straight for the human on the floor. Fangs rip through her neck so deeply that they nearly tear her head from her shoulders. Benson doesn't bother drinking her blood. With crazed eyes, he turns to the others, ready to do the same thing to them.

Five minutes. I'm giving them five minutes before I end this. I let the solutions bounce around my head before I realize there is only one way to end this, and I dread it. But as a lord, I don't have a choice. It's my responsibility. I fought for this. I won the title, so I have to do what has to be done.

Two minutes into my self-imposed countdown, Benson turns, sniffing the air, and I know time is up. I can't give them any more freedom to work through their affairs.

"Enough," I say in a deep, commanding voice that rattles off the walls.

The room falls silent, eyes slowly turning toward me as if seeing me for the first time. And then, one by one, each vampire in the room begins to bow. "My lord...my lord...my lord." Each of them says one by one as they bow their head in reverence.

Even Benson bows, making what I have to do next that much harder.

I clench my jaw as I watch them all bow at me. I knew I had earned their respect, but I hadn't expected this level of respect from them. I expected them to still fight me. Still look at me as less than them, even though I fought to earn the title.

My stare cuts across each of them one by one, the flicker of surprise locked away, replaced by the ruthless authority I must wield. Out of the corner of my eye, I spot her. She thinks she has hidden well in the shadows, but nothing can hide the delicious scent of her blood. All creatures have a unique smell that is intoxicating to vampires, but hers is unlike anything I've ever smelled before—a rich perfume of sweetness and tangy warmth that turns me primal. And I don't trust any other vampire here to resist her.

Benson turns his head in her direction. He's already

locking onto her divine fragrance. But I can't let him realize she's here. If any others notice, they'll demand her blood be spilled for breaking into a vampire court. I have to tread even more carefully now.

"Benson, come forward. I have decided your judgment," I say, letting my voice carry as I ignore the strong scent of Lumi's blood lofting through the cave. I'm not sure if he will listen to me or not; I'm still unsure of the power I wield. But he steps forward, accepting his fate. Even in his cursed head, he listens to me as his lord. The ropes are no longer necessary for him to obey. My words hold that much strength over him, much like my mind control.

"Yes, my lord," he says, bowing his head low.

I stand for a moment, knowing her eyes are on me. This moment is about to change everything. If she wasn't terrified of me before, she will be now. She'll think I'm a monster, and rightfully so. She'll realize we have no chance of being mates, and the only reason there is a bond between us is because we are both so desperate to break the curse. There's no way we could be each other's better half. We aren't destined to be anything but enemies forced to work together to end this.

I leap forward, my fangs sinking into the flesh of his neck as I viciously tear at it in the same way he ended the human life. He doesn't flinch away or fight. He lets me rip into him. He wants me to end his life—his suffering.

And so I do in the most painless way I can. In seconds, it's over. I can see the life draining from his eyes as Talonis hands me the stake, and I drive it through his lifeless heart.

The cave is silent, watching me. No one fights me. No one says I did the wrong thing, even though half the cave wanted to give him the freedom to let the curse run him ragged until it was the one to end him instead of me. Benson didn't deserve to let the curse drive him even madder, to lose everything that made him him before he died. He deserved to die with dignity. I gave him that. But I'm not sure half the vampires gathered will understand or agree.

I wait, assuming there is at least one vampire who will speak out against me. Instead, a quiet hush has fallen so quickly that all I hear is the tiny drips of water from the stalactites. It stretches into what feels like a moment of silence for our fallen vampire. Maybe there wasn't so much disagreement as I first thought, and no more blood will be shed tonight.

Finally, one of the vampires steps forward. He looks me dead in the eye. "I smell a human."

Murmurs break the silence around the room as they all scent her.

Fuck.

Red eyes greet me as I look out through the crowd. Now that the cursed one has been dealt with, their blood lust is the focus, and with a human in their midst after such heightened emotions, none of them will be able to resist her. I have seconds to get them all under my control. So, I do the only thing I can think of to save her in this moment.

"She's not a human, she's a wolf shifter," I say, but the red eyes darken. That won't deter any of them from draining her dry.

With a whoosh, I move unnaturally through time and space, grabbing Lumi from the shadows and yanking her to my side faster than any of them can blink.

"And she's my mate."

CHAPTER 10
LUMI

I'm standing in a dark cave surrounded by dozens of vampires that are looking at me like they want to drain every drop of my blood from my body, as Nyx pulls me tight against his hard frame. My heart is thundering in my chest, but it's not the vampires I'm afraid of —it's Nyx's words.

"She's my mate."

There is no way he actually believes his own words, is there?

I shudder at the thought of this dark, alluring man, with chiseled features, whose skin feels cool under my touch, whose eyes turn from black to red, whose wolf looms large, and moves with lethal precision, is my mate. He can't be my mate.

I don't want a mate. Not anymore. I don't want to be the key to breaking the curses.

"I'm not your mate," I snap into his mind.

"Now's really not the time, love."

"Then maybe you shouldn't announce something that isn't true to your entire court!"

"Maybe you shouldn't have snuck in, and I wouldn't have to save your ass."

I frown, looking around the room at the hungry vampires. Nyx's words have barely changed their reaction. The blade that Nyx gave me is burning a hole through the side of my leggings where I tucked it against my hip. I should be holding it in my palm, but it won't do much good against these bloodthirsty monsters. At least none of these vampires appear to be the vampires I've fought before.

"You're quite impressive. When Nyx said you would escape, I didn't think you would in a matter of minutes," Talonis says as he moves to stand on my other side and slightly in front of me in a protective manner.

I cock my head at Nyx. "Nyx said I'd escape? He knew I would?"

Talonis grins from out of the corner of my eye. "He knows you quite well, I'm afraid."

"Hmmm," I say.

"Can you two stop? Now isn't the time to be discussing how Lumi got away from three of my most trusted pack members," Nyx says.

"Maybe—" I start, but Nyx shoots me a hardened look that has me slamming my mouth shut. But I'm not done speaking to him. *"Then maybe we should talk about how you became a vampire lord?!"*

"Later."

I narrow my eyes at him in frustration. We will be talking about it later. *How can they accept him as a vampire lord if he's also a wolf shifter alpha?*

But they did, they do. They bowed to him with all the respect his title earns him. And they did it willingly, all with a look of awe and reverence on their faces. No one questioned his authority when he decided the fate of the rabid vampire. Even though moments before, they had been split in two, ready to fight each other to the death. When he decided to kill the vampire, they respected his decision.

I admit, watching him kill the vampire, a quiet hush fell over me. One moment, I was in awe, just watching his aura grow around him in his inhuman stillness, and the next, he was gracefully moving with lethal speed. He struck so fast, so fluidly, that I know the vampire felt nothing when he died. A jolt of horror crashed down on me as I watched how dangerous Nyx really is.

You should be afraid of him. He would kill you just as easily if given the chance. But then why am I staring at him with a blistering heat burning in my eyes?

One of the vampires steps forward, "Respectfully, my lord, we know who she is. She can't be your mate. She's the alpha wolf's mate."

Nyx growls, a deep guttural sound that silences every breath in the room, including my own. The vibrations seem to swell over our bodies in almost magical, forceful waves that nearly knock me on my ass. Ancient, feral, inhuman. I've never heard a sound like that before. And I have no idea what it means. *Was that sound real, or was it meant to intimidate the other vampires?*

"Lumi isn't Ambrose's mate. She's *mine*," the way he says she's mine is like he's using mind control and his alpha command combined on every person in the room. With how convincing those two words are, I almost believe for a second that he's telling the truth.

Nyx pulls me tighter against his side, his hand splaying over my hip as his thumb runs circles over my inner hip bone, in a driving a person mad sort of way. It's an obvious display of dominance and control over my body. And I don't like it one bit, despite how the butterflies start dancing in my belly, wondering what else his touch might feel like if I let myself go there.

Maybe in a different world, I would play along with his games, try to convince them I'm his mate. Or at least, not fight him about this. But after what Ambrose did to me, I'm done playing games. I'd rather die here and now by these vampires than pretend another second or let him touch me like he owns me.

I grab his hand, yanking my body free. "Nyx is mistaken. He's not my mate."

The vampire closest raises his eyebrows, and there is a collective gasp as I dismiss Nyx.

Nyx doesn't move. He doesn't try to pull me back in. He doesn't speak to me in my mind, demanding that I shut up. He doesn't command me to shift with his mind control to get me to stop talking. He lets me step away.

Is he so unconcerned about my safety? Or is there a reason he's not fighting me?

The handsome vampire stalks closer, his eyes fixed on me in unrelenting focus, yet even as he advances, I sense him tracking Nyx out of the corner of his vision—calculating, studying, as if weighing predator against prey.

"So then, beautiful Lumi, who is your mate if not Nyx?"

"I have no mate. I belong to no one."

He chuckles. "You sure are a fiery one. I think your name should have meant fire instead of snow."

I glare at him as he inches closer, but I don't tremble in fear. I'm done being afraid.

Nyx doesn't move to block the vampire's path toward me. But I notice Talonis inching closer until Nyx puts up a hand, stopping even him from getting close enough to protect me from the threat.

"Every wolf shifter has a mate. You have a mate. You just have to be smart enough to find yours."

I shake my head. "I don't care about finding mine. And I'm not sure I'm even a wolf shifter. I'm a human for all that matters."

I feel Nyx's gaze laser-focused on the back of my head. But still, he says nothing to me out loud or in my head. For once, I'm not sure if the silence in my head is comforting or not.

"Why does Nyx think he's your mate then?" he asks slyly.

"Because Nyx is an overconfident male who thinks just because he can slither his way into my head, then he can get into my pants as well. When in reality, I'm sure his alpha shifter and vampire lord powers give him plenty of abilities to speak into others' heads. That doesn't mean I'm his mate."

The vampire's eyes cut from me to Nyx and then back to me again. The others in the room trade glances and hushed whispers that are too quiet for me to hear.

"You don't fear him or me. Any of us," he says it more like a fact than a question.

"No, I don't fear. Not anymore."

In a second, he's at my throat, fangs brushing against my skin. The next second, he's flat on his back, a stake millimeters from being thrust into his heart. Nyx grips the stake with coiled, vicious intensity, barely resisting the urge to strike.

The vampire chuckles, looking deeply into Nyx's eyes before raising his hands. "I concede."

Nyx drops the stake.

"She's your mate," the vampire says. "You convinced us. But you're going to have to do a lot more to convince the vampire king."

Nyx drapes his arm over my shoulders, turning me to leave, but he freezes at that word as if just now realizing the truth of that and what that means for him.

"The curse will be broken long before I have to convince the king. Once it is, there will be no need for persuading anyone."

"For both your sakes, I hope so."

CHAPTER II
NYX

You're going to have to do a lot more to convince the vampire king. Orson's words send a chill through my already frigid body—already a sensation to which I'll never get accustomed. When I was only a wolf shifter, I was full of warmth—my body blazing with heat. Now I am nothing but cold, frigid shadows, and unyielding darkness.

I have an inkling of what we would have to do to convince the vampire king we are mates and therefore earn his protection. It's not something I'm interested in, and I know Lumi definitely won't be interested. But we might not have a choice if we don't get answers by the next full moon.

As we exit the cave, I give Talonis a look that tells him exactly what I plan on doing and that he has his own job to be doing: cleaning up the human village mess. We can't stay here. My vampires may have given us their blessing, but that's because it's what they want to believe. They are desperate to have the curse broken, and as I'm their lord, they are easily persuaded by me.

But the other vampires—ones who have seen Lumi with Ambrose won't see it that way. They'll just see her as another meal.

Talonis nods. Without a warning, I scoop Lumi into my arms and run. In the moment, I figure it's better to save her life and ask for forgiveness later rather than risking a vampire taking a bite out of her. I'm all for free will and control over your own destiny, but right now, I just want us all to get home in one piece.

Lumi scrambles in my arms, trying to get her blade somewhere against my skin that will do damage. I commend the fight in her; she's going to need it. It seems the damage Ambrose has done to her has only intensified her will to battle, but she lacks the skill to use the knife effectively.

"Put me down, you bastard!" she wrestles in my arms.

I tune her out, easily carrying her despite the surface-level scratches she produces on my arms until we are back in the living room of my house. Only then do I put her down.

"You're welcome, love," I say, knowing it's going to get a reaction out of her.

"You're welcome? I didn't ask you to carry me."

"No, but I did save your life."

She narrows her eyes at me, defiance blazing in her gaze as she lifts her blade and thrusts it in my direction.

"I didn't ask you to save my life! Now your entire vampire court thinks we are mates, and we are going to have to prove it to the fucking vampire king, whoever that is. I don't need your help! You aren't my mate!"

I cock my head as I watch her crumple in front of me. I want to kill Ambrose for the harm he caused her. She loved him—no, she still loves him. Her heart can't switch off as fast as she wants it to. The pain consumes her so completely that it seems she would rather die than live with another moment of her agony. She truly doesn't want to be saved. She wants to either fight her own battles and win, or lose and not have to live with the pain anymore. I can feel it, and I'm not even in her head.

"I'm going to make sure the house is cleared so you two can have some privacy. That is, if you each promise not to kill each other," Talonis says.

We both snap our heads in his direction.

He chuckles. "I'd let you kill me if it meant you two would work together for a few minutes. But I'm not sure it would change anything." And then he looks at me. "I'll make sure the humans are dealt with discreetly—make it seem like a fire got out of control."

Before either of us can say anything else, he vanishes, and the silence in the house tells me he's taken Sylara, Riven, and Brax, instructing them to leave. It's just the two of us in this castle.

We stare at each other, the tension high. Until finally, I unbutton the top couple of buttons on my dress shirt before sinking into the leather chair.

"Kill me if you must, I won't fight you. I've killed enough for today," I groan.

Her eyes flicker at me in confusion. "You killed a vampire who had gone mad. It seemed like a mercy to end his life quickly and honorably."

"Was it? It still ended his life. But he's just a vampire. So I'm sure you don't weigh his life as much as a wolf shifter or human. He deserved to die. All vampires do. We're killers, predators that need to be eliminated."

I close my eyes as my head falls back against the cushion, the weight of what I had to do hitting me in full force. I hate killing. I hate ending a life. I hated watching the humans' lives end. I hated playing the game just to maintain my power. I hated watching Lumi put her life at risk like that.

She doesn't respond to my comment about vampires being predators. "It's the curse, isn't it? That's why the vampire was losing his mind."

I nod.

"What would have happened if you didn't kill him?"

I raise my head, finally looking her in the eyes, trying to decide how much to tell her. "Vampires used to live for thousands of years. An immortal lifespan if they weren't killed by another creature. The curse shortened that lifespan considerably, making us mortal. Every time we feed, our lifespan shortens and our minds weaken until the curse takes hold of us.

Once it does, there is no reversing it. We lose everything that makes us us. We lose control over our minds. We become rabid animals who only want to feed and feed and feed. We want to feed the curse. Our curse only wants blood. It wants to use us to wipe out the world. If I didn't kill him, he would have tried to kill everything and everyone in his path until he went so insane that he would have driven a stake through his own heart."

She stares at me for a minute, processing. "How long do you have before that happens to you?"

I chuckle. "Worried about me, love?"

She doesn't answer. "How long?"

"Longer than most, as I'm a half wolf shifter. I don't usually have to feed on blood at all, and not feeding seems to keep the curse from starting."

"Why did some of the vampires not want you to kill him? It seemed like a mercy."

"They hoped he could be saved when the curse is broken and reversed. But death is final; there is no coming back from that."

She nods slowly. "You did the right thing, ending his life. He wouldn't have been able to live with himself even if his curse was reversed."

I don't respond even though I agree with her.

"How did you become a vampire lord? I wouldn't think they'd trust a filthy half-breed."

I watch her as she walks around the room, running her hand over the fabrics of the chairs and down the lines of the curtains as if she can't stay still. The fabric of her shirt, my shirt, wafts as she walks, until our scents mix in my direction.

I hold my breath, not allowing myself to smell us together. She's not mine, and the longer I spend with her, the more I know she'll never be. She's destined for far greater things than the likes of me. She can't be tied to a man fated to die a cruel, savage death like that vampire I killed.

"There are seven vampire lords. When one dies, anyone interested in becoming a successor goes to the king. He's the one who decides who the next lord will be," I reply.

She watches me closely, waiting for me to say more. When I don't, she asks, "And what did you have to do to prove to the vampire king that you were worthy of becoming a lord?"

My body tenses as if remembering alone will put me back in that place. "Enough."

"Why put yourself through it?"

"To protect my pack."

Her eyes soften a little as if she understands me better. But I don't want her to understand me. I don't want her to be unafraid of me. I'm capable of killing her without any remorse. She needs to realize that.

"How did you escape?" I ask her.

"Quickly," she says, throwing a one-word answer at me like I did her.

But unlike me, she's screaming her thoughts at me. I can see how she tricked Sylara into thinking she had womanly problems, for which she needed help retrieving supplies. How Brax was distracted by an ask to retrieve wine for her, which left her and Riven alone. How she just straight up told him her plans, and he allowed her to walk right out the door, thinking it was the right thing to do. He's always had the biggest heart when it comes to allowing others free will. Flashes of her following my scent and her intuition led her to me. I saw her watching me, in awe of my power. I feel her fear and how she pushed past it to confront the vampires. How she's truly not afraid of death, and how tired she is of being controlled. How she won't allow herself to be controlled ever again.

"*Get. Out. Of. My. Head!*" She yells so loudly, trying to shove me out. Instead, she just sends her thoughts even louder to me.

"*I can't, not unless you block me out. You're screaming your thoughts so loudly, and our connection is so strong that it's as if you are talking to me.*"

She frowns. "*Get out. I know you can. Stop getting in my head.*"

I force myself out. I try to sever the connection, but it

feels like cutting off one of my arms. It feels wrong not to be in her head.

I frown at that.

"You claim you're my mate, but you're not better than Ambrose. You're both controlling assholes."

I wince. "I'm not controlling anything when you send your thoughts to me. Learn to block me if you don't want me in your mind."

"How would you feel if I could read your thoughts?"

Relieved. Like a burden has been lifted. Like I don't have to decide what to share and what to keep secret. She would just know everything, and then maybe we could figure out what this connection is between us and use its purpose, or end it once and for all.

"You can, I you want to."

"No, I can't."

"It's a two-way connection. You can get into my mind just as easily as I can yours. You can probably do the same with Ambrose."

She freezes. "Can he get into my mind like you can? Has he been able to this entire time?"

Her fear is palpable in the air. I don't need a connection with her to feel it. "My best guess, yes."

"Fuck," she screams, yanking on her silver hair to rip us both from her head.

"When I rejected his bond, did that sever my connection with him?"

"I don't know."

Finally, she collapses into the couch opposite me. She's finally had enough of this madness and needs time to just think. And then she looks at me. Her eyes squint, locking on me with a fierce intensity, as if she's trying to burn straight through my mind.

"What are you doing?" I chuckle.

"Trying to read your mind."

"It's more of a mental thing than a physical one. You don't need to squint your eyes at me."

She huffs. "You can't believe I'm your mate. We are worse together than Ambrose and I were."

"I don't believe we are mates."

"Then why tell the vampires that? We are no closer to breaking the curse than Ambrose and I were."

"Because you are seeing visions, prophecies, so am I. I think our connection is because we are both seers. Together we can figure out how to break the curse." I don't tell her that my theory would also mean that Ambrose is probably a seer and has visions, and that's why the three of us can talk to each other in our heads. That would be too much for her to accept at the moment.

"And telling them you're my mate means they won't hurt you. You're safe, and yes, I'd like to protect you so we can find a way to break the curse," I continue.

"That's it? You just want to break the curse? You don't want to mark me as your mate?"

A primitive growl creeps up my chest, but I quickly push it down before I make an audible sound. One that screams, *she's mine! You're mine! I want you spread before me while I feast on your flesh and drive my thick cock inside you as you orgasm over and over in blissful ribbons until every painful emotion you've been through vanishes and we are the only two souls left in existence.*

But I don't say any of that. It's just the curse fucking with me. She's not my mate. She's still in love with Ambrose for fucking sakes. He's probably her mate, but the gods put a spell on him to fuck it all up so he wouldn't break the curse until we've all been punished to their satisfaction. Only then will they allow them to break the curse.

"I just want to break the curse."

"I'm not sure I care about breaking the curse anymore. And I definitely don't want your protection."

"Prove it."

"What?"

"Prove that you don't need or want my protection."

She narrows her eyes at me as if she knows it's a trick.

I rest my arms casually on the armrests, widening my legs in the most relaxed manner that I can.

"Attack me. Survive for one minute. Sixty seconds to prove to yourself that if you can survive that long, then you can survive long enough when faced against an enemy vampire or wolf shifter," I prod.

"I don't need to prove anything."

"Not to me. But you do to yourself."

She hesitates, thinking it through, but I know she still wants to kill me. She still dreams about it after Rowena's death.

"*Take your revenge,*" I say in her head.

That does it. Her rage overwhelms her thoughts as she runs for me. For a second, I'm not even sure she bothered to pull her weapon from where it was tucked between her hip and her leggings, but she does. Pulling it free from the sheath, she leaps toward me.

I don't move. I let her attack. I want her to see the damage she can do, but also how much more she could do with proper training. Despite her wanting to be independent and fierce, she's going to need me and my pack to teach her how to live that way.

She does have one thing I don't have to teach her—guts.

Her blade slices down hard as she aims for my neck, but the angle is all wrong, and the swipe of her forearms sends the blade against my shoulder, slicing into my deltoid muscle rather than across my neck. She yanks her arm back, aiming for my chest. She doesn't hesitate; she drives the knife down with both of her hands through my heart.

She releases her blade with a heavy breath before looking me in the eyes. She blinks several times, as if she can't believe what she just did.

"I'm—I'm so sorry. I'll grab Riven. You're going to be okay. Just—"

She tries to pull away, intending to hunt down Riven, but I catch her wrist before she can climb off me.

I grab the handle of the blade and yank it out with a hiss before tossing it on the floor. The wound immediately starts healing itself. The mix of vampire and wolf shifter blood in me is tending to my wounds. I rarely, if ever, need a healer for my body to heal.

"Lesson one—don't ever sink your weapon into an enemy unless you are sure it will kill them. Lesson two—only a stake through the heart can kill a vampire." In the next blink of the eye, we've switched positions. She's beneath me, her warm body melting my icy exterior as I press my canines against her throat, giving her a view of the wound that is already mostly healed.

"You're brave. Possibly the bravest of us all. And you're mourning. You want revenge. You want to make all the pain go away. But letting me or another vampire or witch kill you isn't the answer you're looking for. That's just letting us win."

Her heart thunders in her chest as she stills with my sharp teeth brushing against her flesh. She swallows as if taunting me, like she knows I won't actually bite her. She doesn't know me very well.

"We both need each other—"

"I don't need you," she protests.

"You do if you want to stay alive. If you want your wolf back. If you want to be able to back up that bark with some bite and teeth of your own."

She growls.

I grin. "I want to make a deal with you, one we cast in blood this time."

"No, I'm not making any sort of magical deal with you."

"Even one that assures I won't kill you? That gives you back some of the power in our dynamic? And that ultimately ensures you have the power to survive in this world?"

"No deal can give me all of that."

"I need the information to break the curse. You need that knowledge as well—it will give you back your own power. Power to control your own fate again, instead of Ambrose or me assuming you are our mate. And you want your wolf back. We agree to share any knowledge we gain about the curse or how to get your wolf back, through our visions and by consulting other seers together. We won't stop until we find out how to break the curse and you have gained your wolf back."

"It's not enough."

"I vow to protect you, no matter the consequences. I will do everything in my power to keep you alive, including sacrificing myself if it comes down to it."

"And I would have to do no such thing for you?"

I chuckle. "No, you don't have to protect me. In fact, you can continue to actively try to kill me."

Her lips curl up at that. "What happens if we don't honor this deal, if we seal it with blood?"

"Depends on the transgression, but usually the magic of the deal would try its best to force you to honor it. If you still didn't, then it would cause you physical pain. And if you really broke the deal, you'd die."

"So all I have to do to honor it is tell you about my visions and go with you to see seers?"

"Yes. And I'd do the same, plus lay down my life to protect you."

Her eyes narrow, searching mine as if she wants to ask more of me, but isn't sure how to ask it. "And you promise not to use your mind control on me."

I wouldn't anyway, so it's an easy yes. "I promise not to use my mind control on you."

She thinks as if she is searching for one last thing to ask me. Her brows furrow, and the lines at the corners of her eyes deepen. "You also have to promise not to kill Ambrose."

I flip us back around so she's straddling me, and I can look deep into her eyes, searching for the reason for her ask. *Is it because she's still in love with him or because she wants to kill him herself?*

I can't see the answer there, but she has the upper hand in the negotiations. She knows I'll agree to any of her terms because I'm desperate to break the curse. She saw a little bit of the reason for that desperation tonight, but not enough to fully understand.

"I promise not to kill Ambrose as long as our deal lasts," I add.

She purses her lips, but then nods, her long hair

sweeping over her shoulder and brushing against my chest as she does.

"Now what?"

I lift her left hand from where it's gripping the armrest, my eyes never leaving hers as I lift her index finger to my lips.

"Can I prick your finger with my fang to draw blood for the deal?"

"Yes."

I nick her finger against my fang before doing the same to my own finger. I hold out my finger, giving her one last chance to back away from our deal. She doesn't hesitate. She smashes her finger against mine, our blood mixing together.

"I will honor the deal and terms we have agreed to with each other until my dying breath," I say.

"I will help you break the curse as long as I'm breathing," she says.

A jolt sparks between us as the magic mixes and seals us together, like a shockwave running through our bodies.

She yanks her hand back.

"What the hell?"

I raise an eyebrow. "Sorry, I should have prepared you for that."

"I thought you weren't a witch?"

"I'm not."

"Then how?" She stares at her finger, then mine.

"When two magical creatures enter into a deal like this, magic is formed."

"But I'm not—"

I shake my head. "The universe thinks you are still a wolf shifter, even if you can't control your wolf yourself."

Her eyes widen.

"Do you regret our deal yet, snow wolf?"

"No." Her eyes twinkle at me, and my heart skips a beat. I'm terrified I'm going to live long enough to regret it, though.

AMBROSE

"What happened?" Emeric asks as I stand before him and the rest of the Moonlight pack and the entire Moonfire coven. There is no hiding the truth from any of them. Without me even speaking, they can see that I failed in bringing back my mate.

"I reject the bond. You aren't my mate!"

"I reject the bond. You aren't my mate!"

"I reject the bond. You aren't my mate!"

Those words won't stop playing in my head. They have become my own nightmare song being played exclusively for me. For the entire time I ran back, I've been analyzing her words. Her body language. Everything that happened. And I still don't know that truth. *Were they really her words? Her thoughts? Or were they Nyx's words that he forced her to speak with his mind control?*

I don't have the answer, but if there is even a chance that Nyx is the cause of her words, then I have to do whatever it takes to break her free of him.

She's still my mate. Even if she rejected me. Hates me. Wants me dead. Nothing has changed.

Silence spreads through the clearing where everyone is gathered around me, but my mind is still spinning. Still haunted by her never-ending words.

"I reject the bond. You aren't my mate!"

"I reject the bond. You aren't my mate!"

"I reject the bond. You aren't my mate!"

I reach for that connection with her, tentatively, afraid that if I tug on it too hard, it will completely unravel and sever the remaining fragile twine. My heart stops beating as I close my eyes and try to find her in my head. That's the only way to know for sure if her words are true or if Nyx controlled her.

A cool, snowy trail of snowflakes drifts along the edges of my mind, flickering like a fleeting winter flurry. I follow the soft snowflakes that are slow to fall...one... two...three...each one falls so slowly that I'm not sure the next one will fall at all. But I follow them one by one in my brain. I follow each chilly flake that brings me closer and closer to my answer.

Suddenly, the snowflakes pick up speed, falling faster and faster in my head. My mind runs along the path that has started to freeze over. Colder and colder, I keep push-ing, knowing exactly what I'm going to find when I reach the end.

Her.

Lumi—snow.

She's still there. She hasn't severed the connection. It's just lighter than before. But I feel her presence as strong as ever. I only allow myself a moment in her head. Just a moment to ensure she's okay and that I shouldn't send the entire pack and coven to Nyx's doorstep to immediately save her despite the unstoppable war it would create.

She holds a quiet sadness in her mind, but beneath it, I feel an undeniable strength that refuses to break. Suddenly, a biting cold sweeps through me. She's trying to push everything and everyone out.

I pull back, letting her be for the moment.

I want to go to her, get her back. But I can't, not without fixing what I broke first.

"Lumi is safe, for now. Nyx believes she's his mate, so he won't hurt her. And Lumi is strong enough to protect herself and gather information against our enemy while she is there," I answer Emeric. "I plan on helping her escape before the next full moon. Nyx is wrong; he's just trying to hurt me like he has before. Lumi and I still plan to break the curse on the next full moon."

Emeric smiles, but it's a half smile. He was expecting me to return with Lumi and a dead Nyx after what he did to Rowena. I wish I had, too.

"Isolde, I need to speak to you in private."

She raises an eyebrow at me, but says, "Of course."

I motion to Emeric to join us.

"Where the hell is Lumi?" Kael asks, jumping in front of me as I lead Isolde and Emeric toward my house.

"She's with Nyx and his pack."

"His pack or his vampires?"

"Whoever keeps him company as of late."

Kael grabs my arm, keeping me from walking. I could end his life in a second, but he's Lumi's best friend, and I don't need to do anything else to hurt my relationship with her.

"Is she really safe? Or was that all a load of crap to keep everyone from overthrowing you as alpha?"

"Come into my office, you should hear this too," I answer.

I lead Kael, Emeric, and Isolde into my office and shut the door. The main reason I'm having this conversation inside instead of out is to keep the rest of the pack and coven from hearing. But if all of the walls are still intact by the end, it will be a miracle.

I slam the door closed with a flick of my wrist. Kael, who has never seen my magic before, gasps, while Emeric raises an eyebrow at me as if to say we aren't hiding anything anymore, are we? I want to share everything with both of them, but I have a bigger issue to deal with first.

A blast of my magic shoots from my hand, aimed at Isolde's chest. She brushes the magic from hitting her body like it's a bothersome fly.

"I gave you your magic. You really think you have the skills or talent to go up against me, boy?" Isolde says.

A low growl rumbles from deep in my chest, my teeth and claws sharpen into razor points, ready to tear her apart. "If I wanted you dead, you'd be dead."

"Same," she says, the fierceness in her eyes cutting through me like a shard of glass.

"Why can't Lumi control her wolf? Why do I have power over it?"

The room goes so silent I can't even hear the beat of their hearts or the whiff of their breathing. For a moment, it feels like the entire room has vanished, and it's just me and Isolde left.

"Why do you think?" she hisses at me.

"I think you intervened! I think you weren't patient enough for Lumi to figure out how to gain her wolf on her own. I think you tried to control her. I think you didn't think she could do it on her own before the full moon, so you used your magic to—"

"Ha, you think I forced her to shift? Then why can't I control her wolf? It's not me you should be mad at. You were the one who was impatient, not me."

I growl again, my body beginning to shift into my wolf. I have no control over it at the moment. He wants to rip out her throat.

"I would never do that to my mate!"

"Not even to save yourself? Not even subconsciously?"

"Never!" I snap.

She shakes her head, a cackle in her grin. "And yet, it seems like that's exactly what happened."

"I would never do that. I would never control someone like that."

"And yet, you did."

My eyes widen in horror. "How do I fix it? How do I give her her wolf back?" *How do I make her stop hating me for what I didn't mean to do?*

There's a pause that extends forever. "You can't."

I collapse, falling to my knees, all hope draining from me with her words. The world tilts and blurs around the edges. I know Isolde is telling the truth. There is no fixing this. No giving Lumi back what I took. No healing her. No healing the relationship. She'll rightfully hate me forever for what I did.

And she's my mate.

I still know that's true. It doesn't matter that she doesn't love me and that I can't love her yet. We only get one mate at a time. She's it until one of us dies; only then will one of us get another.

She's my mate, and she'll hate me for the rest of her life. She'll never stop rejecting the bond. The curse will go stronger instead of us being able to break it. I've destroyed everything.

"She'll forgive you. Tell her the truth. Tell her you didn't mean to do it. That your magic did it, not you. Never use the power against her. Tell her how much you love her, and she'll forgive you. Lumi is the most caring, loving person I know. She's forgiven me countless times. She'll forgive her mate for this if it means breaking the curse," Kael says.

I look up at him from where I'm on my knees on the floor. He's right. But the problem is, I can't show her that I love her. I can't tell her. As it is, I'm balancing a very delicate dance, trying to keep myself from loving her.

"Even if that's true, I think Nyx might be using his mind control against her to convince her to reject our bond and accept him as her mate," I say.

"Fuck," Emeric says under his breath, punching the wall and leaving the first mark.

"Then we kill Nyx," Kael says, looking from Emeric to me.

"Nyx has done this before. Used his mind control against someone Ambrose loved. It didn't end well," Emeric says.

I stand, eyeing Emeric. I guess we are just spilling all of my secrets to everyone in this room.

"Then we definitely need to kill him," Kael says.

"You and what army, kid? Don't you think we've tried before? Why do you think the Moonfire coven joined forces with the Moonlight pack? It's not because we get along so well. We'd all be better off if he were dead, but that's harder to do than you'd think," Isolde says.

"We have to try. We have to get Lumi back. If that means we have to find a way to kill Nyx, then..." Kael stops, then takes a deep sniff, his eyes darkening into balls of rage as he stares at me.

"What did you do?" he growls at me, the first slowly starting as his canines lengthen and his claws begin to form.

"I already told you."

"You fucked her! I can smell her scent all over you."

I narrow my eyes at him. "Yes, I fucked her. We're mates. She loves me, or did until Nyx fucked everything up. We are two consenting adults."

"No, you fucked her when you could have been saving her," the deep tanner of his voice so intense that words rattle the room. He shifts into his muddy brown colored wolf.

I sigh. I knew I should have brought them to the back-yard and magically soundproofed it. But this felt like there was a chance we'd be more civilized.

Isolde folds her arms and smirks at me. Emeric braces for the impact he's about to endure as well. Kael is right. I should have been saving Lumi instead of fucking her.

Kael pounces with all the rage he rightfully feels. I don't move. I don't shift. I don't build my magic in my veins. I let him tackle me to the ground. I let his teeth get one sink into my neck and his claws one swipe at my face. There's a sharp sting in my cheek as blood drips and an even deeper twinge in my neck.

With a wave of my magic, he's across the room, frozen to the spot on the floor.

"I deserved that. But killing me now won't save Lumi. And every time you hurt me, you hurt Emeric. That's his curse. He didn't do anything to Lumi. I won't let you hurt him."

Emeric growls at me. "I can speak for myself. And you

could have fallen in love with her while you were fucking her. You could have let a slip of your tongue kill her. How dare you!"

He shifts into his majestic sandy-colored wolf.

This time, I brace harder, knowing that when he hits me, it's going to do far worse than just leave a scratch like Kael did. Kael has only had his wolf for a few weeks. Emeric has had years to harness his skills.

Emeric grabs onto my arm and then throws me with all of his might, right through one of the walls. The sheet wall scrapes against my skin, cutting me in several places, and my body hits the ground hard, knocking the wind out of me.

I'm slow to get up, not just from the pain, but because Emeric knows in a situation like this, I won't fight back. Emeric could kill me right now, and I'd do nothing to defend myself. Not after everything we've been through together. It used to be the four of us: Emeric, Amara, Rowena, and me. Now there's just the two of us left. The only time I'll ever fight him is on a sparring mat. And in the end, I always let him win.

When I finally bring myself to stand, I expect to see Emeric already attacking again, not letting up. He'd do it for Lumi. For Rowena. For Amara. For how foolish I was being with her after everything we've been through. He'd be right, but he wasn't there. Didn't know how badly Lumi needed that connection, that safe place. It was almost as if she knew we'd never get away. The best she could hope for was a quick reprieve. A moment where she felt safe. A moment when she could stay connected to me when we were apart.

Instead, he stands just as frozen as Kael. Isolde walks forward, standing in front of the opening in the wall.

I narrow my eyes in a glare at her.

"What? As fun as it was watching you beat each other up and destroy your home, we have more important things to worry about, and time is quickly running out again before the next full moon. I didn't agree to our deal with you to watch them squander it," Isolde says.

"Stay out of it, Isolde."

"No. We have a deal, you and I. I can't stay out of it."

"Release Emeric now, before I make you."

"Not until we are done talking. Then I'll release him, and you three can go back to killing each other all you want."

"I'm going to kill you one day."

She smirks. "If one of us is to end up dead at the hands of the other, it will be you, alpha. Now, what are we going to do about getting Lumi back before the next full moon?"

"It doesn't matter if we can get her back without breaking Nyx's mind control and giving her her wolf back; she'll reject the bond. She won't complete the marking ceremony."

Magic races over her skin with glimmering sparks. "She will. You worry about getting her back. Let me worry about her accepting the bond."

Before I can respond, she vanishes.

I growl, slamming my arms down. No way in hell will I let Isolde or any of her coven force Lumi to do anything. The growl I let out echoes through the house and is enough that when both Emeric and Kael are released, neither of them attacks me.

Silently, I walk forward back into what's left of my office and then slide against the wall onto the floor.

Emeric sits on my right. Kael is on my left. We are all lost in our own minds.

"What are we going to do about Nyx?" Kael asks at the same time Emeric asks, "What are we going to do about Isolde?"

Fuck—two enemies. And a mate who hates me. Rowena's loss. The pack and the coven are both losing trust in me. *How did I fuck this up so much?*

"Emeric, you tail Isolde. Make a plan to sever my deal with the Moonfire coven."

He nods.

"What's the deal?" Kael asks.

I shake my head. "Later. I'll focus on figuring out how to give Lumi her wolf back and breaking Nyx's mind control so we are ready when the opportunity to get her back presents itself."

And I look to Kael, knowing I'm asking a lot of him and putting a lot of trust in him. "And you will ensure that Nyx doesn't hurt a hair on Lumi's head."

"And how will I do that?" Kael asks.

"By joining the Bloodmoon pack."

CHAPTER 13
LUMI

"We should really get you in the weight room. Twice a day every day. And you could use some conditioning too. Sylara loves to run every morning before the sun rises. You should join her," Brax says.

I can hear Sylara's scoff from the side of the room where she's watching my scrawny, sweaty ass lying on the floor staring up at Brax as I grip my blade like it's my lifeline.

"It would all be pointless," Sylara says.

I tend to agree with her. Brax has been going through the basics with me all morning, trying to find any hidden strengths I might have that could be used against a magical creature. Or even another human. So far, I'm pretty sure I have no strengths. Brax couldn't find anything. Emeric couldn't. Ambrose couldn't. There is no hidden talent that is going to give me an edge in a fight. Nothing that will help me to survive. If it comes down to a one-on-one battle with anyone, I'm dead.

"Not helping, Sylara," Brax says.

"Just saying you're wasting your time." Her voice is sharper than any blade.

I'm still lying on the floor, not bothering to move. Maybe she'll just kill me now and end all of my misery.

"You could get in the ring with her. See if you discover any strengths I'm missing," Brax suggests.

"Hell no, Sylara won't hold back. Lumi will end up hurt, and Nyx will kill you for it," Riven says.

"Just kill me," I mutter.

Riven sighs like we've been through this a million times. "You don't mean that."

I sit up, resting my arms on my knees. "Maybe I do. If I die, whether my real mate is Nyx or Ambrose, one of them would get a new mate. A better mate. A stronger mate. And I would be—"

"Dead," Nyx says plainly, making me jump. I didn't realize he'd come downstairs to the basement gym.

I look at him in his cold eyes. "It would end my pain and be better for the world."

"If you say so, but I suspect it's just a way to get out of our deal," he says.

"Out of my head," I say out loud, not bothering to respond to him when he talks in my head.

"She's got a point; there is no way she's fit to survive an attack. What's the point of keeping her alive if one attack will end her? She can't possibly be either of your mates," Sylara says.

"So pragmatic, that's why you're my beta. But you're wrong in this instance, Sylara," Nyx says.

I study him closely as he glides across the floor. I have no idea why he believes what he does so strongly. But he doesn't seem to be bothered by my complete lack of fighting skills, or that the others find me completely incapable of improving.

"You'll get better. But you don't have to worry about protecting yourself as long as you're with me. Our deal ensures your survival."

I look down at the small scar still on my finger where he nicked me so we could make a magical deal together, marked with our blood. Even now, I can still feel the shockwaves from that moment deep within my body, stirring around in my stomach like they have a life of their own.

"Out," I say again.

"Force me out."

"Out," I say.

"Push me out," he says again.

I sigh. Hating this dance we've fallen into. *"I can't just push you out, just like I can't just become good with a blade in my hand. I'm not a killer."*

He blinks. If there is any sign I hurt him by inferring that he's a killer, it's not clear on his face.

"Both are skills. You can learn to become better at both with time and practice."

"Does it matter if I'll never be good enough to defend against a vampire? A witch? A shifter? Does it matter if I can learn to block you only for you to blast through my walls when you're angry enough?"

And then he starts speaking aloud. "Yes, it matters. It all matters. There is a reason you were the one chosen to break the curse. Your strength is your bravery. You faced down a dozen vampires without a drop of fear in you."

Talonis nods. "You did. I've never seen such bravery before."

"It didn't do me any good. If they decided to attack me, I'd be dead."

"But they didn't attack because you were brave. Because they saw in you what could make you a mate with someone like me. They saw your bravery and chose not to fight you. That's your strength, but it's not your only strength."

I open my mouth to argue when he speaks again. "You believe the curse can be broken. You believe in mates. In love. In forgiveness. In the kindness of others. You're willing to do whatever it takes, make any sacrifice necessary, to break the curse for others. That's incredibly selfless." He switches into my head. *"Don't let one heartbreak take your strength away from you."*

I look him dead in the eyes. He's right. I shouldn't let Ambrose take anything from me, but my heart hurts. It aches for something that never was and never will be again.

"Push me out," he says in a mental stern whisper.

I grind my teeth, having had enough of his pushing. He feels cold in my mind, like winter's breath mixed with a tinge of blood. It's nearly impossible to untangle him from my mind and discern where he stands in relation to my own thoughts. The scent of metallic blood is the easiest clue to find him. I hunt that thread as hard as I can, finding where he's clawed into my brain.

"Push me out, snow wolf."

He's everywhere. I don't know how to push every thread out, every drop of him out of my mind.

"If you can push me out, you'll be able to push him out. Destroy the bond for good if you want."

He's trying to taunt me, to motivate me. I don't know

what the others think is happening as we talk to each other in our minds. But none of them speaks.

I still don't know how to do it when he seems to be everywhere, with so many threads to break or push out.

"Just find one. Just this one," Nyx whispers.

I follow it, tasting the cool metallic taste on my tongue as I grab onto that thread for dear life, and then instead of pulling on it, I push. Shove. Throw.

Everything is black. I realize in the moment of concentration, I also closed my eyes. I gently open them and stare at Nyx, who is smirking at me in smug satisfaction.

"Well done, love," he says.

I roll my eyes, hating the nickname he gave me as much as I hate it when he calls me snow wolf. But I did it. I pushed him out, at least for a moment. I can still feel his threads, and I know if he wanted to, he could easily wiggle his way back into my mind, but he won't. He'll let me have this win for a second.

My mind drifts over all the little traces of him still there. As much as I want to find all of them and work on getting those parts of him out as well, my mind is exhausted. I have no mental energy left to try again. And then there's that other thread. The one that smells like evergreens and moonlight and...

I shake my head. I'll deal with those threads in due course. For now, I did it.

My win is short-lived, though. I start to get a strange tingling in my body. It starts off as soft and then quickly builds until I want to throw up.

Dream, your dream, your dream, your dream...

I don't know who is speaking the words. It's not Nyx.

It's not any voice I know at all. The words feel more like a beat in my chest than in my mind at all.

I hold my hand over my mouth to keep from vomiting. "I...uh...dream. I need to tell you about my dream," I force the words out. As soon as I do, a little of the tingling stops.

Nyx narrows his eyes on me as if realizing what's happening. Then he looks around the room at the others. I'm unsure whether he prefers I speak with him in front of the others or in a more private setting, but I need him to hurry up before I actually puke.

"You can tell me later, whenever you're ready," he says.

I frown. "No, I need..." But all of a sudden, I don't feel sweaty, my heart isn't pounding out of my chest, and my stomach has settled.

"It's the deal we struck. It can have some side effects that are a little too pushy until the magic truly believes you will honor the deal. Since we haven't really spoken yet, it will be a bit more pushy. My granting you permission to speak to me later should help the symptoms subside for now."

"What about you? Do you feel this way?"

"Yes." Which means he has something to tell me, too.

Feeling everyone's eyes on me, I say, "Let's get it over with, but I prefer not to have an audience."

Nyx nods, about to dismiss everyone, when suddenly, he goes still.

"What is it?" Sylara asks Nyx.

"We have an unexpected guest," Nyx answers, looking at Sylara.

Sylara and Riven vanish. Brax and Talonis move into position on either side of me with Nyx in front, as if they are all willing to put their bodies between me and whatever danger is coming.

Suddenly, the sweat that just vanished is dripping down my neck, and I get the nausea feeling all over again. I stare at the door that leads into the gym, waiting. I'm sure they all know who is coming by now. They can smell them and hear them. But none of them clue me in.

Vampires?

Witches?

Ambrose?

I'm not ready to face him yet. *Fuck, why would I rather deal with vampires than Ambrose?*

Sylara and Riven appear, gripping the biceps of a male.

My eyes widen as I stare at him. It can't be. I have to be dreaming.

"Kael?" I ask, not trusting my own eyes.

"Let me go, Sylara. You know I won't hurt her," Kael says, annoyed by she's holding onto him. Riven has already released one of his arms, determining he isn't a real threat.

"I know no such thing," she snarks back.

He rolls his eyes, but then turns to me, "Lumi! Are you okay? Are you hurt?"

I grin. It's been so long since I've smiled, genuinely smiled.

The three protective males are still standing in front of me, guarding me like there's an entire troop of vampires standing in front of me instead of my best friend.

I shove Nyx and run toward Kael, not caring why he's here, just that he is. I sling my arms around his neck, throwing my entire body into the hug.

He grabs me, lifting me off the ground with his arm wrapped tightly around my body, with a promise that he'll never let me go again if I don't want him to. He'd fight everyone here to get me out of here if I just gave him the word.

Tears begin to fall, and I don't care. I don't care that everyone is watching me fall apart. I have my best friend back. The only link to home. The part of me that no one really knows.

"Really, you can let go of my arm," he growls.

I lift my head from his shoulder to see that Sylara is still gripping his other arm.

"Not going to happen," she hisses.

"Let go of him, Sylara," I say, despite knowing she won't listen to me; she'll only listen to Nyx. To my surprise, as soon as I speak the command, she releases him.

I pull Kael tighter into a hug that feels like it lasts for hours, and yet still isn't enough as I sob into his chest. No one speaks. But I know they are all still in the room. No one leaves. No one trusts me alone with him.

"What happened? How are you here?" I ask, through a hiccup, as I keep my arms wrapped around his waist. He has his wrapped around my shoulders.

"First, you—are you okay? Has anyone touched you?" He glares over my shoulder at Nyx.

It takes me a second to realize what he's insinuating.

"I'm fine. No one has touched me," I say as reassuringly as I can.

"You're just being held against your will, right?"

Well, yes. And no. It's complicated. I choose not to answer him. Because I'm not even sure how to answer it myself.

"How are you here? Did Ambrose let you go? Did he send you?" I'm not sure how I want him to answer. *Do I want Ambrose to care about me? To want to ensure my safety? Or do I want to imagine that he's been holding Kael captive, and he somehow escaped?*

Kael seems to notice my turmoil in my eyes, confusion ringing out in his own. "I wanted to make sure you were okay. Ambrose doesn't know where I went. As soon as I realized you might be in danger, I came."

"You can't stay," Nyx says firmly, and in an instant, I hate him again. I remember why I wanted to kill him. *Why the hell did I agree to a deal with the asshole?*

I turn, my hand slinking down to hold Kael's as I do. I watch Nyx's eyes follow down to our linked hands, and I recall Nyx's earlier words to me, thinking that Kael and I were lovers. *Good, let him think that. Let him hate me. But he doesn't get to order me around.*

"He stays," I growl back. "If you want me to honor my deal, he stays."

Nyx shakes his head. "You can't amend the deal, not at this point."

"Like hell I can't."

"You can't actually. We inked it in blood and all of that."

"You what?" The room erupts.

"What do you mean you made a blood deal with her?" Riven asks.

"Are you mad?" Brax asks.

"What are the terms exactly?" Talonis asks.

"You made a deal with that halfbreed?" Kael asks me.

Everyone talks over the previous one so that all of their question blend together. But I get the general gist of it; none of them are happy that we made a blood deal together. The only one who doesn't seem surprised or angry by it is Sylara. She stands against the wall, casually watching all of us. *Did Nyx tell her, or is she just not bothered by the idea of it?*

"I'm not explaining the terms of the deal to any of you. It's between me and Nyx, but you will allow Kael to remain here with us if you want my cooperation."

"The blood deal ensures your cooperation, or did you already forget the nausea from earlier?" He raises his eyebrows.

"I'll kill you and then the blood deal won't matter."

He folds his arms across his chest and smirks. "I like that your confidence has built quickly, and you believe you're capable of killing me now."

"All I had to do was mark you first during the marking ceremony and prove you aren't my mate."

The room chills into an icy silence. All eyes turn to Nyx. To see what he'll say. If he'll call my bluff.

"All I was going to say is that Kael can't stay without joining the Bloodmoon pack. For an outsider to stay with us, they must either belong to an ally pack or pledge themselves to us through initiation. Since the Bloodmoon pack currently trusts no other packs as allies, his only choice would be to join the pack." Nyx looks from me to Kael. "But as he's already had a stay with us, he knows the rules already. It's why last time he stayed—"

"You mean kidnapped!" I interrupt him.

He nods. "Last time he was here, I had to have a guard on him at all times, day and night. We don't have the resources to do that again with the impending war that seems to be brewing. So if he stays, he has to initiate first."

"Done," Kael says.

I blink at him. "Are you sure?"

"Yes, I don't care what pack I belong to, I just want to be with you."

I grin up at him and nestle into his side as his broad arm wraps over my shoulders. Nyx studies the movement but says nothing.

"Tomorrow then," he says.

"Tomorrow," Kael answers.

"Did Ambrose send any messages along with you when he sent you to act as a guard dog?" Nyx asks.

"No," Kael answers.

I'm about to say that I'm done training for the day and want to return to my room with Kael and catch up, when I feel the warm thread sparking to life in my mind. *"I'll do anything for you, my mate, my queen. Anything. I'm still here."*

I close my eyes, trying to block the warmth from spreading through my head just like I did with Nyx, but end up shedding a tear instead. I'm not ready to face the warmth. Not ready to follow that thread and learn how it intertwines with mine to block Ambrose out. I'm just not ready to deal with him at all.

I open my eyes and see Nyx staring at me as if he knows. But he can't know. I said nothing. And yet...

"How?" I ask in his mind.

"Sometimes I can feel him in your mind when I'm here, too."

I frown, and the nausea returns. I want nothing more than to hide away with Kael. Hide away from the world. But the fucking deal I made won't allow it.

"Clear the room so we can talk about my dreams."

CHAPTER 14

NYX

Sylara moves to my right side as we watch Kael and Lumi embrace again.

"Disgusting, isn't it?" she says, wrinkling up her nose like she just tasted something sour.

I ignore her, listening in on Kael and Lumi's conversation.

"I need to talk to Nyx, but are you sure you're okay?" she asks him.

He nods. "Are you okay? Really okay?"

"Yes."

"Then why did you make a deal with him? Were you under duress? Did he threaten you?"

"He's tasted my blood. He can control my mind. He doesn't need to make a deal with me, but he did. Making a deal was the right decision."

Kael frowns but doesn't say anything more as he eyes me watching them. Instead, he pulls Lumi tighter, his hand sliding dangerously close to the curve of her ass. "I'm just so happy you're safe." He kisses the top of her head.

She closes her eyes and smiles into his side. "I'm happy you're here. I've missed you. We have so much to catch up on."

And then he whispers so low that I think he believes I can't hear him. "I'll help you escape. I won't let anything happen to you. I love you."

I turn to Sylara, shutting them out as heat bursts through my body in powerful waves. I want to strangle that male's neck, but I won't. "Escort Kael to his room and make sure he has everything he needs."

"Which room should I put him in? The dungeon or—"

"The room next to Lumi's."

She looks at me like I grew two heads. "But they aren't mates, you shouldn't be encouraging their feelings to grow for each other. She—"

"I trust Lumi, and right now, she needs him."

I swallow hard, pushing the strange thoughts racing through my brain, telling me I should listen to Sylara and put him in the dungeons, but not before ripping his throat out and cutting his hands off so he can never touch what's *mine* again.

I shake my head at the ridiculous word that floats around my brain—*mine*. She's not mine, not my mate.

Sylara says something to Kael that earns her a swipe from the male. She dodges the move easily and twists his arm behind his back.

Lumi's eyes go wide, but Kael just cackles, and Lumi backs down, watching them curiously.

I motion with my head for the others to leave behind Sylara and Kael, who we can hear bickering the entire way up the stairs, until it's just Lumi and me left in the gym.

"Is Kael really safe with her?"

I shrug. "They were both like this the last time Kael

was here, and they both survived. I expect the same this time."

She frowns. "Promise me you won't hurt him."

"I already told you the blood deal doesn't work that way."

She shakes her head. "No, just promise me with your words."

"I'll do my very best not to hurt him. But I can't guarantee anything if he keeps putting his hands all over you like that."

A slow smile creeps over her lips as she stands with her hands on her hips, her tight shorts and tank top still glistening with sweat from her workout. She swings her silvery hair back and forth in her ponytail.

"You're jealous? You can't be serious."

Trust me, I wish I weren't. But I don't respond to her.

"Kael is nothing to me. He's my best friend. The only connection I have left to home. I thought he could be my mate once, but I was wrong. And he doesn't share any romantic feelings about me."

"He does, but that's beside the point. What matters is where he puts his hands, especially around other vampires who might think I can't keep my mate in check."

"But I'm not your mate! Even you said you don't believe I am."

"Doesn't matter. All that matters is that they keep thinking you are to keep you safe."

"Well, Kael hugging me isn't going to change their thoughts."

"Him grabbing your ass will."

She glares at me, about to protest, and then she realizes where his hand was and that she has no grounds for arguing anything with me. A second later, her face starts to turn green again.

"Tell me about your dream so you can stop looking at me like you want to puke."

She sighs and then slinks to the floor, putting her head between her knees as if she can't until she pukes first. "I'm really regretting the deal we made."

I slide to the floor next to her, offering her a cup of water.

She takes it and chugs it.

"The symptoms will ease soon enough. And you got plenty out of the deal, mainly the promise that I won't use my mind control on you, remember?"

She nods, breathing heavily. "Just tell me about your dream."

"I don't know where to start or even if it's a prophecy."

"The deal obviously does, so just start anywhere."

I put my hand on her back, gently rubbing to try to relax her.

"In my dream, I was running through a thick forest, running from something that was chasing me. I run so fast that I'm barely able to stay upright."

"Are you in your human or wolf form?"

"Human."

I nod, waiting for her to continue. "Toward the end of my dream, I come to a fork in the road. To my left is icy cold snow. There's a trail of blood through the path. It's nightfall with only a sliver of blood red moon shining on the path. To my right, the night is lighted with a bright full moon lighting the warm path that feels warm, almost too warm."

I swallow the lump in my throat. "Which path do you choose?"

"I don't. The dream stops before I choose."

She's lying; she's not ready to share more. But the deal won't let her lie without consequences.

I don't want to know which path she chooses. Neither is a good choice.

I'm not ready to know, I tell the universe.

I watch her carefully and see the color in her face returning as she lifts her head from between her legs. The symptoms will return, but by sharing some of the dream and expressing my reluctance to have more, it should ease the symptoms for a while.

"I had a dream too. We should go north soon. There is a seer there who has more of the prophecy."

"North it is then, after Kael is initiated and I know he's safe."

"None of us will be safe until the curse is broken. Restlessness is growing in the packs and covens. A war will break out soon if the curse isn't lifted. Even if it is, if the curse is only broken for one species, then an all-out war will definitely happen. But maybe that's what the gods have been wanting all along—a war to entertain themselves with."

"What will Kael's initiation require?"

"His loyalty mainly. He'll have to pledge it in front of the entire Bloodmoon pack and any vampires who decide to show up, which I suspect will be many now that they think I have a mate with whom I can break the curse."

"The vampires—"

"Will behave. I'm their lord. They will do what I say."

"The vampires that attacked me before."

"Weren't mine—they belonged to a different house. Only Nightfall vampires will be in attendance."

"Do you really believe we could be mates?"

"I believe anything is possible. Mates are not based on love. They are based on strengths as a unit. How equal and balanced a pair is. How it would change the world, that sort of thing. So sure, we could be mates. You and Ambrose could be mates. The gods could have paired you with any man they desired. They could be cruel and decide your mate is the man you hate most in the world, a killer, someone who killed someone you loved."

She stares at me, thinking my words over before staring down at her hands. "In my dream, I always go right. I always go toward the moonlight, the warmth, the evergreens, the magic. It feels like home to me. But after everything, I'm terrified of choosing that path. If he's my mate, then I'll spend the rest of my life being with a controlling monster."

"But if you choose left, you'll be with a controlling killer. I get it."

She looks up at me. "You've both done unforgivable things. I don't like either of my choices."

"Maybe the two of us aren't your only choices."

She shakes her head. "It's not about having a choice at all, though, is it? My mate was decided by fate, by the gods. I don't get a choice. To break the curse, I have to accept my mate."

"There's always a choice. Maybe you were given two mates because the gods wanted you to choose."

"How do I do that, though?"

"I can't answer that for you. All I can say is that I don't think you really believe that either of us has done anything so unforgivable that you wouldn't accept us as mates to break the curse."

"Why do you say that?"

"Because if you did, you'd sever our link with you. You wouldn't be having dreams that allow you to choose. There would only be one of us in your head. You still have a choice."

CHAPTER 15

LUMI

Three outfit choices that couldn't be further apart from each other are lying on my bed. Leggings with a black shirt, jacket, and tennis shoes—casual and practical. The second option is an off-the-shoulder black jumpsuit that would fit my body like a glove, paired with boots. And the third, I gasp when I see. It's a black lace gown with golden swirls that look like the runes that mark my body etched into it. It looks low cut in the back and is paired with stiletto heels.

I'm drawn to the third. I want the third. But it seems entirely impractical for an initiation. I need to be prepared for anything.

Nyx laid out these choices to remind me that I have a choice in who is my mate, at least until I sever one of the bonds. But just like my outfit choice, it's fake. There's only one option that will break the curse, but I don't know what the correct choice is at the moment.

I put on the jumpsuit. The only option that allows me to feel attractive and powerful, while still being prepared for anything that could happen. All the while I'm getting dressed, my heart still aches for the dress that I'll never get to wear.

The bathroom is just as gorgeous as the bedroom, with floor-to-ceiling windows that overlook an incredible view of the forest. The room is bright, with white marble and gold accents. I'm brushing my sleek, silvery hair back when I hear the knock on my door.

My heart freezes. I thought I had a few more minutes to get ready before someone would come and get me for the initiation ceremony. I walk to the door, trying to maintain my composure through my trembling legs. I fumble for the door handle and push it open before I change my mind.

Dark jeans, a crisp white shirt, and a trimmed brown haircut meet my gaze, and I stop trembling as my smile draws upward.

"You look incredible," Kael says, "and a little too relieved to see me. Are you okay?"

I swallow. "Yes, I wish you would stop asking me that." I lead him inside, and he inhales sharply at the large window inside.

"That's quite a view."

I nod. "I can't believe the vampire has a house built of glass when he can't even enjoy the sunlight."

"I assume that means he built it before he turned into a vampire. But it's shocking that he didn't have his own room redesigned. Or at least turn one of the other rooms into his room. But then again, it's hard to destroy a view like this."

"What do you mean, his room?"

Kael cocks his head to the side. "This is Nyx's room."

I frown. "How do you know that?"

"Last time I was here, I slept in the room next door.

The same one I'm in now. That way, Nyx could guard me overnight. He'd hear if I tried to escape. He hasn't been sleeping in here with you?"

I laugh. "Gods, no. It's not like that between us. We don't have feelings for each other. And we're pretty sure we aren't even actually mates, that our connection is just because we both have information that needs to be shared to get the curse lifted. He killed one of my closest friends. I won't ever be sharing a bed with him."

"Is that how you feel about Ambrose?"

I turn from Kael and look out the window. "I'd rather not talk about Ambrose. I don't want to know how he's doing, or if he's the reason you're here. I'd rather not know about anything regarding him after he took away my choices."

Kael bites his bottom lip as if he wants to say more, but is holding back.

I sigh, running my hand through my long hair. "What is it?"

"Nothing. It doesn't matter about these idiotic males. What matters is that you're safe. That's why I'm here, to keep you safe. I won't leave your side again."

"And you're okay initiating into the Bloodmoon pack to do that?"

"I'd rather be concocting an escape plan, but I know you won't leave without answers, and whatever idiotic deal you made with him won't allow you to leave. So yes, I'll join his pack. I've never had a problem with the Bloodmoon pack. For the most part, they treated me well during my time here. It's the vampires you have to watch out for. They don't operate under the same civilized rules as the wolf shifters do. They can seem human one minute, and then the next, their bloodlust or curse will take over, and they'll go rabid, completely out of control. They'll kill you even if they like you and consider you an ally. No vampire is to be trusted."

"Does that include Nyx?"

"My understanding is that Nyx has learned to control his bloodlust. As long as he's not drinking blood, he's in control of his own mind."

There's another knock, so I open the door and find Sylara in a red dress, her curls pinned on top of her head, and her makeup flawlessly painted onto her face, which makes her even more breathtakingly beautiful. Gone is any trace of the dangerous beta who usually looks like she's ready to attack at a moment's notice. All that is left is soft, feminine beauty. For a moment, I'm envious of how good she looks and regret my decision not to wear the dress.

Sylara's eyes look me over from head to toe. "You'll do."

"Thanks? Was that supposed to be a compliment?"

She shrugs. "It was supposed to be exactly what I said." She looks past me to Kael and then frowns. "How did I know I'd find you in here? If you want to keep all your limbs, I suggest you stay out of Nyx's bedroom with her."

I raise an eyebrow. "Really? You think Nyx cares that he's here? He's not jealous. I'm not his. He doesn't even like me."

Sylara ignores me. "Don't find yourself alone in his bedroom with her again if you want to keep breathing."

Kael just nods.

"It's time, but don't worry, you can always change your mind. You'd just waste everyone's time, and you'd have to go back to the Moonlight pack or whatever pack would take you."

"I'm not changing my mind," Kael says.

"Good," she answers and then makes a swift exit.

"Are you really sure? I know they say that you won't be required to do much besides make an oath, but still, you'd be making an oath to be loyal to the Bloodmoon pack, to Nyx."

"I'm sure. I'll do anything to protect you, Lumi. You're the only thing that matters to me."

Without another word, he exits the bedroom and starts following Sylara. I run to catch up, my mind whirling with thoughts of what could happen if Nyx is lying.

I'm not sure exactly what to prepare for as we walk outside. Dusk has begun to settle over the horizon as darkness blankets the town. The other pack members I know—Riven, Brax, and Talonis—flank each of our sides as we walk, while other pack members start coming out of their homes. We walk through the center of town, my heart beating a million miles a minute as we do. I'm sure everyone around me hears my anxiety pumping through my body.

We head towards a small amphitheater with a stage at the edge of the pack's town. Nyx has already taken the stage, and as we walk down the stairs, I notice more and more people taking their seats. Some of the visitors are vampires.

I force myself to stand up straighter as I walk toward the stage. Taking a deep breath to try to ease my heartbeat, I'm not sure if we are all going up on stage or just Kael until we get there, but we don't slow down as we reach the stage. We all climb up the stairs next to Nyx.

Tonight isn't a full moon, and I doubt there are any witches here, so I'm curious as to how the initiation will go.

"We have a new member of the Bloodmoon pack who would like to be initiated," Nyx says to the crowd. He motions for Kael to step forward, while I stay standing next to others on the side of the stage.

I grab Kael's hand, giving him a gentle squeeze before releasing him and watching him walk toward Nyx. I try to focus on his steps, but a haze washes over my eyes, my skin becomes clammy, and my body trembles where I stand.

"Are you okay?" a voice whispers in my ear, but I can barely hear it, and I definitely can't make out whose voice it is.

In an instant, I'm taken back to my own initiation into the Moonlight pack. To seeing Ambrose in that tree, unable to speak. To the fear of running. To the spell I was under. To the male pack members surrounding me, each looking at me like they wanted to fuck me.

My eyes fall shut as if it is happening all over again, but this time, I know that I don't really want them to fuck me. This time, when I'm stripped of my clothes, when I am held and spread bare, when they touch me...

A hand goes around my shoulder, pulling me against his chest. I struggle, trying to fight off the hands. No one can touch me! Not again!

"You're safe, it's not really happening. You're safe, love," his words push against the haze in my mind, and his cool body touching me instantly brings down the fever burning through my body. I stop struggling in his arms.

"You're safe, Lumi. It's not really happening."

His words break through the nightmare I'm reliving.

"The initiation is over. Everyone went to celebrate."

"Even Kael?" I ask, shocked that he'd leave me in this state.

"I told him I needed to show you something before we went to the party. No one realized what was happening except me, not even my own pack."

"Why? How did you notice then if none of them did?"

He runs his hand over my hair, smoothing it down as if making sure I'm really back with him, my mind not still lost to the nightmare.

"Because you were sending me image after image of what your initiation looked like. I've never—" he shakes his head, cutting himself off. But I can see the veins popping on his neck and his clenched fist. He's holding himself back.

"Are you okay now?" he asks, tenderly, his voice soft.

I nod. "I'm fine."

He looks away for a moment, like he's trying to say something but unsure. Finally, he says, "Now isn't the time to make the decision, but you don't have to stay a Moonlight pack member forever. Their magic is more complicated. It might take more to break the bonds you have and take away the runes on your body, but it can be done. You can always become a Bloodmoon pack member."

"I'm not sure I'm ready to go through another initiation again anytime soon."

He frowns. "You didn't even see what happened with Kael, did you?"

"What happened? Is he okay?"

"Yes, he's perfectly fine. Ask him yourself."

"I will."

"Good. Now, do you want to go celebrate with everyone, or do you want me to take you back to the house?"

I contemplate for a moment. "I want to see Kael." I need to make sure he's okay.

"Can I carry you?"

I frown. "No."

He sighs, rubbing the back of his neck. "The party is over a mile away. You can see Kael much faster if I carry you."

I huff. "Fine."

No sooner has the word left my mouth than Nyx scoops me in his arms and runs. It feels like a split second between when he scooped me up and put me down.

My jaw comes unhinged as I stare at him. I still can't get over how fast he is.

He cocks his arrogant head before nodding in the direction of the lights and music. We start walking through the edge of the treeline when I gasp for a whole other reason.

Beautiful music filled with laughter floats out to meet me at the edge of the dance floor. Flickering lights hang from the trees. I spot the band on the far side. A bar on the other. And everyone else is on the dance floor together—wolf shifters and vampires.

Kael is easy to spot. He's being lifted over the shoulders of several pack members, as if he had just won an important game.

Brax and Sylara are dancing together. Her dress shimmers brightly with every spin.

Riven is talking animatedly to someone on the edge of the dance floor, nothing but smiles.

And Talonis... "Is that a vampire Talonis is dancing with?"

Nyx nods.

"How? How are they getting along so well? How did you do it?"

"Neither wolf shifter nor vampire can resist a good party. The curse doesn't give us a lot to celebrate, so when we have a chance to, everyone pushes their own hardships aside and just has fun."

I know I'm missing something, something important that Nyx isn't telling me. But if it had anything to do with our deal, he'd be doubled over in pain right now or about to vomit. So whatever it is, it can't be that important.

Before I can ask more questions, Nyx is swept away onto the dance floor. A mix of both shifters and vampires is dancing with him.

The second he's whisked into the crowd, Talonis appears next to me.

"Are you my guard for the night?" I ask him.

"More like a protector. You don't need a guard. You're free to leave if you want."

I don't respond to that when we both know that isn't true.

Nyx smiles, genuinely smiles, and I soften toward him for a split second. For a second, he's not the asshole alpha who tauntingly calls me love or naive snow wolf. He's not the vicious vampire lord that kills so easily. He's not the monster who killed one of my closest friends or invades my head whenever he feels like it. He's just a man dancing with his friends.

"I don't need a protector either." I move through the dance floor to find Kael. The second he spots me, he quickly untangles himself from the woman he was dancing with, grabs my hand, and yanks me to him.

I giggle as he pulls me into an embrace like we're

lovers and then spins me before dipping me like you see in the movies. When he yanks me back to his body, I ask, "How does it feel to be a Bloodmoon member?"

His eyes sparkle as he looks at me. "It feels like I'm right where I belong."

The dance floor vanishes when I'm with Kael. All my troubles. All the mate and curse talk. All of my own trauma is gone. It's just me and my best friend.

"Do you ever wonder what would have happened if we had stayed with the Wintermoon pack instead of running?"

"We didn't have a choice. My father's alpha command—"

"I know. I just mean, if we had gone back..."

"Then we would have witnessed their deaths first-hand. And probably died right alongside them."

"Or maybe I would have been able to shift and saved you. Saved some of them. Maybe I would have saved you all the grief and pain and trauma you've had to go through since."

I shake my head before resting it on his shoulder. "It doesn't matter. I'm just glad you're here now."

He spins us around, holding me tight to his body. "I don't want you to suffer any more. I don't want you to have to be the one to break the curse. I don't want you to have to be mated or marked by either of these bastard alphas. I don't want you in danger."

"I can handle it. I'm strong enough. And I'm done letting either of them control me. The deal I made ensures that Nyx can't control me. And breaking my bond with Ambrose ensures that he can't."

"But you still carry the weight of the world on your shoulders. You still think you're the only one capable of breaking the curse, when for us wolf shifters, it's not even that bad. Who cares that we can't find our true mates? From what I've seen of mates, they are overrated anyway."

"We can't reproduce either. Without it broken, there will be no more wolf shifters. We'll die out."

"Maybe that's for the best. All I know is I don't need to know who my mate is when I'm perfectly happy being with my best friend."

I don't know what to say to him. I understand where he's coming from. I don't need to find my mate or the love of my life either. I'd be perfectly happy spending the rest of my life with Kael, but he doesn't realize that that could never happen. Too many know that I'm the key to breaking the curse. I'd be hunted forever. We'd always be running. Not to mention, if I can break the curse, I feel a responsibility to do that. To end the suffering of at least one species. To try to prevent a war and more destruction.

"I don't understand. Why initiate into the Bloodmoon pack if you just want me to run away with you?"

"So Nyx can't kill me when I do this." Kael dips me again, but this time his lips come down hard and heavy against mine in a claiming kiss.

CHAPTER 16

NYX

Staying out of her head is damn near impossible as she dances with her so-called *friend*. Her *friend*, whom she doesn't have feelings for, and he doesn't have the hots for her. Her *friend*, who just initiated into *my* pack to be near her. Her *friend*, who keeps grabbing her ass and holding her so flush against his body that I'm sure she can feel his erection pressing into her stomach.

If he's just her *friend*, then she and I have very different definitions of the word.

"Want me to kill him for you?" Sylara asks.

"No, they are just friends."

She scoffs. "You're delusional if you think that."

"Lumi's just trying to relax after the trauma she went through. Tonight brought up some bad experiences for her." I still can't get the images of her spread naked, Isolde making her think she wanted to fuck the entire pack, while underneath, Lumi wanted nothing to do with them. She was almost repeatedly raped by the entire Moonlight pack, all so she could prove her loyalty. *Fucking disgusting.* If I didn't want to kill Ambrose before, I do now. No one deserves to go through that.

"We've all been through shit. It doesn't excuse her behavior," Sylara says.

"Trust me, it does."

Her eyes snap from me to Lumi.

"Whatever she needs to bury her trauma in tonight, she gets. Drinks, Kael, other men, I don't care."

"Fine, but she needs to at least do it behind closed doors. Everyone thinks the two of you are mates, and you'll break the curse. If they find out that's not true—"

"I know. I'll send them to the house soon. I just... fuck."

It's too late.

I watch in slow motion as Kael dips her like he has a dozen times before. But this time, when he dips her, his lips seal against hers.

I jolt out of her head, not allowing myself to feel a single thought of what she's feeling right now. I'm not sure if she wants the bastard or wants to sucker punch him for kissing her when her trauma is so bright tonight. Either way, I'll end up making a bad decision that isn't thought through.

"Fucker," Sylara says.

Talonis, Brax, and Riven are at my side in a second. "What are your orders, sir?" Brax asks, already all business-like, like he knows a battle is about to happen, and he's about to command a squadron in a fight.

Maybe no one noticed. Maybe he kissed her so quickly, and I, being the only one in tune with her, was the only one who noticed.

But when I look back at them, they are still kissing. She hasn't pushed him away. *Fucking hell.*

"Kill him," Sylara says, breaking me out of my head.

"No. Just get them both out of here as discreetly as possible."

"Too late, boss," Talonis says.

There is a shift in the air. The celebratory mood has now sobered, and the room begins to spin into slow chaos. The whispers start...

"I thought she was the lord's mate."

"Is that why he initiated? Because he's in love with her?"

"We have to take her hostage. Torture her until we get the truth. The lord has been lying to us."

"No, we kill her. She's a distraction."

"No, we take her."

Godsdammit.

"The vampires want to kidnap and torture her. Stop them," I give the orders, ignoring the fact that even many in my own pack are upset by what's happening. But they are loyal to me no matter what and will fight on my side. The vampires, on the other hand, will deem me unfit to rule and serve me on an open platter to the vampire king.

Orson grabs onto Lumi's arm, yanking her free of Kael's kiss. I leap across the room, landing on top of him. My canines are elongated, and my wolf claws are beginning to sprout from my fingers as I pin him down.

"She's mine. Don't you dare lay a finger on her."

"It seems to me, she's *his*. And if she's his and not yours, then she has no need for protection. She's not a Bloodmoon pack member. She's the enemy."

"She's. My. Mate." I sink my teeth into his neck, but he's fast, having lived as a vampire far longer than I have. He slips, my teeth dragging across his skin.

We circle each other. I shouldn't kill him. I shouldn't

kill anyone, but my heart is out for blood. I want to kill. It's my instinct as a vampire to kill. But my conscious brain says it would only make things worse.

"You're nothing but a scammer. You lied to us."

I swipe at him, hitting him across his shoulder as I pull my wolf back and let the vampire side of me take root in my body. "I've never lied."

"Then you're willing to share your mate? You shared her with a wolf, so it's only fair you also share her with a vampire."

I snap my teeth at him. "Get the fuck away from her. If you touch her again, you and the entire House of Nightfall vampires die."

He smirks. "I don't believe you. None of us do."

He points to the others, where fights have broken out. Vampires against shifters. I don't know how to stop it, but I have to try.

I notice Lumi is safe, surrounded by Sylara and Riven, but I'm puzzled as to why she's still here, given that I gave the order to get her out. Kael is also nearby.

"It doesn't matter what you believe. All you care about is us breaking the curse, and we will on the next full moon."

"Not until I get a taste..."

He lunges for me at the same time three other vampires make their move toward me. But that's not the movement that catches my eye. Lumi is running toward me after leaping between Sylara and Riven.

Fucking hell. How do I get her out of here unharmed? They are going to tear her to pieces.

I grab her, turning her so that the vampires attack my back instead of her flesh. I cry out as they sink their teeth into my back.

"Stop! He's my mate!" she screams. She fights in my arms, but I only hold her tighter. They don't stop attacking me. Their lashes are getting deeper and deeper into my flesh to the point that I know I'm going to need Riven's help to heal properly if I survive this at all.

"Stop! I'll do anything you want. You can kidnap me. Rape me. Torture me. Whatever, just leave Nyx alone," she says.

My heart freezes as I try to understand why she would say that. *Why would she offer herself up to save a male she loathes and has proclaimed many times she wants me dead?* But it gets everyone's attention enough that attacks on my back stop.

"I'm the only one who gets to kill you," she mutters as if that explains everything.

"I'm not letting them take you."

"I know."

"So this was all a bluff? You weren't ever really going to offer yourself to them? You have a lot of faith in me, especially since I haven't actually saved your ass yet."

"I saved your ass, though."

She's right. She did. The attacks have stopped. Slowly, I rise from my hunched over position, but I'm careful to keep my body between Lumi and the vampires.

Orson looks at me expectantly, as if I'm about to hand her over to him. *Not going to happen.*

I snap my teeth and growl at him, which only makes him laugh. But he looks to Lumi.

"You have to make this right. You kissed another male. You almost started a war between our species. Almost got your supposed mate killed. You either let us take you or figure out another way so that we can all leave here peacefully," he says to her.

"Do you have any ideas on how to get us all out of here?"

"I'm working on it," I reply.

I can feel her roll her eyes at me in her head. *"Looks like I'll be saving your ass again, then."*

"Then take me. I offered myself up to stop you from killing my mate, and I stand by that offer. Take me, but you'll be taking away your only chance at breaking the curse. I'm the snow wolf that all the seers talk about breaking the curse. Whether he's my mate or not, it doesn't matter. If you kill me, you kill your chance at breaking the curse, and you'll be starting an all-out war. Because if you take me, there is nothing this man won't do to get me back or avenge my death."

"Except we don't believe that. If he were your mate, he wouldn't let you go around kissing other males."

She glares at him. "Nyx doesn't let me do or not do anything. I'm my own person. I make my own decisions. But you didn't give me a chance to let everything play out before you attacked Nyx."

"And what were you about to do?"

"This." She starts to walk out from behind my protection. I grab her wrist.

"What are you doing?"

"Trust me."

"I'm not going to let them take you. I'll kill them all first and start an all-out war."

She stares at me intently, like she's realizing something for the first time. But doesn't say anything else in my head. She starts moving again, and I hold onto her for as long as I can before I'm forced to make a decision. Hold onto her or let her go and trust her.

I hold on with every fiber until I'm forced to let her go. She keeps her eyes on Orson as she struts with all the confidence that has been bubbling inside her. I think she's going to walk straight for Orson, straight into his arms. I almost lose it and snatch her back before she makes a hard left and turns toward Kael and the others.

What is she doing?

She walks right up to Kael, and my stomach knots. If she gives him any warning about what she's going to do, it's unnoticeable. Raising her hand, she slaps him hard across the cheek. "Don't kiss me, don't touch me without my permission. You'll be lucky if Nyx doesn't immediately kick you out of the pack. And if he chooses to, I won't stop him. I don't care that you're my childhood friend. I don't care how drunk you are, I'm not fucking *yours* to play with. Do you understand?"

Kael nods solemnly.

She spins on her heels and marches right back to me like she doesn't have an audience ready to kill her if she makes one misstep. She beelines it back to me, and then, without a word of warning, she rises on her tiptoes, reaching her hand up for a moment. I think I'm about to get slapped, too, but instead, she reaches around the back of my neck and pulls down.

I don't fully grasp what's happening until her lips crash into mine. The moment they touch, it's like a spark igniting dry tinder—sudden, wild, consuming. There's no hesitation, no gentle testing of boundaries. She kisses me with a fierce certainty, like she's done this a thousand times before. Like she's claiming what's already hers.

Her tongue doesn't ask—it demands, slipping past the seam of my lips with bold intent. Mine meets hers instantly, a hungry sweep in answer. She tastes like ice, like snow melting on my tongue, shockingly cold even against my already chilled skin—and I'm addicted. The way her fingers tighten around my neck, the way her tongue commands mine with ruthless precision—I could unravel from this alone.

She releases me far too soon, but it's probably for the best. She looks up at me with heat in her eyes.

"Take me to bed," she purrs.

CHAPTER 17

LUMI

What the hell did I just do? What the ever-loving hell did I just do?

That kiss—that motherfucking kiss. I just...I... it was...it...

Even my mind has gone speechless. I can't process my thoughts.

And then what did I say? 'Take me to bed.'

My cheeks blush with embarrassment. I shouldn't have said that. I shouldn't have kissed him. I'm so truly and incredibly fucked. My words were meant to be a bluff to save us, but I wouldn't be mad if he took me to his bed.

No.

He killed Rowena. Killed her. He's a killer. And he did countless horrible things to Ambrose. And he's a vampire. And he used mind control on me.

But...

No buts.

Gods, that kiss was powerful, earth-shattering, life-changing kind of kiss. A kiss that parallels every kiss I had with Ambrose. A kiss that screams mate all the way down to my bones. A kiss that never should have happened.

Turmoil is spinning out of control in my head. My embarrassment strengthens when I realize that Nyx can probably hear every thought I'm having. But when I do a quick scan of my mind, for once, I find it empty. No Nyx. No Ambrose. Just me, thank heavens.

Nyx stares at me, a picturesque statue not giving away any of his own emotions. I have no idea what he's thinking, and I'm too terrified to try to slip into his mind to figure it out.

I have no idea if my plan worked. But we aren't being viciously attacked right now, so I'd say it had to have worked at least a little.

Nyx gives me a silent command with one look, but just like me, he doesn't try to get into my head. Either to give me privacy, or he's just as terrified by what just happened as I am.

I nod like I understand, but in reality, I'm a puddle of emotions I don't want to process yet. So, I'll do anything to avoid thinking too hard about what just happened.

Nyx releases my arm, and it's then that I realize he's been holding me this entire time. He takes a step away from me, and my lungs forget how to breathe. Nyx's back is painted red with his own blood, to the point where his shirt looks like it was always red. Large slits cut through it, though, revealing his open flesh. I don't know how he walks so smoothly, like he's not in any pain at all. For any mortal, he'd be near death at this point.

Orson looks up at Nyx, like he's expecting what's about to happen. But I don't have a clue.

Nyx grabs Orson by the throat and lifts him into the air, as if he's just lifting air. "You don't get to question my decisions again, and definitely not my mate's. You don't get to threaten her life. I'm showing mercy for her sake, but if you threaten her life in any way ever again, it will mean permanent death."

Orson stares at him, not even trying to fight, like he knows at this point it's futile.

"Do you understand?" Nyx growls ferociously.

"Yes, my lord."

And then Nyx snaps his neck, dropping him in a limp pile on the ground.

Everyone stares at him. He's dead.

Killer...killer...he's a killer. The words whisper through my head like a strong breeze. He killed Rowena. He'll kill everyone you love.

It takes me a minute to remember that he's not really dead, at least not permanently, unless Nyx drives a stake through his heart. Which he doesn't appear to be doing. I'm not upset if he does, though. That vampire deserved to die for what he did to Nyx's back.

Nyx turns to face me, as if to ask if what he did was enough or if he should take it further. But I suspect the reason he didn't kill him outright is that Orson is popular with the other vampires, and it might start an uproar and a revolution against Nyx that could overthrow him as a lord.

I nod, letting him know I think it's enough.

His lips twitch in response. He walks back to my side and interlocks his fingers with mine. A movement that feels comforting and yet so strange at the same time. Intimate, almost as intimate as kissing. But I know it's what would be expected of us if we were truly mates.

"Go home, the party is over. My mate will decide

Kael's punishment." With that dismissal, Nyx leads me through the thick clearing.

"Can I—"

"Yes," I answer before he even finishes his sentence. I just want to be far away from here as fast as possible. I don't know if in Nyx's current state if he's going to be able to carry me or if his vampire speed will work. But one second I'm in the woods, my feet on the ground, the next I'm on Nyx's doorstep, cradled in his arms.

He's silent as he slowly carries me into the house and up the stairs. As my heart begins to thunder in my chest, I realize he's carrying me to *his* bedroom, not mine. I'm not sure if he knows my words were said mainly to get us out of there in one piece, but heat spreads in delicious antici-pation. I can't shake the feeling that sleeping with Nyx might be the best damn idea I've ever had.

Nyx places me in my bed. "In bed, love, as you requested." There's a teasing glint in his eyes. The first words he's spoken to me.

"I didn't mean...I mean, I meant...I—"

He chuckles. "I know what you meant and why you said what you said. Thank you for saving my life. For preventing an internal battle among the vampires and my pack. And stopping an uprising among the vampires."

I bite my lower lip as my cheeks pinken at my response to kissing him.

"We don't need to talk about it. I forced myself to stay out of your head, so I have no idea what you felt or thought during the kiss. It was done under duress. It doesn't mean anything. And it doesn't change anything. We aren't really mates, we both know that."

"Right," I say, doing my best to keep the disappoint-ment out of my voice. I shouldn't feel disappointed. He's right, of course. It means nothing. It changes nothing. It doesn't mean we are mates. *But then why does it feel like it changes everything?*

"Why am I in your bed? Why not any of the other hundred rooms?"

"Because this is where you are expected to be, as my mate and all."

He means give everyone the illusion that we are fucking all the time.

"And where are you then if I'm sleeping in your bed?"

"Elsewhere."

It's not an answer, *but then why does it disturb me that he might be sleeping somewhere else? With someone else? Sylara perhaps? Or another pack member? A vampire?*

He stills for a moment, as if he read my thoughts. But I still don't feel his icy threads in my mind.

"The vampire that you sort of killed. He's not really dead, is he?"

"No. As much as I'd like to have killed him permanently, I knew it would start a war if I did."

"How long will he be dead for?"

"Depends on whether a healer helps him or how recently he's fed. If a healer helps, it could be a day. If not, up to a week to fully heal from that on his own."

I nod.

"We need to go see a seer tomorrow. We can't put it off any longer. We have until the next full moon to figure out how to break the curse," he says.

I nod. "When do you want to leave? Do you have anyone specific in mind that we should go visit?"

"Dawn, and yes, I've been having my own dreams. We need to go north. There's a small coven about six hours from here."

A coven of witches. It sounds worse than the vampires, but we don't have a choice. We need answers, and our dreams alone don't seem to hold enough.

There's a soft rap on the door. Nyx doesn't glance up from me. "It's Sylara with Kael."

I stiffen.

"I'll leave you to handle him as I promised. Unless you want me to—"

"No, I'll handle him." I glare at the door, still not believing what Kael did to get into this mess. "I'm sorry about what he did. I didn't see that he wanted me before. You were right. I should have seen what he was up to and stopped him."

Nyx shakes his head. "Don't blame yourself. It's not your fault. And I don't even really blame Kael for tonight. He was doing what he thought was best to save you; however, foolish his actions were."

Nyx turns, and I get a look at his back again. "Your back," I almost sob the words out. It looks so tender, so raw, so painful that I don't know how he's standing without wincing in pain.

"I'll have Riven look at it. I'll be ready to go at dawn." He dismisses my concern for him and then vanishes from the room before I can ask more questions or show more concern. But I won't be able to forget about his pain or what caused it anytime soon. He didn't deserve that.

"Come in," I shout to the door.

It opens slowly. Kael is standing in the doorway looking somber, while Sylara stands behind him. She doesn't say anything to me.

"I've got it," I say to her.

She nods, for once, not arguing with me as she vanishes. Kael walks into the room and shuts the door.

I get up from the bed and walk over to the large windows, where I find a door that leads out onto an expansive balcony that goes all the way around the circular room. I don't have to say anything, but Kael follows. I don't know why, but I don't want to tarnish the room with this conversation. It needs to happen outside.

I walk to the railing and lean against it. Kael hesitantly walks next to me and does the same. He doesn't dare speak. He waits for me, which is the only smart thing he's done all day.

"Why? Why did you kiss me? Was it to hurt Nyx? Because Ambrose asked you to? Or because you love me?"

"Ambrose asked me to come, to protect you. But he didn't tell me to kiss you. I doubt I'd still be breathing if he knew what I did."

I turn and face him. "So why? To hurt Nyx?"

"Not to hurt him, but I don't think he's your mate. He can't be, he's a vampire for fucking sakes! A killer. He kills just because, for no reason other than he wants to taste blood. He killed one of your friends. I don't care what he's pretending to be around you; that's not the real him."

"Did you see him do atrocious things when you were held captive by him?"

He hesitates.

"Did you?" I need to know.

"No. He mostly just had his pack members follow me around and keep me mostly isolated. I saw him once with some vampires before he turned into a lord, but I've heard the rumors. I know who he is. He's a killer, a monster."

"Do you love me?"

"Of course, I've known you my whole life. You're my best friend. The only thing left of my real pack. Of course, I love you."

I shake my head. "Are you in love with me? Do you think I'm your mate?"

"I don't know. The curse has all of my feelings all mixed up. I don't know how I feel. I just know you don't belong with Nyx, and I'm not exactly happy with how Ambrose has treated you. So maybe you and I belong together like you thought from the very beginning. I'm not sure I believe in fated mates or that even breaking the curse. But I don't need babies to make me happy. And I know you don't either. We don't need to break the curse. We just need to be happy and safe. We could have that together."

"The curse has to be broken, or a war will start. One we will never be able to run from. We won't be able to escape, no matter what you think." I stare back out at the vast darkness, only lit by the smallest of moonlights. "And I don't want safe. Even if there was no curse to break, I want real love. The kind that doesn't happen often. The kind that roots itself deep in your soul and you'd whither and die if anything happened to your partner kind. And maybe I do want babies. I don't know." I picture little kids with Ambrose's golden eyes, Nyx's black hair, or even Kael's messy hair. But I can't picture any of them fully.

Fucking curse.

"It's hard to explain to you, to anyone, but I know I'm the only one to break the curse. I've felt it. I've dreamed about it."

"You've had dreams about it?"

"Yes. Dreams, visions, I don't know what to call them. But I know that I will break the curse. I will change everything. I don't have a choice."

He frowns. "You have a choice."

"Maybe in a lot of things, but I don't have a choice to

not break the curse. I can't live with myself if I don't try when I see the suffering, the carnage, the death that will come as a result of doing nothing."

"Then that's your choice."

"It is." I'm silent for a beat. "As is my choice in what to do with you."

"Lumi, I'm sorry. It won't happen again."

"You're right, it won't. I won't allow it."

His eyes search mine, but I've already made up my mind about how to handle him. I can't trust him, but he was just doing what he could to protect me.

"You're going to let Nyx bite you."

"What? Hell no, I'm not."

"If you want to stay, you're going to let Nyx bite you. You're going to let him drink a drop of your blood. He'll be able to use mind control on you."

"His alpha command is enough. I'm a pack member. I'll have to do what he says anyway."

I shake my head. "You can fight that. You can join another pack. You can denounce your membership. I want a guarantee that you will not risk his life again. If you want to stay, these are my conditions."

"Okay," he whispers after a nervous gulp.

CHAPTER 18

NYX

I wait on the back porch for Lumi. I know she's awake, I heard her earlier moving around. But I won't rush her. She knows where to find me when she's ready. Instead, I sip one of the two coffees as I watch the lightest pink of the sun begin to rise.

I hear the squeak of the sliding glass door opening and two sets of footsteps stepping onto the deck.

"He's not coming," I say in a clipped tone. I can't believe she has the audacity to bring him after everything he did.

"No, he's not. But you are going to bite him," Lumi says.

My head whips in her direction, causing a slight soreness in my back where Riven spent the night healing me, still tender to the touch.

"Why would I bite him?"

"So you can control him."

I look from Lumi to her asshole friend. She can't be serious. But from his expression, it's clear she's dead serious.

"I'm not going to bite him or control his mind. That's not something I just go around doing. If I really need to control him, I'll use an alpha command."

"We both know wolf shifter powers are growing weaker, and wolves can fight an alpha command. Your mind control is more absolute. Kael could initiate into another pack, where you'd have no control. We need to be certain he won't do something that gets you killed or run back to Ambrose and tell him all of your secrets."

Lumi is looking at me with pure determination on her face, and I know I'm going to do whatever she wants. There is no fighting with her. She is my weakness.

"Do you understand what you are asking me to do?" I look directly at her, making it clear that I will do this if she wants me to, but there are consequences she doesn't even fully understand.

"Yes," she breathes out.

My eyes cut to Kael, wondering how he's taking all of this. To his credit, he doesn't seem to be at all upset by what's happening or her decision. He will be, though, because an alpha command is one thing. Being mind-controlled by a vampire is another.

"You understand that it will be *me* controlling him, not *you*?"

She grinds her teeth together before taking another breath. "Yes."

"And you still want me to do it? To take away all of his control? He won't be able to breathe without my permission. I could order him to kill himself, and he'd have to obey."

She stares me down before slipping into my mind. I let her, even though I could easily block her out if I wanted to. Her thread is so easy to find in my mind. So delicate and female and snow-covered that it feels like the first frost in my head.

I don't say anything in my head, and she doesn't say anything either. She just feels me. Just exists in my head.

"I trust you not to hurt him."

"You shouldn't."

"Maybe not, but I don't trust him not to kill you. And you could be the key to breaking the curse."

"I killed Rowena. What makes you think I won't kill him, too?" Ask me. Ask me more.

"I don't. But he's a pack member. Alphas don't go around killing pack members. Even ones they hate. You'd be challenged as the alpha."

I look to Kael, giving him a slight choice in the matter. But he'd do anything she asks of him. She, too, is his weakness.

Fuck, he loves her. Does everyone who spends any time with her fall in love with her? I'm doomed if so.

I look at Lumi one more time to ensure this is really what she wants.

She nods.

I move in one quick motion, so quick that Kael never sees me coming. I don't give him time to feel fear or to run. One second I'm in my chair, the next I've leaped to his side and sunk my fangs into his neck until I've tasted one single drop. The next blink of an eye, I'm standing across the deck, carefully holding my breath so the scent of his blood doesn't tempt me into drinking him dry.

"It's done. Cover your wound. We should go."

"Give him a command first," Lumi says.

She doesn't know how hard this is on me. How much it pains me to do this.

I look to Kael with sharpened eyes. "Don't take any

action that will hurt Lumi." I can feel the magic working, his mind bending to me as I speak. I have ultimate control over him. Ultimate power. I fucking hate it.

I can't stay here any longer. I need a minute away. Quickly, but without using any of my vampire or wolf shifter speed, I grab my backpack and climb down the stairs and out into the forest. The sun has just begun to peak through the forest leaves. I should shift soon, so I don't have to hop around through the shadows.

A few seconds go by before Lumi joins me. "Thank you. I needed Kael to see how serious I was. I won't make you use the mind control on him again unless it's absolutely necessary, but Kael tends to make stupid decisions when it comes to my safety."

"Don't we all," I mutter under my breath.

"What?" she asks.

"Nothing. Are you ready to go?"

She nods.

"It's several hours north through the forest. I'm going to shift into my wolf form. You'll ride on my back."

She frowns. "Can't we take a car?"

"No, there aren't roads to this coven. They prefer isolation deep in the forest."

"Can't you just vampire run us there?"

I shake my head. "Too much sunlight to dodge going that fast."

She sighs.

"Do you have a problem riding on my back?"

"No, I just hate that I can't run alongside you. Seeing you in your wolf form just reminds me that I can't."

"I'm sorry."

"It's not your fault that I can't shift. You have nothing to be sorry for."

More sunlight starts to creep in through the branches of the trees. I begin to undress, and she blushes before turning around. *"You can watch, you know. Wolf shifters aren't modest, and I know you like looking at my body."*

She just shakes her head but doesn't turn around.

I shift, letting my muscles strengthen, my fur glide over my skin, and my nails lengthen. Nothing feels better than being in this form. I hate that she can't feel this way whenever she wants.

"You have a coat in that bag of yours?"

"Yes."

"Put it on and then add my things to your bag so we only have to carry one bag with us."

"For a male who hates using alpha commands or mind control, you sure are bossy."

"Efficient."

"Whatever." But she does as I ask, putting her coat on along with gloves and a hat before quickly shoving the clothes and sandwiches I packed into her backpack.

"Climb on, love. You know you like riding on me."

Her cheeks pinken again as her silvery hair blows in the breeze. "Actually, it's my least favorite thing." She reluctantly climbs onto my broad back, gripping onto my fur.

"I'll make sure you have a good time this time, I promise." And then I take off. It takes her a while to settle in and relax. I'd guess it's a lot like riding a horse; she has to get used to how her body moves as I move. But to me, running through the forest with her on my back is instantly incredible.

I may also be a vampire and sometimes enjoy the perks of being one, but nothing beats running in my wolf form. It's the most freeing, joyous thing I've ever experienced. And her fingers digging into my fur, her thighs clenching around my back, only adds to my experience.

It takes her close to an hour before I feel settled in. Neither of us has spoken to the other thus far. I've just been enjoying running, and she's been focused on not falling off my back.

"You enjoying the ride yet?" I run with an extra bounce in my step as I ask her.

She huffs. "Not particularly."

"Liar."

"Fine, I'm enjoying myself. But it's still not the same as when I'm in my own wolf form."

"I know. I'm sorry. We'll ask the seer about how to get your wolf back, too."

"I know, but it doesn't mean she'll have any answers for us."

"We won't stop until someone does."

"We might be searching for the rest of our lives then."

"Then that's what we'll do. I made a deal with you that I can't back out of, even if I wanted to. But this is one I won't want to ever."

"You sure?"

"Yes, everyone deserves the freedom to shift and to be able to run through the forest whenever they like."

We return to running in silence, but I can feel her joy as her muscles relax more and more on my back. I can't give her control over her wolf, but I can give her this.

We stop for lunch in a shady spot so I can gulp down my food quickly in my human body before returning to running.

"We're almost there," I say as the coven's scent tickles my nostrils.

"So, uh, I've been avoiding asking this the entire time,

but what is going to make the seer want to talk to us? Witches hate every pack except for the Moonlight pack. And they especially hate vampires. How are we going to get any of them to cooperate with us?"

"I'm going to offer them something they want."

"Which is?"

"You'll see."

"Ah, vague answers. I love it when you do that. It definitely means I'm not going to like whatever it is."

"Did you hear the key word in my sentence? *I'm*—I'm going to offer them something, not you. You have nothing to worry about."

She sighs. "I hate witches."

"And you have every right to. But just like shifters and vampires, it's not being a witch that makes someone unlikable. It's the individual witch. And this coven is mostly peaceful. They prefer to be secluded and keep to themselves. That's one of the reasons I chose it as the first place we went. Less likely to run into problems this way."

"Still don't like witches."

"Maybe they'll change your mind. But you still have that blade?"

"Yes, it's strapped to my thigh."

"Good girl."

"Not that it will be any use against magic."

"You'd be surprised what a normal weapon can do when it's wielded by the right person."

"Stop trying to convince me that we are going to walk out of here alive. The only positive thing about dying here is that I won't have to ride on your back all the way home —" I fling her off my back. She lands on her ass on the soft mossy grass.

And then I shift back to my human self. My naked human self.

She gets an eyeful, not turning away as she takes in my body. Her eyes slowly travel up my muscled legs and quickly land on my cock that is beginning to strain and grow in her direction. Her eyes never leave that spot.

I chuckle. "I don't think you'll be able to say you don't enjoy riding me much longer."

That breaks her attention, and her head snaps up to meet my gaze. "I'm not fucking you or riding your damn cock. I don't even like you. And as you've said many times, I'm not your mate. So stop teasing me."

"Then stop ogling it like you can't decide if you'd rather ride it or wrap your lips around it."

"Gods, you're insufferable. Put some damn clothes on."

"I need the backpack first."

She tosses it to me, and I quickly don the dark jeans and crisp buttoned-down black shirt.

"I'm dressed. Let's go before you get any second thoughts about seeing them."

"Your damned deal wouldn't allow me to. I'm already feeling a bit queasy just because I'm having doubts about going to the coven. I can't imagine what I'd feel like if I said I didn't want to go."

"You're safe with me. I won't let them hurt you."

"They're an entire coven of witches. We are in their territory. I'm not trying to downplay your skills or anything, but you being an alpha and a vampire lord are no match for a dozen witches."

"Well, then get ready to be impressed, love. Because I can take on an entire coven of witches if I have to. Haven't you heard the rumors? I'm a killer."

"You're an asshole, is what you are."

I chuckle. "Let's go." I hold out my hand to her, but she just scoffs at it. She does let me lead her through the forest into the clearing where the witches have made their home.

A dozen houses sit in a large circle. Each house is exactly the same, all facing a giant interior where they are all gathered. There's music and laughter and tables for eating. Nothing about this setup screams that they're cursed. If you asked them, I'm not even sure they would care about the curse being broken or not, from the amount of laughter I hear here.

Everything suddenly stops as they see us intrude on their space.

"You're not welcome here," the oldest says, her hair mostly gray now.

Lumi stills beside me, like she's already ready to flee. But I'm proud of her for remaining still instead of running.

"I brought an offering," I say.

"Her?" the oldest asks.

Lumi's heart stops beating as she waits for her answer.

"No, me."

And then her heart leaps out of her throat. *I thought you said I was safe with you. How am I going to be safe and get home if you offer yourself to them?*

"Just watch. And trust me."

The witch looks to the others, and they all nod. "We will accept your offering. Come forward."

Lumi grabs my bicep, trying to stop me.

"Trust me," I say.

She frowns with a bit of a pout that I find adorable, but she lets me go.

The witches start chanting in an ancient way. Words that neither I nor Lumi can understand, which I'm sure is making Lumi even more on edge.

"Give me your hand, Bloodmoon alpha," she says.

I hold out my hand, and she waves her hand quickly across my palm, causing a large gash.

"Hold it out so your blood spills."

I do as she asks, letting my blood drop into the collection bowl another witch is holding beneath my hand. When she's satisfied with the blood she's collected, she nods, and I pull my hand back. That should be enough for us to gain an audience with a seer.

"And, the other hand, Nightfall lord," she says.

I hear Lumi suck in a sharp breath. I'm not sure she's going to survive much more of this without giving herself a heart attack. She's forgotten how easily I heal.

I hold out the other hand. She strikes across my palm, and I let my blood flow into the bowl.

"Very well. We accept your offering. You are welcome here for the next twenty-four hours. Your wounds will not begin to heal until that time is up, alpha-lord."

I nod. "Thank you for letting us stay."

Lumi approaches me and starts digging through her bag. To my surprise, she pulls out some bandages. "Give me your hand."

I do, and she wraps it quickly and efficiently. Neither of us speaks in each other's minds or comments on how comforting her touch feels against my skin.

"And the other."

I give her that one too, and she does the same. It's strange to be wearing bandages when a wound like this would usually heal in a matter of minutes. But I'm thankful Lumi had the foresight to pack such items.

Lumi turns her scowl to the witch who cut my skin. "We are here to speak with a seer."

"Ah, you are the snow wolf who is destined to break the curse."

"Yes, can we please speak with your seer?"

"That is not up to me, but the seer herself." The older woman looks through her coven. "Juliette, would you like to speak to them?"

Lumi and I both hold our breath. This is where things will get tricky. I'm not sure if she'll want to share her visions with us or not.

"I'll speak with them, but I'm not guaranteeing them that I will share anything," she says, turning. "Come with me."

The middle-aged woman with long blonde curls that are just beginning to show some grays leads us into one of the small houses.

She heads into her dining room and motions for us to take a seat, while she heads into the kitchen.

"*I don't like that you're still bleeding,*" Lumi says in my head.

"*It's barely a scratch.*"

"*What can they do with your blood?*"

"*Use it in spells. Probably control me. Not really sure.*"

"*You're not sure, and you just offered them your blood like it was nothing!*"

"*I had to get us this meeting. It was crucial.*"

"*Well, maybe next time I should offer my blood. Yours seems too important.*"

"*No,*" I snap. "*I'll be the one offering blood.*"

She narrows her eyes at me in defiance as the seer returns with a tray.

"Coffee with cream for you, Lumi." She places Lumi's drink of choice in front of her.

"And black tea, no milk for the alpha-lord," she says, placing a cup in front of me that is my preferred drink.

"You can call me Nyx."

She smiles. "I'm Juliette. And you traveled a long way to speak with me."

"It wasn't too bad, honestly, the ride was quite enjoyable for some," I say.

Lumi kicks me under the table, and I muffle my pained laugh.

Juliette looks at Lumi. "You're here to ask about the prophecy, I presume? To figure out how to break the curse?"

"Yes, what do you know?"

"That's not how my visions work. Can I see your hand?"

Lumi takes a deep breath and then holds out her hand. The witch takes her hand and closes her eyes. Magic connects the two of them with a jolt.

I'm on high alert. Ready to slit the witch's throat the second she hurts Lumi.

"Are you okay?"

"Yes, she's not hurting me. It feels more like a strange tickle than anything."

"I'm sorry, I didn't know she was going to do that, or I'd have prepared you. I'm right here if you need me."

There's a pause then. *"Thank you."*

With a gasp, the witch releases Lumi. Juliette's eyes glow a bright yellow color, and then she blinks, and they return to the muddy brown color they were before.

"You want to know who your mate is between Ambrose and Nyx?"

Lumi nods.

"Your mate is crystal clear in the vision."

I freeze, unable to move, not sure of the answer I want. Lumi, on the other hand, is having a panic attack; it seems her heart is racing out of her chest. Honestly, neither Ambrose nor I is a good choice for a mate for her. There has to be someone better out there for her.

Juliette eyes me suspiciously, then turns her attention to Lumi. "Your mate is who you've known to be your mate this entire time. The one who controls your wolf. The only one you can have a future with. The one who can help you break the curse—Ambrose."

CHAPTER 19

LUMI

Ambrose—I whisper the single word in my head like a prayer and a curse. When I do, I feel the threads connecting me to him pulling, like I'm tugging him to me.

"My queen," I hear him whisper. The connection is still faint, but it's there.

I slam my mind shut. Shut it all out. Him. Nyx. I even try to shut myself off from my own thoughts.

"Thank you," I say to Juliette and then quickly get up from the table and walk out of the house, needing some fresh air. I don't know if Nyx stays to ask his own questions or immediately follows me outside.

When I step out into the crisp air, I take a long, deep breath as snow begins to fall, hitting the tip of my nose. I left my coat inside, but I'm not cold. The icy flakes seem to bring me alive, if anything.

Home, I miss home. That's what this smells like. The small group living deep in a thick forest surrounded by snow. I miss my dad. I wish I could talk to him. I wish he weren't dead.

The snow begins to fall faster, blanketing the ground in a delicate, glistening layer. I move through it in my boots, each step releasing a soft, satisfying crunch beneath my feet. The witches barely glance my way as I pass, their silence a wall I don't try to breach. I focus only on the cold kiss of snow against my cheek, willing myself not to think, not to feel—just to exist in this quiet, frozen moment.

I don't know how long I wander around their town. But long enough that the snow is a couple of inches thick beneath my boots and the sun has begun to set. Only then do I notice that Nyx has left the hut we were in and is now sitting in a chair by the fire, chatting with a couple of the other witches.

He looks up when he sees me approaching, but he doesn't speak to me, nor does he invade my head to talk to me either. He's let me have my space all day.

There is an empty chair on the other side of the fire, and I take a seat in it. I never got my coat. Never needed it. And now with the fire warming me, I definitely don't need it.

"Soup or wine?" A witch to my left asks me.

"I'm sorry, what?" I ask, not sure I heard her.

"I can tell you're in a frazzled state. Soup would heal you the best, but sometimes we aren't in a place to heal and would prefer the wine to help dampen the pain you're in."

My stomach sours at the thought of food. "Wine would be great."

She smiles and returns a moment later with a glass of red wine.

"Thank you. I'm sorry, I didn't catch your name."

"It's Starling. And I'm not a seer like Juliette is, and I

don't know what prophecy she told you. But I can sense great things will happen in your future."

I take a long drink of my wine. "I would prefer if more average things happened to me. Not everything needs to be this big, massive thing. I'm just a girl—"

"No, you're a snow wolf. One who doesn't need a coat to stay warm. You're a queen, destined to rule other wolves. You're a curse breaker. And you'll become many more things, but I'll let you figure those things out yourself."

I frown. "Has Nyx mentioned when he'd like to leave?"

"Your traveling companion has been very courteous. He's been helping with some physical chores and answering all of our curious questions about what it's like being an alpha and lord. I doubt he'll want to leave until morning, after his wounds heal, when he's already been offered a bed to sleep in here. It might appear rude, and your companion seems to want to make a good impression on us."

"Does he now?" I mutter under my breath, my gaze fixed on Nyx as he smiles and laughs at something the attractive witch to his left says.

He realized I'm not his mate, and that frees him to go sleep with any attractive woman he can find. He doesn't need to hold out any longer.

I down the rest of my wine and then hand the witch back her glass. "Thank you for the wine."

I stand, unsure of where I'm headed or what I'll do, but I know I need to get away from here. I take two steps before I stumble, my head a little dizzy. I frown. I take another step, barely staying on my feet as the ground seems to shake so badly that it must be an earthquake.

"I've got you," he slides into my head as his arms slide around my waist, holding my hands and bracing my fore-arms against his to keep me from falling again.

"Are you sure? It looked like you were getting awfully cozy with that witch. If she sees you holding me like this, she might not let you into her bed tonight," I say back in his head, but I'm pretty sure I'm slurring my words, so I have no idea if all the words get through to him or not.

"I'm not going to respond to any of that since I know how spiked witches' wine can be."

"It's spelled?"

"Most likely."

I frown. *"Are you sure an earthquake isn't happening right now?"*

"Very sure."

I sigh. *"Can you help me find someplace to sit down?"*

He scoops me into his arms, not asking for permission.

"Put me down."

"It will take you all night to walk to our hut if I do."

Our hut—huh.

I stop protesting and let him carry me, mainly because the up is now down and down is now up, and my body is beginning to heat, and he smells so damn good, and...

He sets me down somewhere soft, but I barely register it. Just that his scent seems further away now. But it quickly returns.

"Here, drink this."

My stomach balks at the idea of anything else entering it.

"Drink this, it will help. Just a couple of sips."

I take the small cup from his hand and sip. Once,

twice...it's all I can do, but suddenly the world isn't spinning so fast anymore.

"Better?"

I nod.

I finally glance around and realize I'm lying in a small bed covered in pink sheets. The walls are dressed in frilly lace and adorned with rosy-hued artwork—soft, delicate, and overwhelmingly pink. It's far too much for my taste, like being smothered in cotton candy.

Nyx sits on the edge of the bed, studying me closely.

"I should probably just sleep it off."

"You can in a minute. I need to make sure you're okay first."

"I'm fine after whatever it was that you made me drink."

"It's an antidote, but not enough to actually draw out all of the effects of the magical wine. Just enough to dampen the side effects."

"Well, whatever it is, I feel much better." My eyes draw up and down his sculpted body. A body I'd very much like to climb into my bed and—

"You're screaming your thoughts again."

I glare at him. "I am not."

"You are. Once again, I won't hold your thoughts against you because it's the wine talking."

"It's not."

"It is. That or you just really don't want to deal with what the seer told us about who your mate is."

I slump back in the bed, staring at the ceiling again.

"We don't have to talk about it, but it might help you feel better if we do."

"It won't," I say.

"Okay, then we don't have to talk about it. Try to sleep."

"I can't sleep with you just staring at me like that. Go to your bed."

"You're lying in my bed."

I frown. "What do you mean?"

"I mean that this tiny thing they call a bed is the only bed in the village they gave us."

I groan. "Then I guess we should get an early start and head back now."

He shakes his head. "That would be rude, and you're in no state to go anywhere right now."

I sit up, and the room starts spinning again. I fall back into the bed with another groan.

"Just get into bed then."

He stares at me for a moment as if he's going to refuse me, then stands and flicks off the light before climbing into the creaky bed, fully dressed.

I close my eyes, trying to fall asleep, but the nausea returns. It's accompanied by a pounding headache that has nothing to do with the wine I drank.

I sit up, throwing the covers off me with a sigh.

"You might be okay with me not talking about the curse tonight, but the blood deal we made isn't," I say.

He sits up, and we lean against the pink fabric headboard. "I'm sorry. I can try to say I don't care if you tell me again and see if your symptoms stop."

"No, we should just talk."

He waits silently for me to speak. I appreciate that, but I'm not sure where to start.

"I hate that my mate is chosen for me. To break the curse, I must accept the mate predestined for me. I have no say."

"I hate the mating bond, too. I hate that love or choice don't seem to matter to the gods. It's why the curse was placed upon the wolf shifters to begin with. The mating bond was rejected, and we became cursed."

"So if I reject my bond, another curse will be placed upon us?"

"I don't know."

"It's not fair."

"It's not."

"I'm not sure I can accept Ambrose as my mate after everything he's done."

"Then don't. It's your choice. You don't have to accept the mating bond. You don't have to believe the prophecies. You don't have to break the curse. It's your choice."

I stare at him. "Why can you speak to me in my head? What is this connection we share?"

"I don't know. We can ask the seer in the morning, but most will only tell one prophecy per person."

"Did you ask a question then of the seer?"

"Yes, I asked her how to get your wolf back."

"And what did she tell you?"

"She said it can't be undone. Your wolf belongs to Ambrose."

I grind my teeth, my hands fisting, and my mind sobering instantly. "How am I supposed to accept him as my mate if he can control such a huge part of me?"

"I don't know. But we can keep talking to seers. Keep trying to get answers. There must be other parts to the prophecy that we're missing. I don't believe it's as simple as you completing the marking ceremony and accepting him to break the curse. And if you do it that way, it will only break the curse for wolf shifters, not all magical creatures."

"What if all the seers say the same thing?"

"Then that's an answer."

"Are you just saying this because you want to be my mate?"

"Do you want me to be your mate?"

"Way to make me try to answer that first."

"I would be honored to be your mate. You're strong, resilient, beautiful. I have never seen such bravery—every time I'm with you, you surprise me more, leaving me in awe. But that doesn't mean that I am or that we would be any better fit together than you and Ambrose."

I stare at him, really stare at him, trying to understand how this man killed Rowena in cold blood and yet says such things about me. *Honored.*

"But even if I am, I want you to have that choice. No one should ever have their choices taken away from them."

"Kiss me."

"What?"

"Kiss me, please."

He frowns. "I'm not going to kiss you."

"Why not?"

"Because you're magically drunk, you don't know what you really want right now. All of your inhibitions have been lowered."

"I'm not magically drunk anymore. You gave me a tonic to help with that. And I told you what I want, I want you to kiss me, unless you don't want to kiss me."

"You're drunk," he says again, but it's almost like he needs to remind himself of that fact. He starts to roll over, away from me.

I pout.

"Sleep, the second the alcohol finishes working its

way out of your body, I'll kiss you if you still want me to. I'll kiss you so many times that the gods will realize how foolish they were to pair you with anyone else but me. That after you kiss me, you'll think all your choices have been taken away from you because the way I kiss you will claim you as mine. So stop pouting. Our first kiss was tainted by the life-or-death situation we were in. I won't let our second kiss be tainted by anything other than our desperate need to kiss each other."

My mouth hangs open wider with every word he says.

"Now, sleep, love, so that when you awaken, I can kiss your properly."

I bite my lower lip and try to close my eyes, knowing there is no way I'll be getting any sleep tonight after that proclamation.

CHAPTER 20

NYX

Lying next to Lumi and not being able to touch her is my living heaven and hell. But I did it to myself by trying to be a gentleman and not kiss her until I'm sure it is what she really wants. That wine she drank was strong, too strong. The witches are up to something.

I don't tell Lumi this. There is nothing she can do anyway but try to sleep off the effects of the wine. It takes her a long time to fall asleep; she tosses and turns relentlessly, her heartbeat speeding the entire time, before her soft snores finally fill the room. She needs the rest before we face whatever tomorrow brings.

I lie on my side staring at her, my hands aching from where the gashes were sliced open and still not healing. It's strange to have a wound like this still hurting me when usually my body would heal much quicker. This pain is a never-ending annoyance, but nothing more.

Lumi is heartbreakingly beautiful when she sleeps. Her long hair spills across the pillow in silver strands that look like streaks of moonlight. A soft flush warms her cheeks, pinked by the warmth of the comforter. Her lips are parted slightly, as if ready for the long-awaited kiss I promised.

I should have kissed her. I'm going to regret not kissing her until my dying breath. Ever since she kissed me last, all I've been able to think about is her kiss and how it would feel to let loose and really kiss her, not being held back by the idea that she was only doing it to save my life. But there's a feeling that's haunting me, telling me I might never get the chance to kiss her again. So I should have taken it, even if it wasn't the perfect time or under ideal circumstances.

Suddenly, Lumi jolts awake, sitting up frantically in the bed, sweat dripping from her brow. She's staring straight ahead as if she's still seeing something or someone, but there is no one in the room except me.

"Lumi? Are you okay? What's happening?"

She doesn't answer. She's still locked into whatever it is that she's seeing, not fully present in the room with me yet.

I wait, watching her closely for any signs that the witches have put a spell on her. Any sign that I need to intervene. But her breathing is steady, as is her pulse. She's just lost in a vision.

She blinks, and the room seems to come into focus for her. She turns to me, not surprised to see that I'm already awake.

"They could be false," she says.

"What could be?"

"The prophecies. Some are false. And even the seers don't know if what they are saying is true or not. They could simply be false," she says it with hope in her voice.

Hope that she can choose for herself whether Ambrose is her mate or not. Hope that she can get her wolf back.

I frown. "How do we know when they are false or not?"

"I'm not sure."

"Fucking gods. I hope they find this amusing."

"I'm sure they do, the assholes. If I ever meet one, I'd like to give them a piece of my mind."

"Same."

Our eyes meet again, and it's as if we both recall my words from the night before at the exact moment. Words that promised a kiss as soon as she wasn't intoxicated anymore.

I suck in a deep breath, not smelling a hint of alcohol on her breath anymore. Her eyes are no longer red-rimmed.

"I'm not drunk anymore," she says.

I gulp as I'm propped up on one arm next to her in bed. "Do you know what you're asking of me?"

She smiles seductively. "I'm asking you to kiss me, not marry me. Just kiss me. It doesn't mean anything. It doesn't mean we are mates even if we enjoy it. I just want you to kiss me."

"But what if it feels like more? What if it locks in our bond? Deepens it? Makes it harder for you to tell if Ambrose is your mate or if I am? What if it's just the gods playing more games with us?"

"Then you better damn well make sure the kiss is worth any heartbreak we'll have to endure."

There's no arguing with her there. I lick my lip, her eyes hone in on my tongue, and the heat returns to her gaze. There is no denying that this is exactly what she wants. And my body hardening at even the thought of getting to kiss her again is enough for me to know the same. I need to fucking kiss her.

I grab the back of her neck with my bandaged hand, stroking her lower lip with my thumb, teasing her with the promise of what my kiss will bring. I move closer, inch by inch, like I know she's going to back out and say she doesn't really want me to kiss her at any moment.

But she doesn't. If anything, her eyes deepen and darken with a heat that makes my breath catch. Heat diffuses over her skin, and the pull of desire radiates in thick waves—her scent overwhelms me with its unmistakable plea for how badly she wants me. *Fuck, I want her too.*

I lean forward to kiss her and then...

"Ah!" I cry out as the jolt shoots from my hands up my arms.

"Nyx? What's happening?"

I grind my teeth together as I pull my hand back from her body, refusing to scream in pain again. But it's taking all of my focus not to scream out. I have to let Lumi know what's happening, but if I open my mouth again, all I'll do is scream.

"The witches. Hands. Pain." I punctuate each word even in my mind to keep from screaming into her void.

Lumi's eyes widen, getting the message. She grabs my hands and unwraps one of the bandages. We both glance down and see my blood turning black as it begins to spread from my hand, winding its way like twisted rivers up my arms.

"They're trying to kill you. Why?"

I let out a whoosh of breath to keep another agonizing howl down.

"We have to leave. Can you run? Or shift?" she asks.

I have a feeling their magic won't allow me to leave. But I don't have much time.

"Stay here?" My words barely make it through our connection, but I hope she understands what I'm asking her.

She searches my eyes, trying to understand. "No, I won't stay here. I'm not going to hide while you do whatever you think you can do to stop this from happening. I want to help." Her voice is frantic but determined as I expected her to answer, but I had to try.

I let out a strangled growl. *"Distraction—they won't kill you. They think you are the key to breaking the curse."*

"I can do that. What are you going to do?"

I shake my head, my words hard to get out even through our connection. I jump out of bed, pulling Lumi behind me, wasting no time at all.

"Not to be an asshole, right now, but um...do you really think you are capable of stopping them when you can't even speak?"

We reach the door of the hut, and I'm gripping her hand, keeping her behind me. I turn, looking her dead in the eyes as I answer, "Yes."

Her eyes heat, and she bites her bottom lip at the single-word answer. "Later, love." *That is, if you still want me to kiss you after you see what I become.*

I open the door, shielding Lumi with my body as I'm greeted by the full coven of witches. Lumi doesn't care to use my body as a shield, though, as she quickly moves to standing by my right side.

"Tell me when," she says calmly in my head, no fear or self-doubt in sight.

I stare them down. "I gave you an offering, and this is how you repay me? By spelling me?"

I can feel Lumi's eyes on me with a hint of surprise at how well I'm speaking when I was doubled over in pain seconds ago. But it's a skill I've had a lot of practice refining that I can do under the right circumstances.

"You lied to me," Starling says coolly.

I raise my eyebrows. "I don't lie."

"Juliette has a gift for seeing what people try to hide. And you, alpha-lord, tried to hide that the curse can only be broken for one species. Either the witches, the wolf shifters, or the vampires." She spits out the last word like a curse.

"Get ready," I warn Lumi.

She reaches into the side of her boot and pulls out her blade. I don't know what she plans to do with the blade, but I'm glad she has it.

"And you, alpha-lord, seem to think that you could be the snow wolf's mate. Which would mean you would be breaking the curse for the vampires or the wolf shifters. We won't allow that to happen."

"Now."

I don't look at what Lumi's doing to serve as a distraction. I trust her, and I know the witches won't kill their only chance at breaking the curse.

Instead, I do what I've been trained to do—I kill.

The pain intensifies in harsh waves, traveling up my hands and through my arms. But I don't need my arms to kill them. Only my teeth and speed.

They only see me as a vampire. So that's how they'll die, from the venom of a vampire. My teeth sink into the first neck before their magic even spreads past my shoulders. Before her body even hits the floor, I've sunk my teeth into two more—one wrist and one neck.

A blast of a witch's magic strikes my thigh, but I don't stop running. I've got seconds to get this done before their magic overpowers me. Speed is my strength, time my enemy.

I force my body to move faster, searching for any limb to sink my teeth into as quickly as possible. Wrists, hands, necks, thighs, and even one shoulder, until I've hit all twelve of them with a shot of my venom. It's not an instant killer, but it weakens them all instantly, the first ones getting a stronger dose than the last.

Five of the bodies are already lifeless on the ground. A few more are fading fast, but a handful seem unfazed by the venom in their bodies. Magic blasts toward me, hitting me hard in the chest. I fall forward onto my knees as their magic overwhelms me. If they plan to kill me, they better make it fast, and they better have a fucking stake to do it.

I glance over at Lumi, who has also fallen onto her knees. But it's not the position she's in that has me concerned; it's the pool of her own blood circling her.

"No," I whisper in disbelief. *They wouldn't kill her. Did I do this? Should I have used leverage against one of them instead of injecting my venom into all of them? Did they know they were about to die, and so killed the only way to end the curse as well?*

"Drop the knife," Starling whispers to Lumi, her body shaking as she fights the venom in her body.

"Release Nyx from your spell," Lumi says.

"I can't. What's done is done," Starling says.

That's when I see it—the gaping wound in Lumi's stomach, blood pouring from it in a relentless, dark river. Her skin is ghostly pale, her breath shallow, and yet somehow she's still standing, still holding herself upright through sheer will. Then my eyes catch the glint of her blade, lifted now to her own throat. But there's already blood dripping from its edge... and no wound on her neck. The realization crashes into me with a jolt. She didn't just get hurt—she did this to herself. She drove the blade into her own stomach.

Starling drops as do the remaining witches, their magic fading.

Lumi watches them one by one. Only when the remaining one has taken their last breath does she lower her own blade and apply pressure to her wound in her abdomen.

"Are you insane? Why did you do that?" I scream at her.

"Distraction, right? Starling was about to kill you. This is the only thing I could think of to stop her. A blade wielded by the right person can stop a magical creature, were the words you used, if I remember correctly."

I run to her, scooping her up in my arms. "You'd better hope the witches have some healing tonics, otherwise you're in for a long ride back to the Bloodmoon pack."

She chuckles. "It's a superficial wound. I'm a heavy bleeder. I barely stabbed myself."

I don't believe her from the amount of blood I just saw. I run into the healer's hut, gently setting her down in the nearest chair. There's an apothecary cabinet to the right of the kitchen that I throw open, searching, searching, searching...

I grab the bottle I'm looking for, which has the healing rune on it. "Drink this."

She stares at the bottle as she leans against the open

doorframe leading to the kitchen, refusing to even stay seated, her hand still applying pressure over her wound. "What is it?"

"This rune means wounds. It's for wounds. Let's hope you didn't hit any vital organs that are the cause of all the bleeding because this tonic won't help with that." I'm not even sure how much this tonic will help at all, but since I just killed the nearest healer within a hundred miles of us, this is our only shot at helping her heal for the moment.

She downs the drink without questioning me further. I grab all the gauze I can from the cabinet as I pick her up and help her lie back on the small kitchen table. To her credit, she doesn't wince or protest as I do.

I apply gauze directly to the wound before I start wrapping it tightly to stop any further bleeding.

"I just cut myself deep enough to surprise Starling. It's barely a scratch, and I can already feel the magic working to close my skin together." Lumi sits up, brushing my hands off her body like this is nothing. "It's you I'm worried about."

She stares down at my arms, where my veins seem to have turned a dark, inky color. Now that the adrenaline is starting to wear off, I can feel the pain of their magic coursing through my arms, and I know that it will slowly work its way through my entire body to try and kill me like poison.

"I'll be fine."

She stares at me wide-eyed. "There has to be something you can drink to help—"

"There's nothing."

"How do you know?"

"Because they don't want anyone to heal from this kind of magic."

"So you're giving up? You're just going to die?"

"No, Riven should be able to help. But yes, I might die before we make it back to the Bloodmoon pack."

She freezes. "That sounds like giving up."

"I won't die forever unless someone puts a stake through my heart while I'm out. It will just be temporary. Vampire, remember."

"Oh."

"Now, let me find something for your pain."

She shakes her head. "I'm fine."

"You're not." I try to brush past her to grab for the medicine, but she yanks the gauze off.

"I'm all healed up."

Now it's my turn to stare at her wide-eyed. I'm shocked she healed that fast, even with the tunic. I blink again, trying to convince myself I'm imagining things, but her wound is closed and only a small trickle of blood is oozing from the edge that hasn't fully pulled together yet.

"We should go if Riven is the only one who can help you. I don't want to have to walk the entire hundred-mile journey if you drop dead on the way back."

I smirk. "See, I knew you'd come around to saying you liked riding me."

She rolls her eyes. "I'm not riding on your back with you in that condition."

"Yes, you are because it's still the fastest way back, and you're worried I'll die on you."

"Not really," she retorts.

I open the door, and we both step back outside, silently taking in the carnage I did. I killed them all without a second thought.

"I'm a killer. This is who I am. They didn't all need to die. Killing one would have been enough to stop the rest."

She doesn't say anything.

"Still want that kiss, love?" I ask with melancholy because I already know the answer. If she had any doubts about whether I'm her mate, she just got her answer. She deserves better than a vampire killer.

CHAPTER 21

LUMI

He's a killer...he killed Rowena...he killed an entire coven of witches...he's a killer...a killer...a killer...

The words start strong and then begin to fade in my head as I stare at him.

He's a killer—yes.

I hate him—yes.

He's cruel—yes.

A vampire—yes.

And yet I want to kiss him.

I want to feel his lips pressed against mine again for real, not the forced kiss to convince others. I want to know what his kiss would feel like when he's not holding back at all.

Nyx starts to walk away, not waiting for my answer. He thinks he already knows it because of what I think of him, what the world thinks of him—he's a killer.

He's a killer.

I'm naive. I fell in love with a man who now controls my wolf and can't love me back. And now I want a vampire lord to kiss me. To make me forget who I love.

We all have our faults.

"Yes."

He stops in his tracks. Standing in the thick snow, blood soaks through his dark shirt and pants. He's barely wiped the witches' blood from his mouth. And I fucking want him to kiss me.

What is wrong with me?

But I've never been more certain about what I want. Maybe it's the mating bond between us. Whether it's real or a diversion for the gods to tease me with until they are ready to let me break the curse, I don't know or care.

He could die at any moment, from the dark veins now growing up his biceps and into his shoulders. I don't know how much time either of us has left on this earth. But I know I want to spend a few moments kissing this beautiful male.

Nyx's dark eyes narrow at me, as if he's trying to understand how I could possibly feel this way. Trust me, I don't understand it myself.

"It's the bond. You don't really want me to."

I shake my head.

"It's the adrenaline after almost dying."

I shake my head.

"It's because you want me to wipe him from your head."

I shake my head. "All of those things could be part of it, but the biggest part is simple—I. Want. You. To. Kiss. Me." I pause. "Unless, of course, you don't want to. I don't want to force you to—"

He growls, cutting me off. "Fuck, I want to kiss you. It's the only thing I can imagine doing right now."

"Then kiss me."

I've barely taken a breath, and he's closed the gap

between us. He looks down, I look up. Our breathing synchronizes in delicious anticipation. He waits a beat. One...two...three...

It doesn't feel like he's waiting for me to change my mind anymore. He's drawing out the anticipation. The second we kiss, things will change. The desire will grow. The want, the stupidity on both of our parts.

We aren't mates.

We both know the most likely outcome is that the gods are playing games with us. Fucking with us to make it more difficult for us to break the curse.

I know deep down that Ambrose is most likely my mate. I just need to complete the marking ceremony with him and find a way to forgive him afterward. Or at least, be able to live with my decision because it ended the curse.

But what if Nyx and I are mates?

"Don't think about any of that. Just be with me right here, right now," comes his low whispered breath in my head.

His broad hand grasps me on the hip near the spot where I stabbed myself. The wound is still sensitive as it heals, but I forget all about it when his thumb brushes over it. His other hand sweeps my hair back as he casually places his hand at the nape of my neck.

Fuck, I can't breathe. I can't—

His lips crash against mine in a hungry kiss that steals my breath away. Heat burns beneath the icy surface that links the two of us together. His cold-blooded vampire collides with my frosty snow wolf until something undeniable takes shape. This is always where we were meant to find each other—in this space where fire freezes and ice ignites.

His tongue dives into my mouth, desperate and

ravenous, tasting me like my kiss alone is what he has to survive on. Our teeth clank together, and I feel the sharp point of his fang glide over my bottom lip. The same one he used to inject venom into the witches. The same one he used to kill with. And now it brushes over me, not to kill, but to consume.

I know he won't kill me. I know he won't inject me with his venom. He gave up his ability to mind-control me. He won't hurt me.

My hands fly around his neck, bracing his body against mine as I kiss him back. Sweeping my tongue into his mouth, wanting to taste every drop of him, even the parts that remind me of the killer he is. I don't taste the metallic blood—all I taste is him. He tastes like icy darkness. If it wasn't still dark outside, I'd think his essence alone would force nightfall to descend all around us as he kisses me. It's like the entire sky opens up for us when he kisses me. The night and the stars seem to prickle my skin as he kisses and kisses and kisses.

My hands grip harder onto his neck, not wanting this to end ever. I want more. I want to rip his clothes off. I want him touching me. *Why isn't he touching me?*

He chuckles in my head.

Dammit, I really should learn how to block him out.

"If I touch you, I'll fuck you. You permitted me to kiss you, not fuck you. And unfortunately, as badly as I want to fuck you, this stupid spell that's spreading up my arms might make it a little hard to fuck you properly."

I blush, heat spreading through my body like a wildfire.

"Based on this kiss, I'm pretty sure you could fuck me just fine," I think.

A strangled growl echoes through my head.

I bite my bottom lip. "Sorry, did I say that in your head again?"

"Yes," he hisses. Then suddenly, we are feet apart, and the coldness turns to emptiness.

I'm confused for a second, until I feel the flickers of sunlight hitting my skin. The sun has begun to rise.

Nyx is huddled against the side of the building, standing in the shadows where the sun can't hit him. But his gaze never leaves me. I can feel how badly he wants me burning into my skin. That kiss just lit a flame inside both of us that's going to be impossible to extinguish. Maybe we should have sex to try and get each other out of our systems.

If Nyx heard my thoughts, he doesn't respond to them; instead, he begins to shift, not caring that he rips his clothes to shreds as he does. I'm guessing he considers them ruined anyway, since the witch's blood is stained into them.

"Find your coat and pack the bag. We should go," he says in a deeply commanding way that rattles my brain.

I want to tell him that my coat isn't necessary. I grew up in Alaska. I'm a snow wolf, I'm used to the cold. I don't need a coat, but the mood has shifted, and it's not worth arguing with him at the moment. So I run inside the hut, put my coat on, and throw the rest of our things back into the backpack. Mentally, I prepare myself for spending the next several hours riding on his back.

When I step outside, Nyx stops moving, but not before I catch a glimpse of him limping slightly with his front legs as he walks.

"I can walk. You should run ahead, get back as fast as possible, then send Brax or Talonis to come find me," I say.

"You're not fucking walking, and I'm not leaving you."

"Well, I'm not going to let you die."

He huffs. *"I'm not going to die. This is nothing."*

"It's not nothing! That spell will work its way through your body until you die. Even if it's not permanent, you lying dead in the forest means you could die permanently if the wrong person came along while I was getting help."

"No one is dying. And you are not fucking walking."

We both glare at each other, both more stubborn than the other.

"I don't want to hurt you," I say.

"Having you not with me will hurt a lot more than a little added weight to my legs, trust me. I need to know you're safe as much as you need to know that I am."

I finally climb on his back as carefully as possible. The second I'm on his back, he takes off, running at full speed without so much as a painful misstep.

We don't talk, and I'm careful not to let my mind wander into strong thoughts that could accidentally be sent through our bond. I let him use all his energy and focus on getting us back to the Bloodmoon pack as quickly as possible. The soft snowflakes hitting my cheeks are the only thing keeping me focused as he runs.

Slumped shoulders and aching thighs have me barely still clinging onto his fur as I finally see the Bloodmoon pack village coming into view. I have no right to be tired or complain, though. It's only as the village comes into view that Nyx begins to show the real pain he's in. He's been far too stoic up to this point.

He stumbles once, and I move to get off his back. But with a quick bounce, he keeps me on.

"You're not getting off my back until we are safely with the Bloodmoon pack."

"Stubborn, controlling, asshole."

But I don't fight him. I don't want him to waste any more energy than necessary at this point.

Sylara steps out of Nyx's house first as we approach the village.

"He needs Riven!" I yell at her.

Her eyes darken for a split second, and then she's in and out of the house in the blink of an eye, Riven hot on her heels as they run toward us, with Brax and Talonis making their way out the door next.

I jump off Nyx's back mid-stride, not letting him fight me on this now that they can see us, and I run alongside him. His breathing his heavy with every step he takes. His feet stumble, and he begins to fall, but I wrap my arms around his neck, catching him as best as I can to keep him from falling against the ground.

Sylara and Riven are at our sides now.

"Shift," Riven says.

In a blink, Nyx is human or vampire. I'm not really sure there is a difference.

Sylara gasps when she sees the black veins that are now inked from his fingertips all the way across his chest and face. *Gods, did it hit his heart? How much longer did he have before it did?*

"You can help him, right?" Sylara asks, fear in her voice.

"Yes, but it will be painful," Riven says firmly.

I keep my eyes on Nyx's, refusing to let myself ogle his naked body in this moment, no matter how badly I want to. My desire still hasn't faded despite the hours-long journey here. Despite everything, I want him desperately.

He smirks, as if he knows exactly what I'm thinking. Good, that's good. It means his humor hasn't left. Maybe he's not as bad as I thought.

"Can you even walk?" Sylara asks him.

Nyx gives her a look that says he wants to kill her for even asking that. But for once, I'm with Sylara.

"I just ran hundreds of miles in my wolf form. The spell hasn't traveled below my chest. My legs work fine."

"All the more reason you should let us help you," Sylara says, rolling her eyes.

"Where do you want to work on him?" I ask Riven.

"A bed. Somewhere where he doesn't have to move for a while after I'm done working on him," Riven answers.

"His bed, then. The one I've been sleeping in."

"I'm right here, I can answer for myself," Nyx says.

"Brax and Talonis, are you okay carrying him?" I ask.

"On it," Brax says.

"Again, I don't need—" Nyx tries to take a step, but luckily, Brax is already there, catching his arm before he goes down. Talonis quickly puts one of Nyx's arms around his shoulders. Brax does the same with the other. And then the two of them practically drag Nyx, while he carefully limps along.

Riven stares at him, most likely assessing the damage and thinking of what he's going to have to do to heal him.

"I don't know how he was able to run as far as he did, even in his wolf form," Riven says.

"I know," Sylara says, looking at me.

I frown. "What? I didn't force him. His stubborn ass wouldn't let me walk on my own; he had to carry me."

Riven smiles. "Sylara just meant you served as motivation for him to run back here and push through the pain he was in."

"Oh." I want to say more, ask more, but now isn't the time. We all rush after them, but they are surprisingly fast, carrying him up the stairs to his bedroom. By the time we make it upstairs, Nyx is already lying in the middle of the bed. And in the few minutes since he's shifted and revealed the black veins of the spell, it looks like the spell has grown, now covering his entire abdomen.

"Fucking, gods," Riven says.

"Can you stop it?" I ask.

"I'm going to do everything I can to try. Thank gods he's part vampire or he'd already be dead."

"All of those witches deserved to die for this," I mutter under my breath.

All eyes shift to me for a second, but when I don't say anything else, they return to Nyx.

His eyes are closed now. He's barely breathing, and the jokes he made earlier have vanished. But he's also not writhing in pain, so I'm not really sure how much pain he's actually in at the moment.

We all stand around him on the bed. Riven standing on one side, with Brax and Talonis at his feet, and Sylara and me on the other.

Riven looks up at all of us, then back down at Nyx. "This is going to hurt." He says as much to Nyx as to us to prepare us. Then Riven places his hands onto Nyx's hand closest to him. The spot where there is still an open wound when Nyx offered his blood to them.

Agonizing, jolting pain rips through my body—like a thousand fireworks detonating inside me all at once. I scream, the sound torn from my throat as I collapse, folding in on myself beneath the weight of the torment. It's blinding, all-consuming, as if every nerve has been set ablaze. My hands fly to my head—that's where the epicenter is, where the agony pulses like a drumbeat of destruction. *Was I shot? Am I dying?* It feels like I am. No one could survive this. Not intact. Not whole.

The world tilts and spins, and a wave of darkness sweeps through my mind, cutting through the pain like a silent, shadowed knight. The agony ebbs, retreating beneath the cool, calming chill of night—and in that stillness, I know the presence that holds me—Nyx. It was his pain I felt. And he used all of his energy and power to take it away from me.

"Lumi, are you okay? Can I help you?" Brax asks as I open my eyes and find myself on the ground next to Nyx's bed. He reaches his hand down to me, and I take it, letting him lift me.

"Yes, but Nyx isn't," I say, staring down at him.

"He seems so calm, like he passed out from the pain," Talonis says.

"He's not. He's in there battling it, and it's the most intense thing I've ever felt. He accidentally let it through the bond and then had to slam it shut. It's bad." I look to Riven, who is focused. "Is there anything you can do to make it easier on him?"

"I can kill him and let his body slowly heal on its own, but honestly, with how bad this is, it could take months of him lying in this bed in a coma to fully heal, and I'm not sure if he'd stay passed out the entire time or not," Riven says.

"Drugs? Booze?" Sylara asks.

Riven shakes his head.

"Blood?" Talonis asks, and the room stills.

"It could help him, but you know how he feels about drinking blood. Drinking it could bring the vampire curse on him faster," Riven says.

I stare at Riven. "I have an idea. Just work as fast as you can."

He nods, his power immediately flowing through Nyx again.

I take Nyx's other hand in mine, close my eyes, and then concentrate on that door that Nyx has slammed shut to keep me from experiencing the pain again.

"It's me, Nyx. Let me in."

Silence greets me. But then again, Nyx is the most stubborn person I know. He was never going to let me in easily.

I find that cool, shadowed thread again in my mind, and I follow it, slowly, knowing that it will eventually lead me to another path around the door that he's thrown up. He can try to focus as much as he wants, but he won't be able to keep me out forever with the amount of pain he's in.

"Let me in, Nyx. I want to help."

"Leave," a single word floats back.

I grin. *Taunting him, that will work.* *"No, I want in."*

"Out."

"I'm far too stubborn to leave you at this point, killer."

"Humph."

"Huh, you don't like it when I call you, killer? Then let me in so you can do something about it."

"Leave, tell everyone to leave."

"You're going to leave me unprotected for months while you slowly come back to life? I don't think so, nightfall."

"Nightfall?"

"Yes, you are the Nightfall lord—it's a title that suits you more than you know. You're not the darkness itself, not the void you believe you are. You're the moment just before it—when the last

light clings to the edge of the world. You're the in-between, where shadows stretch but stars begin to stir. You're not despair. You're the promise that even in the fading light... there is still hope."

Silence.

"Let me in. I promise I can handle it, and if I can't, I'll push myself out. Let me help you. It could be the reason we're connected—to help each other."

"I don't want to hurt you."

"And I want to help ease your pain, so let me."

I prod against his mind, gently, but he's still doing everything he can to block me out. I look at Riven, giving him a nod, hoping he understands what I'm asking him to do, because if I say it out loud, Nyx will hear and be prepared for what I'm about to do.

With a flick of his wrist, more magic pours out of Riven so fast that I know it will shock the hell out of Nyx. With Riven providing a distraction, I use all my mental resources to counter Nyx's shield, blocking me out. I push so hard that my teeth feel like they're on the verge of breaking from the strain, and my entire body breaks out in sweat.

I push until I feel a gentle break of glass shattering in his mind. I walk right through the shards, even as they're jabbing into me, and I push inside until I finally feel his pain.

And there is nothing that could have prepared me for it.

CHAPTER 22

NYX

The whip strikes my back, and searing pain jolts through my body like a lightning bolt. A scream tears at my throat, threatening to escape, but I clench my jaw tight—refusing to give him the satisfaction of hearing my cry. Still, with the next strike, a sound escapes—the smallest of squeaks. Then another. And another, until the dam breaks and I'm screaming so loudly that it rattles the walls. It echoes off the walls until everyone can hear. That makes it worse. Now everyone can hear what he did. Everyone knows he broke me. And this is only the beginning. He's only warming up.

"I'm here, you don't have to face this alone," a soft voice whispers through the air, but I must have imagined it. I'm all alone. There is no one to face this torture with.

Chains get slapped around my wrists and ankles, like I'm capable of doing any damage in my current state. My back is torn to shreds. All my bones are broken. But it's not enough for him.

I'm yanked by the chains attached to my wrists and ankles. I stumble, falling, and I don't bother to get up as

I'm dragged by my wrists. There is no point in fighting anymore. My fate is inevitable.

"You're not alone."

I shake off the words. I'm hallucinating now. But with that shake comes a new torture scene.

A lifeless girl lies on the cool ground in front of me. Her features are vague, but I know exactly who she's supposed to represent. The next, she's shifted form. Person after person flashes in my mind, ending in the last one—Rowena.

Killer, killer, killer...

Innocent victims, lost to my bloodlust. To my rage. To the vampire killer inside me that I can't control.

"You're not a killer. You're a protector. You're nightfall— the one that ushers in the darkness and makes it safe to go out into the dark."

I don't know where the words are coming from, but she's wrong. So damn wrong.

The harsh memories of my past start twirling together like a tornado spinning and spinning and spinning. I can't stay focused on any one memory.

Bring back the physical pain, I beg. It's so much easier to block the painful memories when the physical pain is rotting my body. But the pain seems to be diminishing. Leaking out of my body like sweat through my pores.

My breathing becomes slower. My heart beats again, pumping the blood through my body that was stagnant before. I brace myself for the pain as my blood flows through my veins against the wretched spell, pumping poison. But it doesn't come.

The room stills.

Silence engulfs me.

The images stop.

"Can I kiss you?"

Her words are as gentle as silk against my mind. *How could she want to kiss me after everything she saw in my head?*

I'm about to say no. To leave. To run as far away from me as possible when she says, *"Please. I need to kiss you."*

The words are so soft, so gentle, so filled with need that I have a temporary lapse in judgment. *"Yes."*

Her lips are as gentle as her voice when she kisses me. Her tongue carefully parts my lips—but the moment she's inside, the kiss shifts. It's ravenous, like I'm the only man she's ever wanted or could ever want. There's a hunger behind it that floods me with wild, reckless thoughts—ones I don't dare voice even in my head. Dangerous thoughts.

Kiss by kiss, a little of the darkness begins to fade away, and light starts to shine again. But it's not day, it's night. And it's moonlight hitting my skin, not sun.

I open my eyes, and the relief filling hers is over-whelming.

"There you are," she says with a warm smile as mois-ture fills her eyes.

I glance around the room and find it's just the two of us.

"Everyone else left, knowing you should get some rest. I told them I'd take the first shift watching you. I should tell someone you're awake, though. They'll be worried about you and relieved to hear you're okay."

"They know."

She frowns. "How?"

"They can hear us. Wolf hearing, remember?"

"Oh," she blushes.

I grin. "They won't listen now that they know I'm okay."

"Why?"

"Because of what they think we'll do."

"Which is what exactly?"

Dark heat floods both of our minds as I show her a second of what that could be. Of our bodies melding together in...

Her blush shuts off my thoughts.

"Are you okay?" she asks, her voice full of concern.

I hate and love how she's looking at me. "Yes, thanks to you."

She shakes her head. "No, thanks to Riven. He's incredible."

"He's an anomaly, that's for sure. One that we are thankful for every day. But I still have you to thank."

"I didn't do anything."

"You did everything." I study her closely, needing to understand her more. "Why? Why try to ease my suffering when I've done horrible things to you? To others? You've seen what I am? I killed your best friend."

"There's always a reason."

"What?"

"There's always a reason that you kill."

We stare at each other. *Ask me. Ask me why Rowena is dead.*

It's on the tip of her tongue. I know she wants to ask, but I can sense her fear at the answer.

She doesn't ask.

She's not ready. And I'm not sure I have the answer for her yet anyway.

"You're really okay?" She asks again, her eyes running over my arms and chest that are bare to her as the covers are pulled up to my waist.

"It appears so. The spell is gone. No long-lasting damage done."

"Well, I'm not sure how we do that again. And I'm not sure how useful it was anyway. She didn't tell us anything we didn't already know. And the information she gave us wasn't helpful at all," she says.

"What's the alternative? You're just going to complete the marking ceremony with Ambrose in a few weeks and hope it doesn't kill you? That it gets your wolf back? And that it breaks the curse for the wolf shifters and not the witches?"

"No."

"Then we have to get more answers first. We'll have a better strategy next time."

"Or you could mark me."

"What?"

"You could mark me. What if it's all a diversion, my connection with Ambrose instead of the other way around? What if you're really my mate? What if it's more important to break the curse for the vampires than any other creature, and that's why we are mates?"

"I'm not going to mark you unless I'm a hundred percent sure you're my mate. I'm not going to risk your life like that."

She frowns. "There's no way to ever be a hundred percent sure."

"There are plenty of ways to be more sure than you are now about who your mate is. It has to be more than you just running from Ambrose and thinking I'm a good kisser. Even if I am, there has to be a bigger connection between us."

"You still don't think there is even a real possibility of us being mates, do you?"

"I'm a vampire, cold-blooded, and have no heart. Vampires don't have mates. I'm pretty sure the day I became a vampire, I lost any chance at having a mate."

Her eyes search mine before she speaks next. "You're worthy of having a mate. And you're more than just a vampire. You're a shifter, too. What if we're mates and you never explore it with me because you're too busy self-deprecating to explore it—"

I kiss her. I kiss her so fucking hard that there can't be any doubt in her head how badly I want her. I desperately want us to be mates, simply so she can be mine. I don't care about the curse. I don't care about some long-ago fated connection with her. I care about her—about wanting her.

I roll our bodies until she's buried beneath me and I'm pinning her against the bed. Letting all of my feelings flood her head—want, desire, need. I shatter any hold she has on our connection just as I wreck her body with my kisses. I kiss her lips, but I'm a greedy fucker who wants more. I kiss down her jawline, her neck, her ear.

I'm rewarded with every tiny whimper and soft gasp she's capable of making. While her hands dig into the skin of my back, begging me to kiss more, harder, everywhere.

"What do you want, love?" I purr into her head. She wants to explore if we're mates, I'm game. She wants me to kiss the fuck out of her until she passes out from exhaustion, done. She wants me to stop and go to sleep in another bedroom, as if nothing had happened, I can do that, too.

"Fuck me, Nyx. Let's find out if we could be mates."

CHAPTER 23
LUMI

I've lost my mind. There are a million reasons why I shouldn't fuck Nyx, and more reasons we aren't mates. But I can't think of a single one right now with his naked body hovering over mine as he kisses me like I'm the oxygen he needs to breathe.

Nyx must be able to tell how serious my intentions are through our bond because he doesn't question them. He doesn't call out any of the reasons we shouldn't do this.

My fingers dig harder into his back, and he allows a little of his weight to press against my body. The hardness and length of his cock pressing against my lower stomach shock me.

He wants me, too.

A darkness dances through my mind. *"Of fucking course, I want you. You're breathtakingly beautiful. Your long white hair, your red lips, your body, elegant like it was sculpted by the gods, with every curve designed to perfection. You're brilliant, and brave, and impossibly stubborn. You'd give up everything for the people you love. You're everything."*

I rake my teeth over my bottom lip. *Please, let him be my mate. Let this man be real. Let me let go of the pain, the heartbreak. Don't taunt me with this man, only for him to not be my mate and break my heart again like Ambrose did.*

Kille—

I slam my mind shut on those words that like to haunt me about him. He kills, but he's not a killer. I don't forgive him for killing my friend, but I know there's a reason why. It will allow me to forgive, to stop hating him even a little bit. I'm just not sure I'm ready to fall that hard for him yet. I don't need to forgive him to fuck him.

He lowers himself even more, kissing me harder than before with a seriousness to the kiss that tells me we are really doing this, but he'll stop the second I say the word.

"This isn't real. You can't be real," Nyx says in my head. I love that he can keep kissing me while still telling me his thoughts.

"It's real. This isn't a dream," I say to remind myself of that fact, too.

His hands are bracing himself on either side of my body as he kisses me, still holding some of his weight off of me. It's as much to keep his hands from touching me, from exploring my body too quickly.

"Touch me," I beg.

"Where?"

I imagine his hand splayed across my lower belly while he debates whether to palm my breasts or dip his hand into my pants. The second I think it, he starts doing it. He slides his broad hand under my shirt until I can feel it against my bare skin. I can feel his hesitation in deciding to snake up or slither down.

"How can you read my mind so well? Am I thinking the words out loud to you?"

"I don't know exactly. Even if you're not talking to me directly, I can hear some of your thoughts and definitely vibes. Especially if they are about me," he replies.

I kiss him harder, my tongue sliding into his mouth.

"Like right now, I know you want me to do this." His hand slides up my body until he reaches the edge of my bra. He grabs the top of the cup, dragging the fabric down until my breast springs free. He wastes no time palming my breast with his broad hand.

His touch is cool, like ice; his thumb teasing over the peak of my nipple.

"Yes," I say.

He smirks against my lips, his body growing harder as he touches me.

"Gods, you smell good," he says as he kisses down my neck.

I arch into him. *"Smell so good that you want to take a bite?"*

He stills, his fang scraping lightly over my carotid. *"Are you scared if I say yes?"*

"No." My pulse jumps up.

"You are, but you're happy about it. You want me to, just to find out if it will feel good."

"Last time, I was passed out. I didn't like you. I was traumatized. Maybe it would feel different now."

He drags that fang up and down my neck as his heated breath hits my skin, such a contradiction to the icy touch of his fingers against my nipple that he hasn't stopped tantalizing while we speak in each other's minds.

"You'd like it, but I'm not going to."

"Why not?"

He hesitates. *"The most important reason is that I don't want to accidentally kill you. Your blood is intoxicating. I could lose control and drink all of your blood."*

I suck in a sharp breath. *Killer*—that fucking word again. I shake it out of my head.

"I'm not afraid."

"I know, which is why we could be mates. The lack of self-preservation runs deep in both of us." He frees my other breast, and a breathy moan slips out as he sweeps his chilled fingers over my flesh. *"To be completely honest, I'm terrified of you, but in the I want you despite everything sort of way."*

"You, scared of me? You're kidding."

"Not even a little. You're capable of being the most incredible thing that's ever happened to me." He pauses for dramatic effect. *"Or you'll be the one who kills me."*

"Right now, you're the one killing me." My eyes roll back in my head as he pushes my shirt down so he can kiss over my nipple, fang dragging over my peak just enough to send a sharp breath through my body, but not enough to draw blood.

My hands are tangled in his hair as I hold his head to my body, never letting go.

"If you keep doing that, I can't do other things that I know you want me to do."

I bite my bottom lip, stifling another cry, and then release his head just enough for him to sink lower down my body. Grabbing onto the hem of my pants, he slides them down just enough to get a view of my wetness.

His dark eyes look up at mine for just a second, asking for permission.

I nod, too speechless to speak or even think yes. His tongue dips between my folds expertly, finding the little bundle of nerves that instantly has my body on fire. With every lick of his tongue against me, he worships my body, dragging my soul along with it. More warmth spreads over my icy body, melting away the snow that's held me together for so long.

Nyx looks up at me from between my legs, locking eyes with me, and I can see his desire swirling. No one has ever looked at me like he's looking at me now.

And then I'm being flooded with his thoughts and everything he wants to do to me. Starting with devouring me.

Gods, what am I doing? I shouldn't be doing this. I'm going to regret this for so many reasons, the main one being that I'm going to want to do it again and again. It's only going to make the whole 'Who is my mate' debate more confusing.

A cascade of heat ripples up my body, and I tremble in his arms. I'm so close already to spilling over the edge of insanity. So close to exploding with his tongue on my cunt. So close to screaming out something I shouldn't say just because he can do beyond impressive things with his tongue.

Fire electrifies my brain, almost burning me up as it hits my head so fast. I cringe, about to tell Nyx that he's sending his thoughts too fast, when I realize it's not Nyx in my head.

"Ambrose?"

The licking stops. Time stops. My heart aches for the man between my legs when I realize I just called out my ex's name while he was giving me pleasure. *Fuck, fuck, fuck.*

But with how intense my head felt, I know that whatever Ambrose is trying to tell me is going to trump everything else.

"Ambrose, talk to me?"

"War—the Moonfire witches and Moonlight pack are coming. Be prepared. Only one species can break the curse. A war is starting. Five minutes."

Nyx is staring at me intently, already figuring out what's going on. "What did Ambrose say?" Although he's serious in his tone, he's not angry that I still hold a connection with Ambrose, even if I am. It felt like the timing was purposeful.

"He said the witches and Moonlight pack are coming in five minutes. They know that only one species can break the curse. A war is starting."

Nyx nods, looking at me with his dark, chilly eyes. The heat in both of our bodies is stifled but not gone.

"You get to choose. Who you go with. Who you complete the marking ceremony with. You get to choose, no matter what the seers or fate say. I won't let him take you if you don't want to go." He pauses. "And I'll let you go if you want to go. You're not a hostage."

"What about our deal?"

"We can honor our deal whether we are together or not."

He climbs off of me, and I feel the weight of what we just did and almost did being interrupted. Warm shockwaves are still tingling through my body. My body is still aching for a release that I know will never come.

I yank my bra down and my soaked panties up. Nyx vanishes and returns fully dressed a second later.

"Sylara knows. She's telling everyone to prepare. Sending for the vampires, too," he says.

"Now what?"

"Now we prepare for the fight."

"And who wins in a battle between witches and vampires?"

"No one wins until the curses are broken, but we can get them to leave our territory. We can keep our pack and coven safe. We can live to fight again tomorrow, to find a way to break the curse for everyone so there can be peace."

I nod. "They should know that. I want to break the curse for all creatures, even if the seers say that I can only break the curse for one."

"Just be prepared that they might not want to listen. Sometimes the only way to get others to listen is to win the battle."

"I thought you just said there are no winners?"

He sighs. "Don't listen to me, I'm not good with words. I prefer to use the one skill I'm good at—killing."

"Why do you always refer to yourself as a killer when I've never seen you kill any more than Ambrose or any other alpha?" I challenge.

For a moment, I think he's going to answer. And the answer will probably tell me something important about him that I'm missing.

"They're here," he says suddenly. He reaches into his back pocket, pulling out two blades and hands them to me. I grab them, but he doesn't release them to me. He holds on until I'm looking him in the eyes. "Stay near me. You're who they came for. I won't let them take you unless you want them to. And if you want them to take you, you have to convince me it's because it's what you really want, not because you're turning into a martyr and will sacrifice yourself to save the Bloodmoon pack or the vampires."

I yank the blades out of his hand. "I'm not a martyr."

"Good, don't become one."

"I'll do my best to stay close." I swallow. After all, that's what I wanted this whole time, to be intimately close to him. I won't run.

"If you choose him, tell me," he says.

There's an awkward pause as if he wants to say more. He really thinks I'll choose Ambrose right now after everything he's done.

"We're here. Come talk to us, and no one will get hurt," Ambrose says in my head. He feels like he's on autopilot, talking to me. Not like the intimate mate I used to know so well, like he's playing a role right now.

I open my mind as wide as I can, letting the words drift through so that Nyx can hear Ambrose's words too.

"If you try to take her against her will, it will be the last thing you do," Nyx says to Ambrose in my head.

"I'm not the one who can mind control her," Ambrose snaps back.

"No, but you can alpha command her and control her wolf. So both of us suck. She chooses who she leaves with," Nyx growls through my head.

It's chaos having them both speaking to each other at the same time in my head.

"Agreed, Lumi chooses. So release her from any mind control."

"Already done." Nyx looks to me, and I nod, already knowing what he's about to do. One second, I'm standing in the bedroom, the next, we are in front of the Blood-moon pack and coven of vampires staring across a field to where the Moonlight pack and Moonfire coven are waiting for us.

Ambrose is standing front and center next to Isolde, with Emeric right behind him. The twenty or so that make up the rest of the pack and the dozen witches are spread behind their respective sides.

Nyx places me to his right. Sylara, Talonis, Brax, Riven, and Kael stand right behind us, followed by another nine of the Bloodmoon pack and the Nightfall vampires, who number almost double that of the witches.

"We are here to collect the girl," Isolde says, like she can't even be bothered enough to speak my name.

I glare at her from across the field. "My name is Lumi."

"Doesn't matter what your name is, you lied to us. You knew a part of the prophecy and withheld it from us. Others have died for less."

"But you can't kill me, can you? If you kill me, your chance at breaking the curse dies with me," I spit back.

"As soon as the curse is broken, I'm going to kill you."

"Not if I kill you first," I threaten.

Sylara smirks at me in an approving huff. Nyx doesn't take his eyes off Isolde or Ambrose. The others, even Kael, seem ready for an attack at any moment. I don't know whose side Kael is truly on, other than I know he will protect me. And Nyx can control him if necessary through his mind control.

"Come with us, Lumi, and no one gets hurt," Ambrose says.

"No. I told you I needed space, and this is how you give me that? By bringing the entire pack and coven to take me back?" And then I send only to him. *"I thought I had a say in the matter. You agreed that I do."*

"If it were just up to me, then yes. As your mate, you always have a choice. But I'm not just your mate. I'm an alpha, and I have a pact with the Moonfire witches that I have to honor. I'm sorry."

I shake my head. *"Despicable."*

Nyx growls next to me, and I know he heard the conversation I just had with Ambrose in my head.

"You're my mate, Lumi. You can pretend with that abomination of a killer all you want, but you know he's not your mate. His talking to you in your head is just a trick of his mind control and powers. Come with me and let's complete the marking ceremony. Together we can break the curse," Ambrose says.

"No, I don't know that you're my mate, actually. And it doesn't work that way. You already know that the curse can only be broken for one species—wolf shifter, witch, or vampire. Not all three."

"The curse is broken by those who break the curse. Typically, that would be two of the same creature. But Ambrose isn't just a wolf shifter, he's also a witch. So the curse would be broken by both," Isolde says.

"Well, that's convenient for you," I say.

"It is," Isolde smirks back.

Nyx has yet to speak. He just watches the exchange, not speaking for me, which I appreciate. But I don't control his pack or vampires. They shouldn't have to fight on my behalf.

They think you're my mate. They will fight for you and themselves. For a chance for you to break the curse for them since I'm half vampire," Nyx speaks in my head.

I glance at the vampires who have gathered in large numbers, outnumbering us all. They are all looking at the witches and shifters on the other side in a stance that tells me one signal from Nyx and they'll kill without a second thought.

"You're my mate, Lumi, whether you like me right now or not, you know it's true. If you let Nyx mark you, you'll die. I'm sorry, but you don't have a choice. The gods have decided. Please, don't let others die for my mistakes," Ambrose says.

For a second, I consider him. I know his words could be true. He could be my one true mate, but I'm not ready to accept that yet. Not after being with Nyx. Not after what just happened in the bedroom. There's a chance I have two mates. That I can actually choose between them. Or that one is a decoy meant to confuse me, placed by the gods for their entertainment. Either way, I'm not ready to make my decision yet. And as far as only being able to break the curse for one or maybe two types of creatures, maybe there is still a way to break it for all three.

"Whatever mind control he's using, whatever pleasure you think he brought you in the bedroom that makes you smell like him, it's not real. He's just playing with you to hurt me and try to break the vampire curse. He's not your mate. And he's incapable of love," Ambrose says.

"Do you want to go with him?" Nyx asks in my head, his temper barely contained.

I don't want a war to start. I don't want anyone to die. But I made a promise I wouldn't be a martyr. And even if Ambrose is my true mate, I'm not ready to accept that yet or go with him. I need more time to get answers.

"No."

"Lumi is my mate. Not yours. But unlike you, I don't have to beg her to be with me or threaten her or the lives of her friends to be with me," Nyx's voice booms. "She is by my side because she chooses to be. Now I'm giving you one chance to leave before we kill you all for threatening to take away my mate."

"Shift."

The word floats through my head so forcefully that it

hits me like a bullet, harsh and unforgiving. I'm barely able to process who said the word or why until I see Ambrose staring at me intensely a moment before my bones begin to morph, my body bending in excruciating painful ways, my eyes descending into darkness as I shift into my wolf.

CHAPTER 24
LUMI

The torment crawls through my body slowly, like it has all the time in the world to torture me. Each bone, muscle, and nerve takes its precious time shaping and forming my wolf as if an artist is behind each stroke, carefully crafting a masterpiece.

All the while, I'm writhing in agony, and I have no idea if the battle has started around me. I'm incredibly vulnerable until my shift is complete. Which means Nyx, Sylara, Riven, Brax, Talonis, and Kael are all vulnerable too, spending time protecting me instead of on the attack.

But I can barely think about anything except the explosive pain. It's just as painful as the first time, like my mind and body are bending in unnatural ways to the whim of another.

"You're strong enough to survive this. It's almost over. And then you can kill him, me, whoever you fucking want, love. I'll save your blades for when you shift back."

Nyx. I cling to his words, focusing on them instead of the pain.

It's almost over. I'm strong. I can kill him.

Those words are my salvation. That string connecting us keeps me alive when I feel like dying. And another word creeps into my mind—*mate.*

And then the pain vanishes. I'm standing on four legs. I open my eyes and feel the weight of every gaze on me. Everyone else has shifted, probably in seconds instead of the agonizing minutes it took me.

I can easily see across the field to Ambrose, making out every expression and line of his face. His lips are in a tight line across his face.

"Do you expect me to thank you? I'm not going to. This wolf isn't mine to control, is it? You can tell her what to do, whose side to fight on, and she'll fight for you, won't she?"

Nyx nuzzles up against my side in his wolf form, standing several feet taller than me.

"Be ready to run if I turn on you. I think Ambrose can control me now that I've shifted," I say to Nyx.

Nyx growls in Ambrose's direction and snaps his teeth together like he wants to take a bite of him.

"No, I don't expect you to thank me. And I won't control your wolf. You have free will to fight however you want to. I just wanted you to be able to protect yourself and not rely on any man—me or him," Ambrose replies.

Warm light starts to blind me. The vampires behind us scatter to the edges of the woods, seeking refuge in the shadows. Only the shifters remain on either side of me in their wolf forms. Ambrose has both wolf shifters and witches fighting alongside him. The vampires can't fight with us unless we drive the fight into the woods. But then I'd guess that's why they are here at dawn instead of dusk.

"Try to lure the fight to the woods so the vampires can fight too," I say to Nyx.

He nods his broad head.

"Isolde will attack first. She'll hit you or me," he says back.

He's right. Ambrose won't hurt me, but Isolde has no such qualms. *"She'll hit me. He'll go after you."*

Isolde raises her hand. I dig my paws into the ground beneath my feet, preparing myself. I wish I had time to practice fighting in my wolf form. Moving every muscle in my body still feels unfamiliar, like I'm in a stranger's body. I know I belong here, but it's not my body, not yet. It's like I'm borrowing a costume.

I leap just as Isolde blasts her magic in my direction, the blow missing me by millimeters. Ambrose and his pack start running in our direction at full force. The witches stay where they are, their feet remaining planted on the floor.

Cowards. They won't get involved in a hand-to-hand fight. They'll just blow magic our directions and let the shifters risk their lives for them.

"Stay close."

"They can't kill me," I remind him.

"Yeah, but they can kidnap you."

"Even if they do, they can't hurt me. I'll survive."

"Until the next full moon, when they force you to be marked by someone you reject as your mate," his voice shakes with anger at even the thought of that.

"It won't happen."

"No, it won't," he agrees.

Magic pours down on us as the Moonlight pack reaches us.

I hiss at the burns that strike against my fur from the witches, but otherwise, ignore the pain as the pack bounds in our direction. Ambrose leaps at Nyx, and before I can jump between them, I'm hit hard by a pack member I don't know well. I quickly lose track of the others. Flashes of brown, black, gold, and white colored fur all become a blur around me, which makes it hard to tell who is fighting on which side. But I know to go for the wolves marked in the golden colors of moonlight. The blasts of magic seem to strike just as haphazardly, not always striking just the Bloodmoon pack.

A dark colored wolf with a golden stripe down his back circles me before growling, like he's trying to get me to submit.

I growl back, my own voice sounding strange to my ears. The heaviness of my paws hitting the earth with each step is getting more familiar. I snarl, letting my lips curl back around my teeth, and then I strike, lunging for the wolf's neck.

He side steps me easily enough before getting a bite of his own into my shoulder.

I whimper before Sylara hits the male hard enough that he runs away scared.

I give her a thank-you nod, and we both glance toward the woods. Together, we start running, leading the Moonlight pack toward the woods where the vampires are. But the witches are prepared for this move, and we hit a hard, invisible wall yards before the edge of the woods.

Fuck.

"The witches put up a wall. We can't lead them into the woods. What do we do now?" I ask Nyx.

Yelps and whimpers ring out all around me as my friends are injured. We are far outnumbered. But we are the better fighters, so even with the witches hitting us with their magic, we are still holding our own. The lack of bodies on the ground tells me that no one has been killed yet, but it's only a matter of time.

Panic rises in me in hard strokes. I won't be able to live with myself if anyone dies because I wouldn't go with Ambrose. He's not going to hurt me. Or kill me. He wouldn't even force me to complete the marking ceremony.

I'm just pissed at him. I'm so angry, but if it could save lives, that's what matters.

"You promised," Nyx shouts at me, and I realize he and Ambrose are locked in an intense battle. My heart hammers in my chest every time the two of them fight because...

"I won't kill him. And he won't kill me," Ambrose says.

"You both hate each other so much that if given the chance, I know you will," I snap back, running to them. I have to stop them. They need to fight others, not each other.

"We won't kill each other," Nyx promises.

"But we will end this," Ambrose says.

I'm so far away and yet so close at the same time. Other shifters try to grab me, but the Bloodmoon pack members are prepared and fight them off before they even touch me. I'm running full speed to where Nyx and Ambrose have moved far to one side of the field. They are only fighting in their shifter forms. Neither is wasting time shifting to their witch or vampire forms.

I run faster, feeling like my time is running out. I don't

know what either of them is going to do to try to end this. All either of them has promised is that they won't kill the other. There leaves a lot of room for other damage to occur. I don't know the extent of why the two hate each other, but it certainly runs deeper than I will ever understand.

I don't have a choice but to intervene, as I have before. I take a deep breath, prepared to jump between them when a blast of magic hits me hard, freezing my body in place.

It feels like a boa constrictor is slowly squeezing me, coiling all the way around my body from my ankles all the way up to my chest. Slowly, the breath begins to leave my body until it's hard to breathe. My breaths become shallow, and my heartbeat is forced to beat in long, steady beats to push enough blood through my body.

"Isolde," I send out to Nyx, but the single word bounces off a shield and then back to me. She's blocking my ability to communicate.

I try again, this time with Ambrose. *"Isolde! I can't move. I can barely breathe!"*

All of my words are thrown back at me. Both of the guys are too focused on each other to notice what Isolde is doing to me.

Suddenly, she's by my side, smirking down at me like she's going to enjoy the torture she's about to inflict on me.

"You're the chosen one. The snow wolf—protected by the gods themselves. But I wonder..." She taps her finger against her cheek before excruciating pain explodes in my head.

I want to crumple to the ground, grab onto my head, and curl in on myself to try and ease the pain. I want to do something, anything, to make it stop. But I'm forced to stand silently by while she tortures my mind. If anyone looked at me, they'd have no idea what was happening to me. My connection to Nyx and Ambrose has been blocked, so they don't even realize what's happening to me.

"You think that's pain, you have no idea what pain is. You have no idea why I need you to break the curse for the witches so badly, do you? No idea the lengths the witches will go to ensure that you break it for us. We even granted a wolf a witch's power to ensure that the curse is broken."

She lets me into her mind, and I get a glimpse of the pain she's in.

I scream. Gods, do I scream. The pain is unsurvivable. I must be dying. She's killing me.

Just as fast as it starts, the pain stops.

I pant, trying to get my breathing under control. "You have no idea. Each witch endures more pain every second than you endure in a lifetime." She glances over where the vampires pace in the shadows, wanting to fight but being unable to.

"You have no idea the pain they endure, either. You don't understand the gods' wrath against us. The wolf shifters have it easy. So you can't have babies. So you aren't as strong as you used to be. So you can't find your one true love. Ah. Ridiculous to listen to you all whine like that's a curse. *We* are cursed. Every time I use my powers, it's like I'm being burned alive. My powers are growing weaker because using them hurts. Not to mention, each witch was cursed with an individual curse. One to kill us one by one in the slowest, most torturous way."

I don't know what the witches did for the gods to curse them so, but I'm not sure anyone deserves that pain. Not even Isolde. For a moment, Isolde connects me to her thoughts, her memories, her pain, and fires each one at me like a bullet, until I can barely keep up with the images she's sending me. More cries leave my body as each new wave of pain washes through me.

Ambrose's head snaps in my direction as he finally notices that Isolde has me. I'm seconds away from her transporting me to hold me hostage until the next full moon. I can see him try to talk to me, then get frustrated when he realizes he can't.

I try to swallow, but it's difficult to even push my own saliva down my throat with how tight Isolde's magical grip is on me. She hates me. The only reason I'm alive is to break the curse. After that, I don't care what alliance Ambrose has with her; she'll kill me.

What are you going to do, Ambrose?

Nyx still hasn't noticed what's happening to me, or if he has, it doesn't stop him from continuing to fight Ambrose. He attacks Ambrose like I've watched him do countless times, but there is something different about this strike of his paw against Ambrose's side. It hits different, deeper, a more crucial spot.

Ambrose cries out in pain as his body quickly shifts from wolf to human as he lies on his back. Nyx grabs Ambrose by the neck and quickly carries him into the shadows before shifting himself. The vampires surround him quickly.

In a heartbeat, the witches have circled me and Isolde, where I'm still held frozen, unable to even blink without Isolde letting me.

The shifters haven't moved, but I don't hear any growls or snarls. It's as if time has stopped; the fight has slowed.

"I'll trade you Ambrose for Lumi," Nyx says to Isolde from the shadows in his vampire form.

"No. You want us to leave without killing any of you, then we leave with both," Isolde says.

"Ambrose is dying. If he doesn't get a healer to work on him soon, he'll die," Nyx says.

"Lies, he..." Isolde's voice stops as she listens to Ambrose's heartbeat slowing. His breath is becoming even more labored than mine.

She squeezes me tighter with her magic until I feel my ribs breaking.

I try to scream, and this time, she lets me. My cry pierces my own ears, but I can't stop it.

"Let her go. Take Ambrose and leave," Nyx says firmly, like he's giving an alpha command. But I can hear the hint of fear in the undertone of his voice, even if our connection is no longer there.

Isolde squeezes again, forcing more painful howls from me. Tears fall hard, fast down my cheek. I'm trembling from the pain as my voice rings out through the silence. More ribs are broken, and my entire body will be bruised, I'm sure of it.

"Come and get her, killer," Isolde says.

I'm falling. For a second, it feels like flying, but just as fast as I'm thrown upward, my body is descending at a rapid pace. I shouldn't be falling. My feet were just on the ground. But I am. Isolde must have thrown me, used me as bait for Nyx.

The ground is coming at me fast. *Fuck, this is going to hurt my already broken body.*

I hit.

Arms cushion my fall as best as they can, but all it

does is cause him pain too, as we both hit the ground with a large thump.

Tears are burning my eyes as they mix with my sweat. I can't see. I'm human again, as is Nyx. I don't know how he's here as the sun seems to be blasting us both. But that doesn't matter right now.

"You're safe. They're gone," he whispers.

CHAPTER 25

NYX

I'm going to kill her. I don't always like my nickname—'killer.' But in this moment, I've never wanted to earn that nickname more.

Lumi whimpers as I carry her body, covered in red bruises, up to my bedroom. The others follow without me even having to speak to them. It feels like deja vu. We were just here in this room healing, but this time it's *her* healing instead of me. I much prefer it to be the other way around.

"Lumi, where does it hurt the worst?" Riven asks, looking her over from head to toe.

She moans, but can't get any words out. I push inside her head, needing to gather information for him so he can stop her pain. As soon as I'm inside, I'm gasping for air. Each breath feels like I'm inhaling fire, making it impossible to take a deep breath.

"All of her ribs are broken, and she can barely breathe because of it," I say.

Riven nods, placing his hands over her chest. As he starts to work, the runes on her body come alive, lighting up all over her naked body like drawings slowly coming to life.

"What's happening to her?" Sylara asks.

"Her runes are responding to my magic. They are trying to help me heal her," Riven says.

I glance around the room at everyone here, all watching her as worried as they were when it was me on the table. My eyes stop on Kael, who looks like he's about to pass out at the sight of her.

"Lumi is strong. She's going to be okay," I say.

"I know, but I'm tired of her having to be strong. You have no idea what she's been through," Kael says.

"With Ambrose?"

Kael's jaw tenses. "Her entire life."

I frown, having no idea what he's talking about. But now isn't the time to question him. I need to be here for Lumi like she was here for me.

I slip back into her mind, filling it with thoughts of moonlight, snow, crisp air, and nightfall—all of her comforting things. I don't know if it's me or Riven who helps her finally take an easy breath, but the entire room takes a collective exhale when she does. This is the first sign that she's going to be okay.

I continue to flood her mind with things I know make her happy as I sit on the edge of the bed, softly tracing the runes on her arms with my fingers.

Finally, Riven stops and gives me a nod. "Everything is put back where it's supposed to be, but she'll be sore for the rest of the night at least. She needs to rest." He gives me a look.

I growl. "I'll make sure she gets rest."

"Good." He responds. "Now, let me work on you."

"What are you talking about?"

"You carried her in the sunlight back to the house in your vampire form. I know you're hurting. Let me try to help you."

"You can't. Your magic doesn't work on my vampire problems. And I'm fine. I was just in intense pain while I was carrying her, but nothing long-lasting. And it was worth it." I look down at Lumi, whose eyes are still closed, but I know she's listening to our conversation.

Riven hesitates, as if he wants to say more. Then he says, "Everyone out."

"We can't leave them alone, they'll fuck like rabbits and that can't be good for Lumi's healing," Brax says.

Talonis chuckles.

Sylara hits Brax on the back of the head.

Riven rolls his eyes.

And Kael looks at me like he wants to murder me.

"I won't touch her. Scouts honor," I say.

"You hurt her, you die," Kael says with a longing glance back at Lumi, who still hasn't opened her eyes. Although, her cheeks are a gorgeous shade of pink from everyone talking about us fucking.

"Get out," I say.

"Is that an alpha command or mind control? I can't tell the difference," Kael snorts.

"Out," I growl.

Finally, everyone leaves. "You can open your eyes now."

As I say it, Lumi opens her eyes, and I get to see her gorgeous, sparkly blue eyes staring up at me. I don't ask her how she's feeling. I'm still in her mind, still connected to her, so I can feel everything she's feeling.

"Everyone is okay? No pack members or vampires were killed?"

I shake my head. "Everyone survived."

"Good." She hesitates, and I can feel the anxiety rising in her mind, but she's not thinking clearly enough about her question for me to understand what her concern is about.

"What is it?"

She bites her lower lip and then asks, "And Ambrose?"

Oh.

I sit down in the chair next to the bed, giving her space. "I don't know. You should ask him yourself how he's doing." I hesitate before saying the next part, "He's the reason we're all alive, unharmed."

She squints her eyes at me. "What do you mean?"

I sigh. "He let me hurt him like that for me to make the trade for you."

"But he came with Isolde. He's on her side. He thinks you're mind controlling me. He thinks I'm still his mate. Why not let Isolde kidnap me?"

"You'd have to ask him. But from my perspective, he doesn't want you to get hurt in order for him to accomplish his goals."

Her mind grows warm like a small fireplace has been lit in the corner, bringing a warm, earthy scent to her mind. She pushes me back, my cold, shadows coming with me.

I pull myself out of her head, giving her the privacy she seems to want in this moment. I know they are talking, and I try to distract myself, but it's impossible to do so.

"Ambrose is alive."

"Good."

"It was strange being in my wolf form. I don't know whether to thank him for that or still hate him."

I'm silent, letting her process her own feelings.

"We're running out of time, aren't we?" she asks.

I nod. "Two weeks. We have two weeks until the next full moon. Until your next chance at breaking the curse."

Ask me. Ask me everything.

She stares at me, really stares. "What?" I ask.

"I heard that. Your inner thoughts. I know you weren't trying to talk to me, but I heard them anyway."

I'm silent, just watching her decide what she's going to do with that information.

"I can't ask you."

I wait for her to say more, but she doesn't. "What do you mean?"

"I can't ask you. Call it intuition or part of the prophecy, but I've had dreams about both of you. And every time they make it clear that I shouldn't ask you about your history with Ambrose. I shouldn't ask why you hate each other. I shouldn't ask how you became a vampire and him a witch. I shouldn't ask more about your curses. It will interfere with figuring out who my mate is."

She takes a deep breath. "I want to know. I want to know what pain you endured that made what those witches did to you barely affect you. I want to know how you became who you are. I want to know the truth about what happened between you and Ambrose. I want to know, should I side with the witches or vampires, or should I only care about the wolf shifters? But I have to be patient. If I ask those questions too soon..."

I flip into her mind, needing to hear the words she won't say out loud.

"I'm the spark that will start a war. A war that only one of you will survive. And if I choose whose side I'm on too soon, if I choose my mate wrong, it's more than just about breaking the

curse. We will all be doomed by the gods. They'll swallow the earth whole—destroying everything."

"When do you get to ask?"

"After I've figured out and accepted who my mate is."

I want to ask her how close she is to figuring that out, but her not asking any of the questions she wants to ask makes it clear that she doesn't have the answer. And as much as I try to reassure her that it's her choice, the gods have already chosen her mate. What she does with the information about her mate is her real choice.

She should know the truth before she has to make any decisions. But for now, I'll respect that her intuition or prophecy or whatever is telling her she shouldn't ask the questions yet.

Her eyes go up and down my body, heat returning to her eyes as her tongue licks over her lips.

"What are you doing?" I ask her.

"Looking at your body. You do realize you're naked, right?"

"So are you."

She rolls her eyes and pulls the covers over her body. "I was injured and being healed. What's your excuse?"

"I was making sure that you were alright."

"And now?"

"Now I haven't bothered to go get clothes, but if you keep looking at me like that, I'm going to have to because if anyone hears us even doing so much as kissing or the bed sheets wrinkling, they are going to rip my balls off."

She chuckles. "They won't."

"We will!" Sylara shouts from downstairs.

I look at her with a raised eyebrow. *"See?"*

Lumi pouts. "Stop cock-blocking me!"

"Then stop fucking when you should be healing!" Riven shouts.

"We haven't even fucked once!" Lumi shouts back. Then looks at me. "Can't you kick them out?"

"No, unfortunately."

"Aren't you their alpha?" she teases.

"Rest, we have time for that later." I shift in my chair as my cock grows hard at the thought of it.

She sighs. "We don't."

I raise an eyebrow. "Why not?" I try not to sound too upset at the prospect. *Did she choose him? Does she not want to anymore?* All of my self-doubts return in an instant.

"Because as soon as Riven gives me the clear, we are going to talk to every seer we can find. Most witch covens have one, so we are going to see each and every one of them until we find a way to break the curse for all creatures. Until I know once and for all who my mate is. Until I figure out how to get my wolf back. Until I get to ask the questions that are burning inside me."

I nod, knowing it's what we need to do.

"And we are taking them all with us."

I groan. "Do we have to?"

She sighs. "Yes, I'm not letting you risk your life like that anymore. We're stronger together. We need answers." She shifts her tone of voice, making it louder and directed at them downstairs, "And since they are hell bent on not letting us touch each other."

She looks at me. "I'm not sure when we are going to get to be together."

I groan, I let my voice carry, "Everyone, get out."

"No!" they all shout back.

CHAPTER 26
LUMI

"If you don't keep up, Kael, you're going to be the one doing the blood offering," Sylara barks out.

"I'm keeping up just fine. Somebody needs to be in the back to make sure we aren't attacked from behind," Kael says.

"And that somebody is Brax, not you," she retorts.

"You do know that Nyx is in charge, not you, right?" Kael says.

Sylara huffs. "Nyx knows that I could challenge him for alpha and win at any time, I just don't because I love him."

"Riiiight," Kael says real slow.

I give Nyx a knowing look but keep my mouth shut. He just shakes his head.

"Why did you think we should bring them all with us again?" Nyx asks in my head.

"So if you get poisoned again, I don't have to carry your dead body miles by myself to be healed. We brought our healer with us this time."

"I'd rather die than have to keep listening to them bicker."

"I think they're cute together. If they are bickering, then that means Kael can't be hitting on me."

"True, I take back all my words. I love them bickering."

I laugh.

His eyes light up at the sight. *"I really wish we hadn't brought them with us, though."*

"Why's that?"

Heat reflects in his eyes as they run up and down my body. *"Because we never got to finish testing how compatible we are together."*

My panties are soaked, and my body flushed from that thought.

"Knock it off with the dirty thoughts. We're here," Sylara says.

"Such a cockblocker," I mumble and shake my head.

She rolls her eyes. "Now really isn't the time for that."

"Maybe it is, how else are we supposed to know if we are mates or not?" Nyx asks.

"I've enjoyed fucking countless people, that doesn't make them my mate," Sylara says. "It proves nothing."

I look between the two of them, feeling a bit of deja vu all over again. "The two of you haven't...?"

"Gods, no. I wouldn't touch the man. He's like a big brother to me. I'd rather fight him than fuck him," Sylara answers.

Nyx makes a disgusted face at the thought of fucking her. And for once, I believe them.

"They really are the epitome of professionals most of the time. They would never mix business with pleasure, but yes, they aren't each other's type," Riven says.

My voice lowers. "Who are their types?"

"For Sylara, it's men who like to be bossed around but secretly put her in her place." My eyes flash to Kael.

"And Nyx?"

Riven smirks, his eyes going up and down my body. "You."

I roll my eyes. "Before me."

He shrugs. "It's been a long time since he's been with anyone."

"How long?"

"Nyx, you're doing the blood offering," Sylara says, interrupting Riven.

"No, I will," I say, walking toward them.

"You can't."

I cross my arms across my chest. "I can. They can't hurt me, I'm the only one who can break the curse."

"No, but they can kidnap you and use your blood to hold you hostage. The answer is no," Sylara says.

I frown.

"She's right," Nyx says.

"I know she's right." I look from Nyx to the others, but I would never ask any of them to do the blood offering in his place.

"I'll do it," Kael says.

"No," both Nyx and I say at the same time.

"Why not? I'm dispensable. No one needs me."

"No, you're my friend. I would never ask you to do that for me," I say.

"I know, which is why I'm volunteering."

I shake my head and look up at Nyx. "Nyx has this. That's why I brought all of you with us. To help protect him. He's the only one of us who can die and still live afterward. He's the one who has to do it," I say.

Nyx nods his agreement, and without hesitation, he starts walking to the village where the coven of witches lives. We all follow after him, flanking him on either side and behind him. They can take his blood, but we won't let them take anything more.

"I'm here to offer my blood and talk to your seer," Nyx says.

Slowly, one by one, witches come out of their homes to look at us. This coven seems smaller and quieter than others we have seen. *Do they know the truth of the curse? Do they know that it can only be broken for one creature? Do they—*

"We don't need your blood, vampire," a short-haired blonde witch says.

I frown. *Fuck, this isn't going to go well.*

"You're here to try to learn how to break the curse for all creatures. To stop the war that's inevitable. There's plenty of honor in that," she continues.

I let out a slow breath. *Thank gods.*

"Come," she says.

We all follow her as she leads us to the seer.

"This is Zya. She's been expecting you."

Nyx starts to enter, but the woman shakes her head. "Only the snow wolf."

Nyx frowns. *"Are you okay talking to her by yourself?"*

"Yes, I'll be fine."

"I don't like it. I can—"

"I don't either, but I'll be fine. You'll all be right outside, and I can talk to you at any point. And the deal we made will ensure that I have to tell you everything."

"I'm not worried about you hiding things from me. I'm just worried about you."

"I have my blades, and you'll be right here waiting for me. I'll be fine." I follow the seer into the house. She leads me through the house to a dark bedroom with a small full-sized bed in the center.

"Lie down," Zya says with a husk to her voice.

I frown. "You know he'll kill you if you hurt me."

"I know, which is one of the many reasons I don't plan on hurting you. I know what happened to the Mystic coven—how he killed all of them. I have no intention of my coven ending up that way. Now please, lie down. I can get a better reading if you're relaxed."

Reluctantly, I climb up on the bed and lie down as she continues to talk.

"Usually, seers can only get one or two questions answered, but as you can see by the wrinkles marking my skin, I've been doing this a long time before the curse. We used to be able to get many questions answered if we were patient. You're important enough to try to get more answers."

"Are you okay? You feel anxious," Nyx asks.

"I'm fine."

"What's happening?"

"I'm lying down on a bed. She's going to try to get multiple questions answered. She said to be patient. This could take a while."

"I'm not going anywhere."

"I know."

"Clear your mind, no more talking to vampire boy."

I do as she asks, clearing my mind as her magic gently seeps inside me. She's probably learning everything she can about me, not just trying to see the future. But I let her get whatever information she wants because I'm desperate for someone to see a different fate. Even if the cost is her learning my secrets.

"You can get up now," she says suddenly.

My head is foggy, and I yawn like I just woke up from a long nap. "What happened?"

"You fell asleep."

"How long?"

"Five hours."

I shoot up. *"Nyx, are you okay?"*

"Yes, but it's been taking everything in me not to come barreling through that door to come and get you. The only reason I haven't is because your mind felt calm and safe."

"I'm fine. We're almost done."

I turn to the seer. "What did you learn?"

"Answers you aren't going to like."

"Tell me."

She eases herself back into her chair before taking a long drink from the water glass sitting on the nightstand. She looks exhausted as she stares into my eyes, like she's about to break the news that someone I love has died.

"Your wolf is no longer yours to control. There is no way to get her back. She belongs to Ambrose."

My lungs are being squeezed tight again, but this time it's by my own doing, not a witch's.

"There is no way to break the curse for everyone. You can't even break it for two species—only one. The more powerful of the mating pair decides which species the curse is broken for."

"Who's my mate?" I ask.

She looks at me like I imagine a mother would look at her daughter. "You already know the answer. Being some-one's mate isn't about the person you love the most or are most attracted to. It's about fate, destiny, and what's best for the packs. The only way you stay a snow wolf, a wolf queen, is by Ambrose's side. He's your mate. You can talk to every seer in the world, they'll all tell you the same thing."

Which means Ambrose, being the strongest between

the two of us, would be the one who decides which species the curse is broken for.

I stand, hating her answers, hating the time we wasted.

"You can't keep running from the answers."

I don't respond as I reach the door.

"You still love him. You know you do."

I look back at her with clenched teeth. "Why can Nyx talk to me in my head if he's not also my mate? Why is there such an intense connection between us?"

She doesn't answer.

"If there are three curses, then there have to be three ways to break the curses. Curses always have a loophole, a way to break them. There is a way to break all three, you just haven't seen the answer," I tell her.

"You're probably right, but you snow wolf, are only destined to break one curse. You get to break one, not all three."

"Watch me."

"So cocky. It will be the death of you," she bemoans.

"I'd rather die than accept the torment of so many, than accept the inevitable war."

"The Nightfall vampire isn't yours to save. And he definitely isn't yours to love."

"What if you're wrong? What if the gods didn't want the curse broken, so they sent you all the wrong visions? What if he's my one true mate, not Ambrose?"

"Are you willing to bet your life on that? Because if you choose wrong, if you let the wrong man mark you, you'll die."

I turn and walk out the door, not bothering to look back. Nyx is by my side the second I walk outside. He doesn't even bother to ask me a single question; he can see it all on my face. He knows the answers I got amount to nothing new.

I don't want to stay here tonight. We don't have much time. We need to keep moving. Keep trying.

The others follow behind us, none of them questioning my decision or complaining about the trek ahead.

We repeat the same motions five more times.

Five more covens.

Five more seers.

Five more times, getting the same answers.

Five more times of losing hope, over the course of weeks, until there's only one seer left to see.

CHAPTER 27

NYX

We have one last seer.

One.

Thalia.

She's already revealed a prophecy to Lumi, but she hasn't revealed one to me. I don't know if she'll help. But she's our last hope that a seer sees a different fate for Lumi. That she has a choice in who her mate is. That there is a way to prevent war. That there's a way for Lumi to get her wolf back.

I'm trying to be wishful for Lumi's sake, but I don't have any hope left. I'm here because of Lumi. I already know her fate without asking Thalia.

Lumi will be able to break the curse for one creature if she accepts Ambrose as her mate. She'll get her wolf back by asking for it whenever she wants it. She'll be an alpha queen.

But a war will still happen. She can't stop it. No one can.

So she has to decide for herself if she can forgive him.

If she still loves him. If accepting him as her mate, even if it doesn't stop the war, is enough.

I'm pretty sure I already know what she will choose. She hasn't completely severed her connection. She still loves him, still wants to forgive him, but she just can't figure out how.

And me, I've always known how I'm doomed. I've accepted my fate as a killer, the enemy that needs to be stopped. She's forgotten a little bit that I'm the villain. The one who took something from her far worse than just control over herself. I took her friend's life, and I did it on purpose. Ambrose took her wolf by accident.

She can learn to forgive him, but she'll never forgive me.

We stand on the small college campus that Thalia attends, standing outside of her statistics lecture hall, waiting for her to get out of class. It's just Lumi and me. We saw no need for the rest to come with us this time since she's not with her coven.

Students start to file out of the classroom, and we wait for the woman with long red hair and green eyes with an arrogance about her that only a talented witch could possess. She's easy to spot. Without glancing at us, she says, "I have thirty minutes before my next class."

"We won't take up more of your time than that," I say gently.

"I know you won't." She doesn't ask us to follow her; she just starts walking. She leads us to a bench along a pathway that is anything but private.

We don't argue with her. If this is where she wants to talk, then this is where we'll talk. She's doing us a favor. We don't want to piss her off.

"I know you've already told me part of the prophecy, but you haven't seen any of Nyx's future," Lumi says.

Thalia looks from Lumi to me. "I had a dream last night. A vision. A part of the prophecy. Every seer's abilities work a little differently, as I'm sure you know. Some see their visions in dreams. Others need to touch you to extract a vision. Some are shadows, and some see clear pictures. Some are false, but not mine. Mine are prophecies, not simply visions. They are always true. That's why they say I'm the most powerful seer of all time. I know the one strand of fate that is absolutely going to happen. I've seen a lot of strands—choices that both of you could make. But the vision I had last night, I know it will happen, no matter what you do. Both of you were in my dream."

We both suck in a breath at that. Hope—that kernel of hope is back. If we are both in each other's futures, then that could mean...

"Would you like me to tell you my prophecy, still knowing everything I've told you? Knowing that it's the absolute future and nothing you do can change it?" she asks, staring at me. It's my choice.

"Tell me your prophecy."

"The Nightfall vampire is the one who stops the war. He finds a way to end the curse for all creatures. He basks under the stars..."

Lumi is smiling, but I see the problem with how Thalia is wording this. There is a but...a downside...

"While he watches the babies of the snow wolf dance in the moonlight."

"What does that mean?" Lumi asks.

Thalia stares at me intensely.

"It means I figure out how to break the curse for all creatures. I stop the war. But you aren't my mate," I say.

"But you're watching my babies, couldn't that mean they're yours?"

I shake my head. "Vampires can't have babies."

She goes solemn, understanding slowly crossing her face. I can't be her mate. If this is the one true prophecy. If this is the one true vision, and if we believe Thalia is the most powerful seer, then this prophecy is true, and we aren't mates. We can't be.

All of the seers point to the same future. The same fate. Ambrose and she are mates, while I stop the war. The details are vague, murky, and unhelpful. But if what she says is true, we all get what we want in the end. I ensure the curses are broken for everyone. The war has been prevented, or at least stopped. And she gets her happily ever after with her mate.

Then why are we both looking at each other like we were just served a death sentence?

CHAPTER 28

LUMI

The living room is packed when we return to Nyx's house. Each person's eyes sweep across our bodies, studying us for any wounds or injuries. Riven, in particular, breathes out a sigh of relief when he realizes his healing services won't be needed tonight.

"Learn anything helpful?" Kael asks, but I know he can tell by my body language that the answer is no.

I shake my head, hanging it low. Nyx doesn't even respond to them. He can't even make eye contact with any of them. He's in a haze. He's been this way since we spoke to Thalia. He's completely lost in his own thoughts, unable to articulate any of them to me.

To him, it's like no one is even here as he walks past the living room to the stairs that lead to his bedroom. I follow after, not bothering to share anything more with the group.

The sun has begun to set, but for now, the room is illuminated with golden light, leaving long streaks stretching across the floor. Nyx lingers at the threshold, the sunlight brushing against the edges of his shoes in a cruel warning. He paces just outside the door, slowly inching inside his room as the light pulls back, retreating slowly from his room. His mind twisted with the words Thalia spoke to us.

I step through the sunlight over to the bed, where I sit on the edge.

"What are you thinking?" I ask.

He doesn't answer. I'm not even sure he heard me. His pacing is relentless. He walks back and forth in quiet resignation as if this is his new destiny—to grind a path into the floor, forever.

I push gently against his mind. He has a shield up, but it's a weak one. He's not really putting much effort into keeping me out, making it easy for me to slide through. Once inside, I feel all of his emotions flooding me.

Killing, death—that's how I end or prevent a war. I kill everyone important. That's always been my role.

Ambrose is her mate. But then, that's always been true. She'll break the curse for at least one creature, and I'll help them break the curse for the rest.

I suck in a breath, realizing the immensity of what Thalia told him. I've always been the one destined to break the curse. But she said he's destined to do something as big or bigger—stop the war. Break the curse for the rest. That's huge. That's a lot of responsibility on his shoulders to figure out how to do that.

"Do you believe Thalia? All of the witches?"

He blinks, as if he's finally realized he's not alone in the world.

"Yes."

"Even though they are witches and might have their own motives?"

"Yes, I believe them. Thalia, especially. "

I nod, my own heart sinking a little.

"That's it then. He's my mate. They've all said so. He's the only way I can break the curse."

"It appears that way, yes," Nyx says with dark longing in his eyes as he looks at me. He knows what could have been but will never be. We could have been good together, so fucking good.

But then again, he's a vampire. I'm a shifter without a wolf. He's a killer, and I'm a fragile human. He has his own baggage, and I still have feelings for my controlling ex. *Could we have ever really worked?*

"Even if he's truly your mate, it doesn't mean you have to do anything about it. You have one week until the next full moon. Take your time deciding. Make sure it's what you really want. If you want to take longer to decide, then I'll protect you as long as you want." He pauses and looks at me with an intense gaze. *"Just because you can break the curse doesn't mean you have to. You don't have to break the curse—ever."*

"Do you think I could live with myself if I could break the curse but didn't? If I could end others' suffering but didn't?"

"Still doesn't mean you have to choose someone who is a controlling asshole. But if you do, maybe you need to make your own blood deal with him."

I stare at Nyx, not sure what to say.

"But it's also okay to give yourself permission to forgive him, to go back with him. There is a reason you never severed your bond with him. You still love him," he says.

I don't confirm or deny it. I just stare at Nyx, still caged by the sunlight across the room from me.

"Ambrose is my mate," I say out loud in a neutral

tone. The words are fact, at least according to every seer we've met. I still don't know how I feel about it, about him.

I loved Ambrose. There is a part of me that still loves him. But what he did...it's not something I can just forgive.

And then there's Nyx. He did something just as unforgivable. I don't love him. But my heart is thumping so loudly in my chest at the sight of him that I think there is something I might be missing about him.

I want the choice.

The wolf shifters never used to get a choice in their mates. They were always predestined, and everyone accepted that. We accepted our mates. We procreated. Lived happy lives in our packs. We followed the rules. Until someone from my pack rejected her mate. She wanted a choice, and it angered the gods so much that they cursed all three magical creatures that walk this earth.

And now, there's a rebel part of me that wants to do the same. I want the choice. I want to pick, even if it means I end up picking Ambrose. I want to decide my own future.

But that's not what the gods want. They want to choose. They want us to dance around for them like the playthings they see us as. Nyx isn't my mate; he just shares a bond with me because he is also destined to end the curses.

The sun begins to dip, the light pulling back from the room inch by inch. Nyx stares at me, and I stare at him. Both of us lost to our thoughts, no longer in each other's heads.

"Lumi could still be my mate. Sometimes the prophecies

are wrong. Sometimes they change. Our connection is just as strong as hers and Ambrose's. There is no denying that. She could be my mate."

I didn't realize I slipped back into his head. Or did he whisper the words through our bond? Either way, I heard them.

The veil is pierced between us as he realizes I heard his words.

"What do you want to do, Lumi? It's your choice."

The sunlight has crept to the foot of the bed and is rapidly retracting from the room now. I watch it slowly retreat across my body until I'm cast entirely in shadow before I answer. My eyes meet his with hooded eyelids.

"Right now, I want you."

His body goes still as stone. He understands exactly what I'm saying.

"I can't promise you how I'll feel tomorrow or what decision I'll ultimately end up making. It's not fair to you. You're an alpha shifter and a vampire lord; you have feelings, too. I've seen them. Doing this will only intensify those feelings for both of us. I doubt it will make it clearer if you're my mate or if Ambrose is in my mind. It will probably just confuse things even more," I say.

He continues not to move, not even blink, as I speak.

I take a deep breath. "But if I don't get at least one night with you, I know it will be the biggest regret of my life."

His lips hit me first, crashing into me with such force that it nearly knocks the wind out of me. It's so fucking worth it as I fall onto my back on the bed. Whether we are mates or not doesn't matter in this moment as he claims my mouth with his. My arms are pushed up over my head, and my hips are pinned by his as he kisses me desperately.

"I'd regret not getting to claim you as mine for at least one night, even if you're not mine to claim forever."

Shivers dance over my skin at his hungry words. I get a haunting feeling in my belly that I don't know what it means.

"Let's forget together," I say out loud.

He kisses me, pushing me deeper into the soft mattress. "I won't forget anything about tonight, love."

My tongue pushes into his mouth, feeling the sharp point of his fangs trailing over my tongue. He fists my hair, pulling my head roughly, and my tongue slides out of his mouth.

"Careful, love, you're playing with fire and you're going to get bitten if you keep teasing."

With flared eyes, I say, "What if I want to get bitten?"

He shudders, but shakes his head. Without any notice, we are across the room, my front is pressed against the window, and he's pushed against my back, his fangs hovering over my neck.

I can see our reflection in the window as the moonlight hits us just right. One of his hands grips my hip, while the other sweeps my hair off my shoulder, exposing my neck to him. His fangs touch just the top of my skin without breaking it.

Fear pulses through me. He could kill me. As a vampire. A wolf shifter. Just a male. He could kill me in a thousand ways.

He'll kill you. He'll kill you. He'll kill you...

The whispered promise of the voice that likes to play in my head at the most inconvenient times promises me. A prophecy of its own making.

But not today. He's not killing me today. He's protecting me.

"You don't want me to bite you, love. If I bite you, I kill you. Vampires don't bite for pleasure, even if, for a moment, it would be intoxicating to you, heighten every emotion you're currently feeling, and more." His fangs tease me, drawing over me. "The only time I get to bite you again is if you want me to mark you as my mate."

"What if I want to be yours?"

He gulps as he covers his fangs with his lips, kissing me softly on the neck. He doesn't have an answer for that. Neither do I. But then he's kissing me so sweetly, finding a sensitive spot behind my ear that I don't care how permanent this is or not.

I watch him in the reflection as the night continues to fade to darkness.

He can move at lightning speed, but doesn't. Time slows with his hands as he drags a sharpened nail down the front of my shirt, slowly ripping it in half, exposing more and more of my skin.

I can't breathe, and my heart is beating so fast in my chest as I watch him take his time undressing me. Slowly, he pulls my shirt over my shoulders and drops it to the floor as he kisses the exposed skin on my back.

He keeps kissing lower and lower until he's kneeling on the ground. He guides my hips to face him, and I see that single nail of a wolf again. He drags it over the fabric of my jeans, shredding them in seconds, which is somehow so much hotter than him peeling them off my body.

Leaning forward, he kisses over my black lace panties at the same time he reaches up, using that nail to cut through the material of my bra until my breasts spring free.

Nyx has seen me naked many times, but this is different, more intimate, and suddenly my entire skin blushes at the thought of him seeing all of me and getting all of me.

"You're gorgeous, Lumi. The most beautiful woman I've ever seen or will ever see again."

"Don't say words that aren't true. Ever is a long time."

His teeth sink into my panties, ripping them from my body with one bite. He leans back on his heels to admire his handiwork. His eyes glaze over my body, sparking at the sight of me like fireworks.

"I can definitely promise those words will be true forever, love."

Without warning, he spreads my thighs and dives between them, his tongue plunging into the folds of my body.

I grab onto his shoulders, barely able to keep myself upright as he licks up my slit, expertly finding my clit.

"Gods, I missed how you tasted. Like delicate snow, you taste cool in my mouth as it dissolves into your warm heat," he says in my mind.

"I love how you can tell all your thoughts while never stopping what you're doing with your tongue." I inhale sharply as his tongue circles my clit before one of his dangerous fangs nips at it without acutely biting. *"Fuck, never stop doing that."*

"Your wish is my command." He keeps doing that exact thing, making it harder and harder for me to stand on my own as my body trembles around him. He guides me backward until my back is against the glass.

"I can't wait to hear what you sound like when you come. Do you call out my name? A whimperer? Or a screamer?"

"I—" Gods, I nearly explode as he slides his middle fingers through my slickness. My body falls forward, almost collapsing on top of him, but he pushes me back, his hand splayed across my lower belly.

His fingers slide in and out of me, curling around into my body with each thrust. His tongue moves faster, superhumanly fast. And I'm—

"Nyx!" I scream out in one long shuddered breath.

His lips curl up in a smirk, but he doesn't stop, doesn't give me a second to catch my breath as he draws out my orgasm until my panting can barely keep up with him.

My legs feel like jello, and I start sliding down the glass, but he catches me, holding me in one arm, and he starts carrying me toward the bed. His other hand yanks off his shirt and pushes down his pants like he's a fucking magician.

I scrape my teeth over my bottom lip as my hand feels over his bare chest. Thin lines of muscled body greet me, as do the scars. I still don't understand how his body is so scared. How a healer or his vampire body hasn't healed him to perfection. But I don't care, he's perfect to me.

He lays me down so gently in the center of the bed before he stands back, admiring me. Worry creeps in.

"Don't you dare leave. I'm not tired, and you don't get to decide what I do or don't need," I say.

His lips curl up in a snicker. "I wouldn't dare leave when you're splayed out naked on my bed like this. And I intend to make you far more sore and tired before I'm done with you."

There's an unspoken fact that stings between us.

Tonight has to last a lifetime. There will be no tomorrow for us. This is a beginning and an ending.

We both push those thoughts away, not letting them into whatever this is between us. But I do feel our minds connecting again. I feel his digging, searching for something in my mind. I don't shut him out; instead, I follow him around my own mind like a lost puppy.

"What are you looking for?"

He doesn't answer, but then he finds it. And he shows me exactly what he found.

I draw in a shaky breath as my own dirty fantasies play out in both of our heads simultaneously.

"You really want this? You really want me?" He asks aloud as he stares down at me. His body is hard and large, so fucking large. Dark scars mark his tanned body. His blood-red eyes and fangs give me all the hints in the world of how deadly and dark this man is. This creature is seen by others only as a killer.

At first, it was all I saw. The heart that barely beats because it belongs to a vampire. A deadly predator that lurks in the night.

"I killed Rowena," he reminds me.

I narrow my eyes at him. "Why are you trying to get me to stop this?"

I try to push into his head, but he's locked me out. All of his shields are blocking me like an impenetrable wall.

"Nyx?" I push again, gently.

He doesn't yield. "Are you sure you want this?"

His eyes swirl, and he's firm in his demand for me to answer aloud.

"Yes, I want this. I want you. I need you to fuck me. No one else."

He sucks in a breath so sharp that it feels like he cut the room in two with it.

"Do you want this? Want me?" I ask.

He's on top of me, his arms holding him up. "I've never wanted anything more in my life."

"Then stop questioning this and fuck me."

He grins. "Yes, love."

I feel his long, thick cock at my soaking entrance. And I watch in waited anticipation, still not sure if he's actually going to take me or not.

His hand gently cradles the back of my head as he kisses me so softly and tenderly that it almost doesn't seem like Nyx on top of me. He slides through my slickness, my walls, until he's all the way to the hilt inside me.

A crack of lightning strikes outside the window as he seats himself inside me, my nails dig into his back, holding him to me like he can somehow possibly go deeper. His kiss captures my cry as I stretch around his enormous length.

Another flash of lightning and the room descends into darkness as the lights flicker off. Thankfully, my eyesight adjusts immediately to the darkness, so I don't miss being able to see all of Nyx's glorious body.

I can't speak. I can't think. But I feel Nyx in my head, reading all of my feelings like an open book. He thrusts hard, filling me completely.

"Open your legs wider," he commands.

I let my legs fall wider, and he thrusts again, somehow getting deeper.

I yelp as he hits that delicious spot deep in my core. A chill dances over both of our skins in opposition to the warmth spreading with each pounding thrust. My hips buck up to meet his each time, my body tightening around him, building us both closer and closer to that release that will have us falling hard back into reality.

Not yet. It's far, far too soon for that.

He palms my breast, feeling the heaviness in his grasp as my nipples pebble into icy peaks.

"You're so cold," he says.

"Sorry."

"No, we're both cold. Both ice and snow, and the chilled night air. You feel like you're part of me. We're the same."

I gasp as he thrusts again hard, while his thumb gently strokes my nipple just like in my dirty fantasies. I love the stark contrast between a man who can be both gentle and rough at the same time.

"Gods, you're incredible. Your gasps, your whimpers, your cries. I could listen to them all night," he says.

He pulls another whimper from me as his pelvis hits my clit.

"And your body..." he growls his approval as he nips at my ear.

My body is humming, on the edge of orgasm. So fucking close, and yet I bite down on my lip and clench my fists at my side, doing anything I can to keep it from happening. I have to stay here in this moment. This can never stop, never end.

"Come, love."

"I can't."

"You can...come." His voice is so coaxing, and caring, and tender, like he's trying to persuade me to jump through a window when the house is burning and he'll catch me at the bottom.

He'll catch me.

So I jump, right off the edge, letting my orgasm

swarm like a hurricane; it hurtles through my body, blasting us both with how strong it is. Another lightning strike, even louder than the first, blasts through, lighting up the room, giving me an even better view of the predator on top of me, coming completely undone at the sight of my orgasm.

A single word floats in my head—*love.*

Yes.

No.

I force my walls up hard and fast. Not allowing the word to leave or for him to hear it. Not until I can process what it means without his thick cock buried inside me.

His body shudders, his own orgasm spilling inside me in cool bursts. His muscles are trembling as he holds me tighter, gripping onto me like I'm about to be blown away from him.

I dig my own fingers into his back until I realize my fingers have shifted into wolf claws and I'm drawing his blood.

"Don't stop," he says.

So I hold on for dear life, just like he's gripping me. Our aftershocks rumble through us as we both pant in each other's arms, our slick cum spilling out of me and onto him.

There's a tingling on both of our tongues. Words we both want to speak but never do. And then my body starts glowing—the marks of the runes lighting up my body.

I don't know what it means. But it puts a damper on any feelings either of us was feeling. Reminding us both of the elephant in the room. The reality we are both facing.

I push into his mind, needing to know what he's feeling when he's not saying anything. But I'm met with a dark, looming wall—one I know I have no way to climb.

I feel him pushing at the edges of my mind with the same desperation, needing to know how I feel. But my silvery white wall is tall and unyielding even against his formidable strength. For once, I know that I can block him out.

I'm not ready to share my feelings. The words that could destroy us, and neither is he.

CHAPTER 29

NYX

The runes on her body have spread. What once marked only her stomach now coils down her arm, winding like twisted golden vines etched into her skin. They've glowed all night, taunting me each time I fucked her.

She's not yours, she's mine...

Gods, I know it all too well. Selfishly, I've been hoping the whole time that I was wrong—hoping everyone was wrong—that Lumi is mine. My intuition was screaming that she was my mate when he was trying to mark her, which meant she really is my mate.

In reality, I was likely pushed by the gods to save her so she could have more time to prepare for Ambrose's mark. She wasn't strong enough to survive the marking ceremony then. She would have died, and the curse wouldn't have been broken. But she's getting stronger each day. Her wolf is stronger, even if it's tied to Ambrose. She's ready now. She'd survive.

But I've been selfish with her. Fucked her senseless over and over again. Made it harder for her to make the right decision. To find her mate through our lust-filled moments together, because that's all they really are—lust, attraction.

It's all going to lead to heartbreak. Hopefully, just mine. Hopefully, she's realized through this that I'm the bad boy who's fun to fuck, but not the guy you marry, mate, and share a life with. I'm doomed. Not fucking her would have been a mistake, but fucking her knowing she'll never be mine is going to wreck me forever.

She's lying on my chest, completely passed out and naked. I run my hand through her hair that sparkles a little as the moonlight hits it, but it won't for much longer. The sky is slowly changing. Soon the sun will rise, and we will have to face reality.

I push against her mind, trying once again to get inside, to prepare myself for the words I know she's going to speak. But even in her sleep, she's blocked me out. Sealed up so tight, there's no way for me to get inside.

I grin, proud of her for finally figuring it out. I just wish now wasn't the moment she did.

As more light starts to creep through the windows, I curse myself for not getting curtains. I had too much hope that I could somehow get rid of my vampirism. *Foolish, foolish man.*

I slide under the covers, pulling them over my head.

She stirs slightly as I yank her thigh so I can get a perfect view of her glorious pussy. I grin at the wetness still spilling out of her. I don't know if it's her or me. I've lost track of the times we've fucked, but I'll remember every single time.

I gently kiss the inside of her thigh, inching my way up to the soft V that joins her leg to her cunt. She shifts her legs, letting her legs fall open, giving me permission and full access.

Fuck, yes.

One long stroke of my tongue tastes the wetness between her folds, spreading them over her sensitive lips. I'm rewarded with the softest of whimpers as she begins to stir a little more from her sleep. She begins to squirm, but I grip her thighs, holding them in place so I can feast on her.

Another whimper, then another. But no words. Not from her or me. There won't be any words. Just our bodies joining like we've been doing this daily for weeks as our morning ritual.

I listen to her heavy pants as I slide my fingers inside her. I curl my fingers up, finding that sweet spot that leaves her breathless. As I pump my fingers in and out of her, my tongue lavishes her clit. She tastes so fucking good. I try to memorize the taste, the sounds she's making, but they'll fade, and they won't always be this vivid.

And then she's coming. It still amazes me how fast she can come after I've brought her to orgasm so many times tonight. But she does. She's so sensitive, so ready for me at every moment.

As she's coming, I flip our bodies until she's straddling mine. The sunlight flashes on my face, causing me intense pain for a split second before she pulls the covers over us again, blocking us from the sun.

She reaches between her legs, finding my cock and easing herself down on me. Her eyes and messy hair tell me she's still half asleep, but as she fills herself with my cock she comes alive.

Her nails shift to her wolf's for a split second before

she pulls them back as she grips my chest and rides my cock.

She'll get her wolf back. She doesn't realize it, but she's already reclaimed a tiny part of it. She'll get it back fully, one day.

She leans down until our bodies are pressed together as she kisses me with everything she has. She tastes like sweet, crisp morning chill. I run my hand through her hair, tangling myself in the mess, hoping I can tangle us together so much that this will never end.

Her thrusts over my cock grow faster, and soon I'm as breathless as she. Her warm wetness drips down onto my lower belly, and her walls grip me tighter and tighter with each rock of her hips up and down my cock.

And then she's coming yet again. She breaks the silence game we were playing by screaming my name.

I cry out her name in return as I come buried deep inside her, pulling her to me with all of my might, digging myself as deep as I can into her.

She collapses her full weight onto me.

"Beautiful," I whisper.

She sighs, and then I feel something. Or maybe I imagined it.

A tear lands on my chest.

"Lumi?" I pull her back to look at her, but as I do, there is no sign of her crying or the tear that I thought I felt.

She smiles at me, a genuine smile, as if I've just made her entire night. But the smile scares me more than the tear.

I nudge at her mind. Still blocked.

My eyes search hers for answers. But she looks too happy, too determined, too hopeful.

Don't give me hope. I'm too fragile for hope.

Then she breaks our silence in a real way. "I've decided what I'm going to do at the next full moon."

I hold my breath, waiting for my world to shatter or come to become whole.

"I need to talk to Ambrose," she says.

CHAPTER 30

LUMI

"*Nyx and I need to talk to you,*" I send to Ambrose. I haven't talked to him or felt for our connection since the Moonlight pack and Moonfire coven attacked us.

I'm still lying on Nyx's naked body. I never want to move. I want to stay hidden in the covers with him forever. But now that I've realized what I have to do, I need to do it. I need to carry out my plan.

Nyx tugs at the door to my mind again, begging to be let in. He wants to know what my decision is—who I chose as a mate.

But he can't know. It kills me that I can't tell him. I have to block him out after what we just did. But I can't have him talking me out of my decision.

"*I assume you mean in private without anyone else knowing?*" Ambrose sends back.

"*Yes. Do you have a place where we can meet safely?*"

There's a long pause. "*Yes, I'll send you the exact coordinates. I have a house in the woods that's about halfway between the Bloodmoon pack territory and my territory. Meet there in three hours."*

"See you in three hours."

I'm shocked that Ambrose didn't make me promise more things. If he thinks this is a trap, he's not even questioning me about it. He didn't ask if he could bring Emeric or anyone else to offer protection for him. He still trusts me.

Nyx is still beneath me, except for his thumb that lightly traces circles over my lower back. He doesn't rush me. He doesn't ask me. He patiently waits.

I'm still processing our night together, just as curious about his own feelings about what transpired as he is about mine. But we've both blocked each other out, and our time is up.

"Ambrose gave me a latitude and longitude to meet at. It's a house somewhere between his territory and ours. He said he'll meet us there in three hours alone," I say.

Nyx doesn't respond at first. He wants to say no, that it isn't safe.

"I doubt we have time for a bath, but we can at least take a quick shower first? Otherwise, we're going to reek of each other, and Ambrose is going to lose his mind before even talking to us," he says.

One second he's under me, the next he's in the bathroom, and I hear the water running. I collapse into the bed with a soft, infectious smile and a blush staining my cheeks. He wanted to bathe with me—so sweet and romantic.

When I walk into the bathroom, I'm not sure what to expect. Nyx watches me with a hungry gaze that he quickly tames with a blink of his eyes, returning to all business.

"You're gorgeous, can I wash you?"

I bite back a smile. "Yes."

He holds out his hand and I take it, like he's about to lead me out onto the dance floor. Instead, he leads me into his shower. Water hits me from the four shower heads that are in here, melting any soreness away. He steps in behind me, his massive frame easily fitting in the expansive shower that three adults could fit in. I don't think too hard about who else might have enjoyed taking a shower with him here.

He grabs a bottle of shampoo and squirts some into my hair, then his fingers start to scrub. He doesn't say a word as he works. He doesn't even speak while rinsing the soap out of my hair. He stays silent as he takes a washcloth and rubs soap all over every inch of my body.

I don't tell him that if the point is to wash the scent of each other from each other's bodies, then showering together might not be fully helping. But I'm enjoying the quiet silence. The slow study of each other's bodies without talking and without sexually touching each other.

I watch as, under his touch, the markings of the runes begin to fade back into my skin. The gold lighting up the edges disappears. He washes the runes away like they're nothing more than a marker drawn on my skin. The runes had spread from my chest to my arms, claiming more of my body for their own pleasure.

I hold my breath as he washes over my chest and breasts, scrubbing the runes away along with the soap. I'm happy to watch them vanish once again. I can't make sense of it, just like I can't make sense of why they became visible when Nyx started fucking me. The water rinses the soap off my body until there is nothing left for Nyx to wash on me.

I take another washcloth and soap and do the same to Nyx's body. I wash over his arms—where thin black scars have darkened almost overnight. His entire chest is the same. I can see every cut, scrape, and hit he's ever endured in his life, and there isn't a part of his body left untouched.

I have questions, so many questions, as does he. But in this moment, neither of us asks them.

"We should go," Nyx finally says after I've cleaned and examined every inch of him.

I nod.

What feels like seconds later, we are running through the forest, me on Nyx's back while carrying a small backpack of clothes and supplies to the spot where Ambrose agreed to meet us.

"Let your wall down just a little," Nyx says as we approach the location. He's shifted back into his vampire form and gotten dressed.

I raise an eyebrow at him.

"I'm not going to read your mind or push to get any thoughts, I promise. But if things go south, we need to be able to communicate easily. You can still block me out from what you don't want me to know. Just let me talk to you in your mind again," he begs.

I study him closely, unsure if I should, but I trust him. And I trust myself, so I lower the wall. A few feet behind where it was before, I build a new wall, still blocking him from most of my mind.

"This better?" I ask.

His shoulders relax a little. *"Thank you, love."*

My heart skips when he looks at me like that. *Fuck, I*

have to get it together if I'm going to be able to make it through this.

Nyx grabs my hand, holding me back as his ears perk up. *"Someone found us."*

"Ambrose?"

"More than just Ambrose."

"He wouldn't betray me by bringing others. He might bring Emeric, but that's it."

"He would betray me.*"*

I frown, knowing that there is no arguing with Nyx about that. But I know Ambrose differently than Nyx does, which makes me proceed with even more caution.

Something hard and fast hits Nyx right in the chest.

"Run!" Nyx screams at me.

I glance back to where Nyx hit the ground and see the vampire that hit him.

"Trust me. I'm fine. Run!" Nyx says again.

Dammit.

I run. I pull my blade out and run as fast as I can, trusting that Nyx is strong enough to take on one vampire by himself.

"Ambrose?" I call out in my head, trying to figure out if he's made it here or not.

"Run," his whispered breath comes into my head.

Fuck.

Unlike Nyx's order, Ambrose's is weak. He's hurt. Captured. In trouble.

I halt running, turning in circles, trying to figure out which way to run. I never saw the cabin when I started running, but my intuition tells me that's where I should go. That's where Ambrose is.

I slam my walls down, opening my mind to both Ambrose and Nyx, allowing them full access to everything. It's risky, but it's necessary for our survival. Everyone will be too preoccupied with staying alive to dig deep into my thoughts for answers.

I start running toward the cabin, to where I know Ambrose is.

"*Lumi, no!*" Nyx shouts. Now that my mind is open to him, he knows where I'm going.

"*I have to. He's hurt.*"

"*I'm coming. Stay alive,*" Nyx says.

But I can tell by how breathless he sounds that he's fighting off more than one vampire now. I don't know how long it could take him to help.

"*Where are you?*" I send to Ambrose as I approach the house. I can sense him inside, but I don't know where or in what condition he's in.

"*Run, Lumi, they're using me as bait,*" Ambrose says again.

"*I'm not leaving. Now, where are you? How many? Anything that could help me save your ass would be helpful.*"

"*Back bedroom. There's a window you can enter through. Hurry, they're gone now, but I don't know when they'll come back.*"

I know Nyx hears everything, so I don't bother repeating Ambrose's location to him.

The cabin is small, so it doesn't take me long to locate the entry. I creep up to the window, raising my head just enough to peek inside. Ambrose is tied to the bed, and he's lying in a puddle of his own blood.

"*Hold on, I'm coming,*" I tell Ambrose.

A light groan is all I get back.

Fuck, fuck, fuck.

I try prying the window open, but it doesn't budge. So I turn backward and slam my elbow as hard as I can into the window. It breaks, but the noise is loud enough that I'm sure the vampires heard. I throw my body through the shattered window, ignoring the burn of glass slashing open my skin as I push myself through.

I force myself onto my feet and am next to Ambrose in the next second.

"Ambrose, I'm here."

His eyes are shut, his chest is rising and falling so slowly that every time it falls, I'm afraid it's not going to rise with another breath again. His limbs are tied to the four posts of the bed. There are bite marks on his neck, wrists, and ankles. He's lost so much blood. The vampires didn't even drink it; they just spilled it out on the bed.

I move to one of his wrists with my blade, and I work on cutting through the rope binding him, but it's slow work.

"Hold on, Ambrose. Hold on," I whisper to him, my heart thumping wildly in panic.

"Our trap worked," I hear an unfamiliar deep voice behind me.

I don't stop sawing, hoping that if I can just get one limb free, then we'll survive this. He'll get free. He'll be able to stop this.

"Your wolf shifter alpha is dead, or he will be in a matter of minutes. Don't waste your energy," the menacing vampire says from behind me.

I saw faster, so close.

"We're not going to hurt you, though. You're the snow wolf. The one who can break the curse. We just need you to break it for the vampires, not the shifters. That's why you'll choose the Nightfall lord as your mate."

"That's not how it works. I don't get to choose."

I keep talking, keep trying to buy myself time. One more strand.

It breaks.

One of Ambrose's arms is free, but he still doesn't move. He can't. He's too weak, too near death.

Fuck.

"Nyx, I need you to make me shift."

"Only Ambrose can control your wolf."

"He's unconscious. But you can control it too with your mind control."

There's a pause. *"I made a blood deal with you that I wouldn't use mind control. I can't do it. I'm close. The vampires won't hurt you. They need you alive to end the curse. I'm almost there."*

"But they don't need Ambrose. He's out of time." A tear rolls down my cheek. *"Please."*

Nyx growls, the sound echoing through my body with a force I've never felt before, and then I'm shifting. Faster than I've ever shifted before, like he's forcing my body to move faster, to bend my frame and turn my skin to fur as fast as his vampire moves.

In seconds, I'm standing in the small bedroom in my white fur with golden streaks and eyes that scream, 'I'm going to kill you.'

At the sight of me, one of the vampires runs. The other stands frozen, like he can't move at all.

Nyx.

Is he mind-controlling them, too?

I don't think. I attack, going straight for the vampire's throat. The vampire starts to move at the last second as I leap. It takes a swipe at me, trying to knock me away, but I'm far more determined to win this fight than he is.

I rip.

I tear.

I don't stop until he's dead on the ground.

I know he's not permanently dead. I'd need to put a stake through his heart for that, but it's enough that I can draw my attention back to Ambrose.

I shift back. Nyx is pushing me back into my human form as quickly as he shifted me into my wolf form.

"Ambrose! You can't die. Don't you dare fucking die!" I scream at him.

I make quick work of the ropes, using what remains of my canines to tear through the thick cords. And then he's free but still not out of the woods. His breathing is labored. There is more blood outside of his body than inside.

"Riven will be here in three minutes," Nyx says.

Thank gods. I tear off fabric from my clothes to start applying pressure to the worst wounds on his neck, trying to keep the remaining blood inside.

"Three minutes. You hold on for three more minutes. Help will be here in three minutes," I keep repeating the words over and over with desperation clinging to every word. I need him alive. I need him to stay alive. I need him. I need him. I—

"Yes, my queen," he finally replies.

CHAPTER 31

NYX

I'm twenty feet from the cabin where Lumi and Ambrose are. I can barely stand. My legs are shaking so badly, but I have to keep moving forward.

The vampires are either dead or gone.

Lumi is safe.

Riven is on his way to save Ambrose.

All that's left to do is go into the house.

But I can't make my legs move.

I used a lot of power, too much.

To send a message to Riven.

I used my vampire lord powers like an alpha command to try to help Lumi—sending one vampire running and one frozen long enough that she could attack.

But the worst offense of all—I used my mind control to make her shift.

I'm nauseous.

Shaky.

Weak.

The headache.

Breaking the blood deal is taking its toll on me. But it's more than that. I fall to my knees as the world starts spinning.

I hear Lumi in my mind begging Ambrose to hold on, to stay alive. She doesn't realize the condition I'm in; she's so focused on *him*.

Her words, which I assume are meant for him but my heart hopes are for me, are the last thing I hear as the world starts to go dark.

"I love you—don't die."

CHAPTER 32
AMBROSE

My eyes snap open, my breath catching in my chest. I gasp for air, like I haven't been breathing any oxygen for hours. I try to sit up, but a soft hand on my chest holds me back.

"Shhh, it's okay. You're going to be okay. You're safe. Take it easy."

Lumi.

I look to her and can breathe again fully. My face lights up at the sight of her.

"You're here," I say.

She takes my hand in hers and gives me a gentle squeeze. She has some moisture in her eyes, like she's spent the entire night crying.

"Are you okay? Are you hurt?"

She shakes her head, wiping away a tear she couldn't contain. "I'm fine. Riven made sure of that."

"Who's Riven?"

"That would be me," a tall man with a thick braid says from behind where Lumi is sitting. He's leaning over the bed beside me, too focused on what he's doing to notice me. "I'm a healer. You were pretty close to death when I arrived. You'd lost over ninety percent of your blood."

I blink in surprise. "You're a healer? But you're—"

"A man and a Bloodmoon pack member, I know. But you're also a witch. It's rare, but a few men are blessed with the gift. At least, I was. My mother was a witch, and my father was a wolf shifter. I was born just before the curses started." Riven finally glances my way. "You should take it easy today, but I expect you'll feel back to normal by tonight. Anything still hurting that I can make better?"

My entire body feels sore, but I know that's normal after what I went through. His tone is friendly but also rushed—it's clear his attention is needed elsewhere.

"No, I'm good."

He nods. "As far as Lumi is concerned, I healed her wounds too, although her's weren't life-threatening, thank gods."

"Good." I look up at Lumi. "I'm so sorry. I don't know how they knew we were going to be here. I didn't intend to set you up. I—"

"I know. It's not your fault. It was risky to meet. I should have known that we'd all be tracked. Until the curse is broken, we are going to be hunted like crazy now that everyone knows only one creature's curse can be broken."

"It's important, though. Whatever it is you want to talk about is important."

She nods, squeezing my hand tighter. For a second, I think she wants to do more than just squeeze my hand.

I hold my breath. *Has she forgiven me for the unforgivable?*

"He's waking up," Riven says from behind her.

She doesn't hesitate. She lets go of my hand and rushes to the other bed in the room, to *his* bed.

"Nyx," her voice breaks around his name.

I turn my head toward the window, trying to give them privacy, but it's hard when we're all in the same room and her mind is still so open to all of us.

"I release you from our blood deal. I'm so sorry, I should never have asked you to use your mind control to help me shift. I release you!" She sobs against his chest.

Blood deal?

He used mind control?

My hands fist, wanting to punch the bastard, but I know that wouldn't win me any points as far as Lumi is concerned.

I block out the rest of their conversation to the best of my ability in my head.

"Are you both up for talking?" Lumi says suddenly, bringing me out of the forced aloneness I'd been in.

Both Nyx and I nod.

Riven looks at Lumi. "I'll be in the living room trying not to listen if you need me. Take it easy, all three of you."

We all watch as he leaves, the air as awkward and tense as one would expect.

I glance over at Nyx, who looks like he's been through hell. His skin is pale, bruises and scars still cover his body, and he looks as if he stands up, he'll topple over.

"You don't look much better yourself," he says to me in Lumi's head.

Lumi gives Nyx a sharp look. "Did you get that out of your system? I need you two not to kill each other until this conversation is over."

Nyx gives her a clipped nod.

She's sitting in a chair exactly between our two beds. I

hate this. I want to get out of this bed for this conversation.

"I agree. I feel like I'm locked in a hospital room," Nyx says.

"Stop listening to my thoughts, asshole."

"Stop shouting them in her head, then motherfucker."

Lumi sighs. "If we move this to the back porch, do you two promise to behave?"

"Yes," we both say simultaneously.

I climb out of bed first, immediately regretting my choice. That is, until I see Nyx moving even slower than I, and I know he's hurting as badly or worse. Neither of us groans nor makes a sound about our discomfort. We both have too much pride for that.

Lumi decides to stay out of it completely and walks into the small kitchen that I stocked when I first arrived. I hear her clinking around the cabinets. Riven says something to her, and her response is, "They're both stubborn assholes, is what they are. I'll let you know if one of them starts bleeding again."

Riven chuckles. "I'm staying out of it unless they're about to die."

"Smart move."

It's then that I realize I haven't thanked Riven. "Thank you for helping me. I know you're Bloodmoon, and our packs are enemies. You didn't have to help me, but I'm eternally in your debt for healing me."

Riven's eyes widen like they are about to jump out of his head. "I would do anything for Lumi. But you can repay me by not killing my friend out there."

"I'll do my best."

Riven nods.

I head outside onto the deck that has an expansive view of the forest as the sun is beginning to set.

Lumi comes outside with a bottle of whiskey and three glasses. She hastily pours the liquid into the three glasses, giving us each several shots worth of the alcohol.

I raise my eyebrows at her. "We're going to need it."

I look back at the door, waiting for Nyx to come out.

"He's waiting until the sun fully sets," Lumi says, taking a long drink.

I nod, forgetting that he can't come out in the sun. Lumi hands me a drink, her eyes skimming my bare chest as she does, but I can't tell if it's because she's looking for injuries or out of lust.

Finally, the door opens and Nyx appears. He takes the chair on the other side of Lumi. She hands him his whiskey.

"*Who was she?*" Lumi starts, not wasting any time or hesitating. She speaks to both of us simultaneously.

Nyx and I exchange glances, both of us as confused as the other about what she means or what she wants to talk about.

Lumi sighs. "*I want to know why you both hate each other. What is your history together? How did you become a witch, and how did you become a vampire? It must have started with a girl. I want to hear it from both of you at the same time so I'm not just getting one side of the story. I want to know everything. I need to know everything.*"

"Raya, her name was Raya." Nyx swallows down a lump in his throat, glaring at me like he's definitely going to kill me during this conversation.

I glare right back. *Yeah, someone is going to die.*

"And she was my sister," Nyx finishes.

Lumi looks to me, waiting for my response.

"She was my first love. I thought she was my mate," I say.

"Raya was bright, a free spirit," Nyx says.

"She was adventurous, with a spunk I'd never seen in a woman before," I continue. *That is, until you, my queen.*

Lumi smiles, encouraging us both to keep talking. She doesn't hold any grudges about me loving a woman before her.

"Raya knew we were mates. We fell in love hard and fast. It felt different than anything I'd ever experienced or seen with others before," I say.

Lumi's eyes widen at the "fell in love" part, already knowing exactly where this conversation is going from my point of view.

"If we were mates, we never found out. Before we could mark each other, Raya was killed." I glare at Nyx, who is silently watching me, his own rage barely contained. I look at him, waiting to see if he wants to do the honor or if I should.

"I killed her," Nyx says.

Lumi gasps, her head whipping to Nyx. She wasn't expecting that part of the story. "I don't understand. You loved Raya?"

Nyx nods. "I loved her more than anything in this world. She was my sister. My best friend. My entire universe. I would have done anything for her."

"Then why? What happened?" Lumi's voice is soft. She doesn't think of him as a killer.

Nyx looks at me with shadows and moisture gathering in his eyes. "Ask him. His magic forced me to kill her. Do you know what it feels like to not have control over your own body? To fight with everything inside you to keep yourself from killing someone so innocent and kind and perfect? I snapped her neck with my bare hands and then cried over her body, as confused as ever about why I killed her."

"I told you I was cursed. I didn't put a spell on you. I didn't realize until it was too late," I say.

"You went to the witches, asking them to become one so you'd be the most powerful alpha in existence. So that you could find your mate. You knew what your curse was. You were so threatened by me and Raya that you forced me to kill her!"

Lumi reaches for Nyx, but then thinks better of it. She's trying so hard to remain neutral in all of this. It's important for her to hear the entire story before she chooses whose side she's on.

"How did you become a witch?" Lumi asks.

"It wasn't my choice. I was kidnapped by the Moon-fire witches. When I woke up, I was a witch and had a deal with them. I didn't ask for this life."

"How did you become a vampire?" Lumi asks Nyx.

"Him—after I killed Raya, he hunted me down, drove me into a house of vampires, thinking they would kill me. But I survived. They turned me."

"And then you killed my entire family and half my pack. You killed my father, my brother, and some of my closest friends. You killed without remorse. And you won't stop killing. You blame me for Raya's death when it wasn't my fault she died. It was my curse that I didn't know existed until she died. You even killed Rowena."

"And I don't regret a single death," Nyx says.

Lumi shakes her head at both of us as she listens to us speaking and mutters under her breath. "Hating each other has all been a misunderstanding."

She looks up, her gaze meeting mine. "Tell him—tell him what your witches curse is."

"No."

She gives me a look that says if I don't, then she will. But I don't want to make him feel any better. He killed everyone in retaliation. It won't make him stop hating me.

"My witches' curse is that when I fall in love with someone, they die. When I fell in love with Raya, she became destined to die. I don't know why the curse chose you to carry it out. But the magic found you and forced you to be the one to kill her. But it was *me* falling in love with her that sparked the magic and stirred the curse. It's why I'm so careful around Lumi because even though I believe she's my mate, I can't fall in love with her. If I fall in love with her, she'd die."

"Why didn't you tell me it was your curse that caused me to kill her?" Nyx growls, his rage overwhelming.

"Because by the time I had realized what had happened, you were already a vampire and had killed so many people in my life that I could never forgive you or myself. And when I told you it wasn't me, it was a curse, even though I didn't give you the details, you didn't believe me. You thought I wanted you to kill Raya. I loved her." My voice breaks.

Silence stretches between us before Nyx's eyes go wide.

"You loved Rowena," he says.

CHAPTER 33

NYX

Ambrose is looking at me like I just kicked him in the nuts.

Lumi is nodding her head, like everything makes sense to her now.

"I killed Rowena, but it felt similar to when I killed Raya. It was an out-of-body experience. I thought with Rowena, it might have been because I was a vampire. Vampires like to kill. It's a predatory instinct. But I killed her because you loved her."

Ambrose looks from me to Lumi, like he's going to have to explain himself. "I guess I did, but—"

"You don't have to explain anything to me. I get it. I know you were trying to do everything you could not to love me, including forcing yourself to feel things about others." Lumi has tears in her eyes. She wipes them away quickly before looking at me. "And it's why you think of yourself as a killer."

I don't respond. My look tells her everything she needs to know.

Lumi slumps back in her chair, looking from me to

Ambrose and then back again. I'm not sure if this conversation has changed her mind about who she's choosing or who she thinks her mate is. But it solidified a lot of things for me.

I still hate Ambrose, although that hatred isn't as warranted as I once thought. His curse really did cause me to kill Raya…

I suck back the tears, not ready to go there fully, to fully process what that means. I stand up with my drink still in hand and pace, already knowing the conclusion I've come to.

Fuck.

I down the drink, not wanting to speak the words out loud. But I have to…

"You have to choose. You have to complete the marking ceremony this full moon. You can't chance him accidentally falling in love with you," I say, looking at Lumi with such desperation in my voice.

All I see is her, how beautiful and brave she is, staring back at me. I want nothing more than for her to say that she loves me, that I'm her mate.

"For whatever reason, the universe has tasked me with fulfilling his curse and making me the one who has to kill those he falls in love with. Don't…don't give him any more time to fall in love with you. I won't survive having to kill you."

"I know. I won't," she promises.

I stare at her, and I know the decision she's made. She's not choosing me, and it's the right decision. I know it in my heart of hearts. I know every fucked up decision he's made has been to try to keep himself from loving her and killing her. They are perfect for each other. My stopping the last marking ceremony didn't save her life; if anything, I almost caused her death by giving him more time to fall in love with her.

Pain builds in my chest, reminding me of the other reason why she shouldn't choose me as her mate. I don't have much time left.

I pry into her mind, trying to find the answer, to see if I'm correct in my assessment.

I feel her anger, her fear, her exhaustion. She is analytically assessing us both, weighing our pros and cons. But how she feels about either of us is locked up tight. Every time I search for the answer, I'm hit with another wall, another lock—she's completely sealed it off.

I pull back quickly before she realizes that I was in her head. Even if she's decided who her mate is, it doesn't seem like she's ready to share it yet. That was the reason she called us together: to get us to share our story, not for her to reveal who she's chosen to us. With all the power left inside me, I push my thoughts toward Ambrose, unsure if it will work or not, *"Lumi's hiding something. Something she doesn't want either of us to know. That means it's risky; it could hurt her. She's too brave and selfless for her own good sometimes. I can't get into her mind."*

"I can't either," Ambrose says. I don't know how we can talk to each other like this. Just like I don't understand why our curses are connected—our lives connected. But I don't have time to question it when there are more important things to discuss with him.

"Fuck. She lives, whatever we do. Whether we break a curse or start a war, Lumi lives."

"How do we keep her alive then?"

"She's your mate. We all know it. Every seer we've seen said so. Every prophecy. I'm just here because I'm a diversion, the villain. Someone to fuck up your love stories. We need to

ensure she accepts you as her mate. That she completes the marking ceremony with you."

"How much longer until the full moon?"

"Three days."

"Fuck, keep her as far away from me as possible. Fuck her. Love her. Make me hate her. That's too much time for me to fall in love with her." Ambrose finishes his drink, and he looks at me. *"Deal?"*

It's not a blood deal, but it doesn't matter. We will both do whatever it takes to keep her alive. I love her, and she's his mate. But I'm going to have to ruin her to keep her alive.

"Deal."

CHAPTER 34
LUMI

I asked my questions and I got my answers. But their story was more heartbreaking and fucked up than I first realized. I thought they had fought over a girl, much like they are doing now. I didn't realize the curses had been working to destroy the division between us for far longer than any of us realized.

I'm glad I asked. I'm glad I waited until they were both together. Otherwise, I wouldn't have gotten the whole story.

Ambrose takes off, agreeing to meet us at the marking ceremony with a witch he trusts. He barely looks at me and doesn't tell me goodbye. He's trying his best not to expand any feelings he has for me, and he's not sure if I'm still pissed off with him or not.

Ambrose didn't ask who I was choosing in the marking ceremony. Nyx hasn't asked either. Instead, he's been silent and standoffish since Ambrose left.

"Tell me what you're thinking about," I say.

After gently prodding in his mind, I realize his shields are once again locked up tight. I suspect that Ambrose and he have a plan involving me that he doesn't want to share. They think I'll martyr myself, or that I'll choose wrong. Whether his shields are up or down, I know them both too well. They are two sides of the same coin. Ambrose is moonlight, fire, and warmth. Nyx is the embodiment of nightfall, darkness, and cool. But they both love me, or as close as either of them will allow themselves to. Both could be my mates.

It doesn't matter what their plans are; I have my own plan.

"Are you thinking about Raya?" I ask.

Nyx closes his eyes as the breeze blows against his face. "Always."

I rub my hands over my biceps, warming myself in the chill air. "Want to talk about her?"

"No." His eyes turn to me, the red turning to blackness, blending in with the night sky. Desire swirls, and I know what he wants. To make the pain stop. I see it, the pain he's feeling. I just don't know why.

Because of Raya?

Or is he still recovering from his injuries?

Because he thinks I'm choosing Ambrose in the marking ceremony?

Or is it the secret he's hiding from me? The one he thinks he's hidden, but I can't help but see?

It's hard to tell, but the pain gets louder with each beat of his heart, seeping through his skin and leaving more ink-like stains on his body.

"You're not a killer. Whatever happens next, know that."

"But I am. If anything, this just confirmed that."

"None of it is your fault."

"It's not Ambrose's either."

I raise an eyebrow. "You don't need to defend him to me. I already told you I loved him and that I think he's my mate."

"Yes, but you still haven't forgiven him."

"Hmmm, and what about you?"

"What about me?"

"I forgive you."

He shudders at my words as I rest my hand over his heart.

"It's time you forgive yourself."

He places his hand over mine. "Oh, yeah?"

"Yeah. You're worthy of being my mate, too. Worthy of being loved."

I expect him to argue. To fight me and say that I'm wrong. That we aren't mates, to try to push me toward Ambrose.

He doesn't.

It makes me even more suspicious.

For all his martyr talk, he's the martyr between us. He's the selfless one. The one always sacrificing. The one willing to make the most significant sacrifice of all.

"I love you, Nyx."

His lips crash into mine. He doesn't fight me, doesn't argue that I'm wrong.

I stop trying to figure out what game he's playing, and I don't think about my own plans or hide my feelings.

Our hands wrap around each other as I rise on my tiptoes to meet his kiss with my whole body. His hand tangles in my hair, gripping my neck so he can angle my head to deepen the kiss.

"Gods, yes," I think.

His tongue sweeps.

My body melts.

He breaks the kiss and, with a dark, husky voice, says, "I love you, too. I've loved you for far too long, love."

Then believe in us. Don't push me to him, I think behind the wall I built in my mind, knowing he won't hear my words.

Neither of us speaks the word mate.

He doesn't believe we are. And the word holds no weight for me in this moment.

My hands rake over his bare chest, slinking between us to grab the waistband of his jeans. I get the button and zipper undone while keeping my lips locked on his. I've never been so hungry for him. So needy to have him thrust inside me, trying desperately to show him that we belong together. That we're more than just lovers. Or if love is all we have, then that's enough.

His hands are just as frantic on my body as he rips my shirt, pants, bra, and underwear from my body in the time it takes me to slide his pants down his legs.

We're outside and the air is cold, but neither of us is bothered by it. Not when we're together.

Before he gets a chance to protest, I've knelt before him in the grass, my mouth wrapping around his thick cock, humming my lips as I pump him, knowing he's fully under my control right now. I feel powerful as he fists my hair and watches me through hazy eyes, looking down at me as I pump my lips along his cock.

He lets me do it for one, two, or three strokes before he starts roaring. Snow begins to fall from the sky, hitting our skin as he yanks me up with one arm. I wrap my legs around his waist.

"My turn," he says before kissing me.

Before I can take another breath, my back is against a tree, my thighs are spread, and he's on his knees in front of me, kissing me like he wants to worship me for hours.

But I give him the same courtesy he gave me. One, two, three...

I shove him hard until he falls to the ground on his back. I dive on top of him, the snow hitting us harder now, blanketing our bodies in a thin layer of snow that we ignore.

"I need you," I pant.

"I need you more." He angles our bodies, easily sliding his cock into me without separating us. I feel like I'm crushing him as he glides in and out of me, gently stretching me as he fucks me.

He kisses me just as tenderly. Sweetly under the stars with the snow frosting my back.

He rolls us until I'm underneath him, shielding me from the brunt of the snow and cold. But the cold doesn't bother me, not with him.

"I'm scared," I admit.

"Me too."

"We aren't supposed to love each other, are we?"

"No."

My breath hitches as he dives deeper inside me, my walls tighten around him, pulling him deeper. We arch together.

"This is a dream," I whisper.

"Or a nightmare."

"You really think there's no chance I'll choose you?"

He thrusts harder, ignoring me. And I have no choice but to follow his lead. My mind can't focus on anything but us.

As the snow falls harder, the flakes start sticking to my eyelashes. Regular people would shiver from the cold, but we're not like them. We actually welcome the cold, the darkness, and the night.

His pace increases, and the friction between us has me hurtling closer to the edge of my orgasm. He shifts ever so slightly, knowing exactly how to angle our bodies to bring the most pleasure.

The runes on my body return, shining bright gold in the darkness. His scars seem to shimmer as well in sync with my own.

"Fall apart, love," he gently coaxes me.

His body, on the other hand, is doing nothing gently. He's hammering into me now, hurdling us both toward that end point that is either a dream or a nightmare.

"Only if you go with me," I pant back.

"Always, my love, always," he rasps.

I fall, disintegrating into a million pieces that only he can put back together as I come. My voice is wrecked as I scream out his name and lose myself completely to him.

His strained voice barely cuts through the air, but I hear it.

Mate.

I heard it in the dark. With the snow falling. The wind howling. Lightning striking. Darkness engulfing us.

I heard it.

He can't take it back.

I wouldn't want him to.

Because he's my mate. I loved Ambrose, but he broke me. Maybe it was unfair since he couldn't love me back. Maybe the universe always intended Ambrose to be my one true mate, but something went wrong or right, because there is no doubt in my mind that Nyx is also my mate. He mended me when Ambrose broke me. Brought me back to life when I felt like there was no reason left to live. Nyx is the only reason I'm alive now.

I love him.

He's my mate. For better or worse. Whatever tomorrow brings. He's the one I choose. The problem is I don't get a choice. And in the aftershocks, Nyx let his guard down; I slipped into his mind. I know exactly what secret he's hiding. I know what I have to do. I don't have a choice.

CHAPTER 35

LUMI

A random location was chosen at the last minute, hoping that it would make it safer and ensure the other packs, covens, and vampires wouldn't be able to find us until after the full moon was over. But we are all on alert—we all know the likelihood that we will be found before the ceremony can be completed. Everyone will hunt us tonight. It's the full moon—the only night that we can complete the marking ceremony. This is the only night when the curse can be broken. And everyone will want to find us, to ensure that we break the curse for them.

The stakes couldn't be higher. Sylara, Riven, Brax, Talonis, and Kael are on security duty. Everyone keeps their eyes peeled as we wait for Ambrose to arrive.

I'm wearing a simple black dress with matching boots and loose curls in my hair. Nyx is in a suit. We chose formal attire to match the mood, but the clothes won't change anything about tonight.

I've run through my plans a million times. I'm ready. Even for the idiotic plan, I know Nyx and Ambrose have most likely planned to try and "protect" me. But I don't need to be protected or saved. This is my destiny. I'm not afraid to face it anymore. Even if it kills me, I know what I have to do next.

"He's here," I say to Nyx.

Nyx shifts next to me, trying to drop my hand, but I don't let him. I keep our fingers interlocked. I don't care if Ambrose sees us together.

Ambrose starts walking toward us through the tree line to the clearing where Nyx and I stand. He's flanked on either side. Emeric is on his right, and a woman I don't recognize is on his left.

He nods at both of us in greeting. Even in this somber mood, Emeric flashes me a smile that's so infectious, it has me grinning right back.

"This is Florence. She's a Moonfire witch that I trust," Ambrose says.

Nyx eyes her suspiciously, but says nothing.

"Thank you for coming," I say.

She nods. "Of course. I think it's silly that everyone is fighting over who your mate is and who you can or can't break the curse for. You are both shifters. It makes sense that you break the curse for the shifters. Plus, I need to see how exactly you break this curse in the hopes it helps me figure out how to break the witches' curse later."

"Well, I appreciate the risk you're taking by being here," I say.

"It's no risk at all. I'll just wait over there until you're ready to start," she says to me.

Tension fills the air between the four of us. Emeric hesitates and then says, "I'm going to do a sweep with the others. But you should do this quickly. We don't have much time before we'll be found." He looks directly at me when he says it, like I don't already know the stakes. Then he runs into the woods that surround the small clearing, shifting as he jumps between two trees.

Ambrose is also dressed in a dark suit with a golden yellow tie. He looks good, too. We look like we're all about to go to a party, not a ceremony that could cause the deaths of any one of us.

"Ready?" he asks me.

I look from him to Nyx. "Yes."

Nyx stands on my left, Ambrose on my right, as we walk toward Florence. We all stop at once in front of her as she turns to face us.

With a wave of her hand, a soft, bed-like mat appears in front of us.

Suddenly, my heart is beating out of my chest.

"Breathe, Lumi," Nyx says.

I take a long breath as I feel Ambrose give my hand a gentle squeeze. I forgot about joining as humans before being marked as a wolf.

I look at the two men I'm being forced to choose between. But it's not really a choice. Mates are not about free will. They aren't about making a choice. They sure as hell aren't about love.

I link my fingers into both of their hands as we step forward—the three of us, stopping just in front of the bed that Florence has created.

She looks over all three of us and then back to me. "It's time to choose. Who will you allow to mark you? Who do you think is your mate?"

"I love you. But choose him, not me. Live, survive, he's your mate. He's the only one whose mark you can survive," Nyx says in my head.

"Now who's being the martyr?"

"I'm not being a martyr. Just facts. If you choose me, I won't accept you. I'll reject you."

I grind my teeth together. *"You don't get to choose for me, Nyx."*

"I'm not. I'm just telling you that I'm not a choice. So choose Ambrose or don't mark. But I'm not going to be the one to kill you, and we both know that if I mark you, you'll die because we aren't mates."

Without warning, Nyx vanishes—uses his vampire speed to disappear into the woods.

I look at Ambrose, who isn't at all shocked by what Nyx just did. "You two planned this together?"

"Nyx doesn't want to watch us together. He'll be in the woods, protecting us."

I shake my head. "I thought it was *my* choice."

"It's never a choice, and you know it. I'm your mate. Every seer says so. You know it in your heart. Complete the ceremony. Break the curse. Live. We can figure out what tomorrow brings together. Please, Lumi."

"Only if you make a blood deal with me first."

His eyebrows jump in surprise, but he says, "Anything."

I look to Florence, who is staring at me intently. I can't chance her knowing what I'm about to say, even if Ambrose trusts her. But I make sure to close off the part of my mind that lets Nyx in when I speak.

"Nyx triggered his vampire curse when he used his mind control to command me to shift into my wolf. He's going to lose his mind, go slowly rabid until he wants to do nothing but kill mercilessly. He won't let himself get to that point. He'll have someone kill him first." I bite my lip, preparing myself to say the next part. *"I'll accept you as my mate; I'll complete the marking ceremony with you if you make a blood deal with*

me that we break the curse for the vampires, not the wolf shifters. We save him." Tears hang from my eyelashes, but I refuse to let them fall. I have to do this. I don't have a choice. Ambrose is my mate. Every seer agrees. He's the only way to break the curse.

But Nyx—I love him. If I do this, I can protect him. I can keep him alive. I can save him.

"How do we do that?" he asks.

"The strongest between us gets to choose who the curse is broken for, which would be you. So when the time comes, you choose to break it for the vampires."

"You love him?"

"Don't ask me that." I prick my finger on my blade, holding it out to him. *"Do we have a deal?"*

I hate what I'm doing. I hate that this feels like I'm rejecting Nyx. That I'm choosing Ambrose. But I'm doing the only thing I can think of to save him. I know Nyx doesn't plan on living after I've completed the marking ceremony if his curse isn't broken. He won't chance hurting anyone he loves.

"You know what this means, right? After we become mates, I don't know if—"

I cut him off. *"I know what it means."* I might not ever be able to be with Nyx again. The bond between us as mates will most likely prevent that. But I'll figure out how to undo my bond with Ambrose after I save Nyx's life.

Ambrose pricks his own finger, holding it up to me, but not making contact.

"I swear to it," he says.

I press our fingers together, sealing our blood deal.

The tear falls. I can't help it.

I reject Nyx as my mate. He's not my mate. I feel the threads connecting me to Nyx severing one by one. Unlike when I rejected Ambrose, I let the magic of my bond with Nyx untangle itself from my mind. I watch as each thread rips, shreds, and severs itself until I can't find even a single inkling of his icy, cold shadows in my mind.

I'll get you back. I'll find a way to get you back. Just not now. I can't force you to live in my mind while I'm mated to another man.

I look to Florence and give her the slightest of nods. The moonlight hits my skin, and it's time. I blink back my tears and steady my mind for what I'm about to do.

"Have you made your choice?" Florence asks me.

"Yes, Ambrose is my mate. He'll be the one marking me," I answer.

She looks from me to Ambrose, a scowl slowly forming on her face. "So be it."

The entire Moonfire coven instantly appears behind Florence, as if uncovering an invisible veil.

"What the hell are they doing here?" Ambrose asks, positioning his body in front of mine.

"I knew you'd betray us," Isolde says, walking up to stand next to Florence. "Florence is an excellent mind reader; some might even say she's the best. She overheard your little blood deal conversation between you two. That just won't do."

"Blood deals can't be undone," I say.

"Everything can be undone. Blood deals, magic, curses—all of it!" Isolde answers. "You can release him from your blood deal, Lumi."

"What blood deal?" Nyx asks, he's flanked by Sylara, Emeric, Kael, Brax, Talonis, and Riven.

"The idiotic blood deal she made to try and save your life," Florence answers.

Nyx looks to me, trying to speak to me in my head.

But he blinks in horror when he realizes that I've severed our bond. There is nothing there. I haven't just blocked him. I've destroyed our connection permanently.

His head snaps back toward the witches. "She has to complete the marking ceremony tonight."

"We agree, but when she does, she'll choose the witch's curse to break, not the vampire's curse," Isolde says.

Nyx's eyes widen as he finally realizes what I've done.

"No, I refuse. And now, because of my blood deal with Ambrose, he has no choice. He has to break it for the vampires, or he will die."

"Foolish girl," Isolde says, turning her attention to Ambrose.

He freezes, his body going completely rigid.

"Ambrose? What's happening?" I prod into his mind.

But when I speak, my words are thrown back at me as if I spoke them into a wall, and not a wall of his own making. Isolde is in his mind.

I growl in her direction. "Get out of his head!"

Her lips curl up. "He's a witch because I made him so. His powers are linked to me and the Moonfire coven. He is under my control."

"You can't kill him. If you do, your hopes of ending the curse die with him. He made a blood deal. He can't get out of it. Saving Nyx is the only way to break your curse now. Let us break the curse, end it for the vampires. Keep Nyx alive. Thalia saw in the prophecy that Nyx is the one who breaks the other two curses. If you help me keep him alive, he will break the wolf shifter and witch curses," I say.

I look at Ambrose, but he hasn't blinked. I'm not even sure if he's taken a breath.

Isolde won't kill him, she won't. But every second this drags on, I'm afraid she's going to call my bluff and end his life.

"Say it," Isolde says, looking at Ambrose with a dark evil in her eyes.

Ambrose's body twitches, his eyes fall closed, and his lips snap shut.

"Say it," Isolde snaps again.

He clenches his fists, and every vein in his body is popping out, straining against her words. She's cast a spell on him, and he's fighting it.

The rest of us are ready to attack. I hope it doesn't come to that. If a fight breaks out, there will be no time left to complete the marking ceremony tonight before dawn approaches.

"Say it," she hisses, a snap of her wrist flooding Ambrose with her magic.

He's fought her. Fought her with every fiber in his being. Fought her so hard, but he can't fight her any longer. He doesn't have a choice.

"I'm sorry," he whispers through our bond.

I shake my head. This isn't his fault. Whatever she's making him do, it's not his fault.

He grinds his teeth together, trying one more time to keep the words inside, but his lips move and he finally speaks the words, "I love you, Lumi."

I feel his curse locking in place. I've been marked for death.

"Now, you have to decide whose life you're willing to save. Your vampire lord or your own. The only way to prevent Ambrose's curse from killing you is to break the witch's curse," Isolde says.

I glance from Ambrose to Nyx, who looks back at me

in horror at what Ambrose just did and how he sealed our fate. My time left is limited. I'm not afraid of dying. I'm afraid of what will happen to Nyx if he's forced to kill me.

The only way to save Nyx now is to break both the vampire's and the witch's curse. But if I complete the marking ceremony tonight, it will only break one. I need more time.

"Run!" Ambrose shouts to me through our bond. He read my thoughts. *"I'll buy you time. Run!"*

I turn and run, leaving everything behind.

Ambrose, my friends, Nyx.

Gods, Nyx.

The world will be destroyed if Nyx actually kills me. They think he's a killer now—I can only imagine the predator he'll become if he kills me.

Nyx's words haunt me as I run. *"For whatever reason, the universe has tasked me with fulfilling his curse and making me the one who has to kill those he falls in love with. Don't... don't give him any more time to fall in love with you. I won't survive having to kill you."*

———

THANK you for reading Bitten by Bloodmoon! The story will continue in Owned by Moonfire, releasing soon! Join my newsletter to find out the release date: https://ellamiles.com/freebooks

MATELESS SHIFTERS
BOOK THREE
OWNED
BY
MOONFIRE
USA TODAY BESTSELLING AUTHOR
ELLA MILES

Also by Ella Miles

TRUTH OR LIES:

Taken by Lies #1

Betrayed by Truths #2

Trapped by Lies #3

Stolen by Truths #4

Possessed by Lies #5

Consumed by Truths #6

SINFUL TRUTHS:

Sinful Truth #1

Twisted Vow #2

Reckless Fall #3

Tangled Promise #4

Fallen Love #5

Broken Anchor #6

LIES SERIES:

Lies We Share: A Prologue #0.5

Vicious Lies #1

Desperate Lies #2

Definitely: The Complete Series

STANDALONES:

Finding Perfect

Savage Love

Too Much

Not Sorry

Hate Me or Love Me: An Enemies to Lovers Romance Collection

ABOUT THE AUTHOR

Ella Miles writes steamy romance, including everything from dark suspense romance that will leave you on the edge of your seat to contemporary romance that will leave you laughing out loud or crying. Most importantly, she wants you to feel everything her characters feel as you read.

Ella is currently living her own happily ever after near the Rocky Mountains with her high school sweetheart husband. Her heart is also taken by her goofy five year old black lab who is scared of everything, including her own shadow.

Ella is a USA Today Bestselling Author & Top 50 Bestselling Author.

Stalk Ella at:
www.ellamiles.com
ella@ellamiles.com